The Stealth Virus Conspiracy

Mary Collingwood Hurst

DISCLAIMER

This is a work of fiction. Although its form is that of an autobiography, it is not one. Times and places have been adjusted to fit with the flow of the story. With the exception of public figures, any resemblance to persons living or dead is coincidental.
The author researched her own hypothesis thoroughly using scientific sources and discussion with experts and the results in this book contain true and factual findings.

Who cares if we're different?
We all shine bright like a STAR.
That's all that matters. Even if we're
UNIQUE , We all shine. Everyone
does.

Summer Hurst, Age 9

Contents

ACKNOWLEDGMENTS

I would like to thank my family and friends who have supported me during the writing of this book.

Special thanks goes to Steven Spiller, who, without his patience and help with the proof-reading and publishing, I would have been unable to release this book.

CHAPTER 1 'SHOCK...'
17th August 1997

The doctor's diagnosis overwhelmed Anna like a tidal wave of fear which hit without warning and with complete devastation. It was as though she were drowning and fighting for breath. From that instant her life changed in so many ways and would never be the same.

She and her fifteen-year-old son Rob had been waiting for nearly two hours for the results of his blood tests.

Searing heat from the August sun in 1997 was melting the tarmac roads outside and engulfed the small isolation room on the paediatric ward where they were held captive.

Despite the intense heat, the very core of her being now felt like a block of ice.

Briefly she glanced at the world carrying on as normal beyond the hospital window. It seemed so remote and distant, as though it belonged in a different time and space. Then she turned to look desperately once more at her teenage son as he lay slumped on the bed. He seemed to be failing before her.

His dark hair accentuated the deathly pallor of his face. His cheeks were sunken and drawn as though his body was dehydrated, and black shadows rimmed his eyes.

'This is not in the right Cosmic order of things,' she thought overcome with panic. 'It should be me, not him.'

That whole day now seemed like a bad dream.

Anna was unaware that she was about to embark on a

journey that would take her through the dark realms of despair and would reveal hazardous truths that were best left suppressed.

Rob had woken that morning feeling too weak to get out of bed – although after a struggle, he had managed to get dressed ready for the lift to a holiday job at his older brother's computer business.

Until the beginning of July he had seemed fit. He was an athletic build and always kept physically active. Just before the school sports day at the end of the summer term he suffered from a sore throat and mild fever, but still managed to win a sprint race with ease.

A string of seemingly unrelated minor ailments followed one after the other. A deep rattling cough and chest infection would not clear up despite two courses of antibiotics. He was continually tired and lacked energy. Endless sore throats and infections from cuts on the hands that would not heal were a constant source of annoyance to him. More recently he had been sick if he ate anything with a high fat content such as ice cream or a milk shake. He had lost a lot of weight and wanted to sleep all the time.

Individually and spread over a period of time these symptoms had not seemed important, but as each new one appeared, they produced a worrying pattern. The most recent addition was that his gums would bleed for no apparent reason.

Anna kept torturing herself saying she should have realised there was an underlying problem but none of the symptoms in isolation were enough to give cause for concern. When she looked at the picture now though, as a whole, it seemed blatantly obvious to her that something was seriously wrong, and she blamed herself for not picking up on it before.

But why should she blame herself? After all, more than one doctor they had seen at the surgery had missed the signs too.

And that locum doctor who breezed in this morning on a home visit and treated them with contempt for wasting his time, announcing it was only a case of 'mild tonsillitis.' Well, he should be shot! She had even mentioned the bleeding gums and he just said, 'take him to a dentist.'

Somehow mothers always blamed themselves for everything though, didn't they? Even when it was not their fault.

Rob was the youngest of her three children. There was a seven-year gap between him and his married sister Alice, and a nine-year gap between him and his older brother James.

As the next school year would be the final GCSE year, Rob had opted for work experience with his brother's computer firm and enjoyed earning a bit of money. He had been determined to go to work that morning. Almost immediately after he had arrived at the premises though, James had rung his mother to say Rob had collapsed and could she go and collect him.

Once back home, Anna called for a doctor's advice and despite not being asked to come around one of the GPs came to visit. She did not believe his dismissive diagnosis though, so after he had gone, she bundled her son into the car and took him to the local hospital.

The doctor who looked him over this time gave a much more thorough examination than the ill-tempered locum who had visited earlier. He pressed Rob's stomach, and asked full details of medical history.

'You've been taking some knocks, haven't you?' remarked the doctor as he inspected Rob's legs. They were covered in bruises.

Anna was shocked to see this. As he always wore jeans and had the privacy of his own room, she'd not seen the bruises before and he had never mentioned them.

'You'd better have a blood test and an expert to examine you' the doctor continued 'but as you're not sixteen yet, you'll have to go to the paediatric unit at the hospital in the next town.'

Rob still had enough fight left in him to be defensive. 'I am not a child,' he insisted. 'Can't they do the tests here on an adult ward?'

'Sorry,' said the doctor. 'Sixteen is the cut off age.'

He gave Anna a sealed letter and told her to hand it to the next doctor and said that they would be expecting them on the ward. He would ring ahead.

Puzzled and anxious she bundled Rob back into the car for the nine-mile journey to the hospital in the next town. She even sneaked a look inside the envelope but all she could see was 'Query AML', and this meant nothing to her.

On their arrival at the paediatric ward they were shown to a single room.

'We think it may be glandular fever,' said a houseman as he disappeared with the files of blood.

Rob looked around in disgust at the pictures of Walt

Disney characters on the walls. 'Damn,' he said. 'Tim had glandular fever and it took him ages to get over it.'

'Well we'll just have to go with what they say,' said Anna. 'After all you've your final year of GCSE coming up, and been elected head boy, it's better to knock this bug on the head as soon as possible before the new term starts.' Then she had turned the television on to take their minds off what was happening.

'I'm still hoping to get out of here in time to go to Ben's party tonight,' Rob said optimistically.

Nurses kept coming in and out of the room to take routine observations.

Over the next hour Rob lay back on the pillows looking totally drained as he drifted in and out of sleep. Then a nurse and two doctors entered the room, closing the door carefully and quietly behind them.

Anna's heart sank. She had trained as a nurse years earlier and read the signs that this sort of behaviour from the staff did not bode well.

The more senior doctor sat on the bed next to her and extended a comforting arm.

'There's no easy way to tell you this I'm afraid,' he said, 'but the tests have come back positive for leukaemia.'

In that moment, the world stood still suspended somewhere above her head in a glass ball, and then it crashed into little pieces around them. Anna had been expecting bad news, but nothing like this.

After what seemed a very long pause, Rob voiced Anna's own fears. He sounded a long way off. 'Does that mean I am going to die?'

Anna's head was ringing, and her elbows tingled with the shock – her brain felt numb.

The doctor rose to get up and said 'The senior Paediatrician will see you tomorrow morning, and he'll decide the best form of treatment. There are two main types of leukaemia – one we can treat here mainly as an outpatient, the other will mean going to the city hospital where you will have to stay as an in-patient for about six months. We won't know until tomorrow which type it is.' He had avoided answering Rob's question 'Does that mean I'm going to die?'

Then taking Anna to one side he added 'He is too ill to be allowed home tonight, his white blood count is extremely high, but you are welcome to stay on that couch next to the bed if you'd like.'

Silently Anna nodded and, in that moment, made a solemn vow that she would not leave her son's side whichever hospital or town he was to be treated in. She would if necessary sleep in a chair, but whatever happened, she was staying with him for every precious moment, and she would fight his corner.

The possibility of losing her son filled her with unbelievable fear. She just prayed that they would find out it was the sort of leukaemia that could be treated locally so that they could have periods at home surrounded by friends and family. What on earth would they do in a city thirty miles away, with no support around them if it turned out to be Acute Myeloid Leukaemia?

Suddenly she felt very alone.

The doctor suggested she get her husband, but Anna explained she was divorced, then added 'but I do have a fiancé who is not far from the hospital. The only thing is we had a huge argument…' Her voice tailed off. She did not add that the argument had been with his fists and she had fled in terror from his home where she and Rob had been staying until recently.

Anna had been advised by her own doctor, who had been picking up the pieces after the event, not to go back until her partner Patrick had received anger management as it was not safe for her or for Rob to be in that environment. Particularly as it was not the first time it had happened.

Using the ward phone, she rang her eldest son James and told him the news. He was a mature twenty-four-year-old and took charge of the situation immediately. 'I'll let Alice know and we'll be with you as soon as possible,' he said.

'Thanks,' said Anna relieved that she would not have to ring her daughter separately. Each time she had to talk about it all, the situation became more real and she was in denial. This was her usual coping mechanism with anything traumatic, to pretend it was happening to someone else as though she was watching a play.

She hesitated. 'Can you let Patrick know as well,' she asked. 'I feel he should be aware. Perhaps he'll be supportive.'

There was a pause. 'Alright I will mum, but you know I don't agree with it. You should really break away completely.' James replaced the receiver.

He was probably right, but once again, Anna was in denial. The extreme emotion and threat of the present seemed to block out the immediate past.

Rob was in a state of shock still reeling from the words the doctor had said, but he was feeling too exhausted to take it all in properly. Anna reached out for his hand.

'You will not be fighting this alone,' she said trying to sound strong. 'We are in this together, in some sort of deep pit, but together we will climb out again I promise you.'

'Thanks mum,' he said and closed his eyes.

Thoughts tumbled over each other competing for space in every corner of Anna's mind.

Mixed with the feelings of terror and disbelief, one thought in particular kept coming to the surface. 'Why has this happened? Why does a young healthy body suddenly tip over into the abyss of such a devastating disease? Rob's illness can't be random, there must be a reason,' she tortured herself. 'Is it something I've done or not done – isn't there some rule in the Universe that for everything that happens there is a cause?' The questions piled up in her mind, tumbling one over the other.

She decided to start asking questions from the consultants as soon as she could. She could not let the matter lie and refused to accept blindly that some random chance had caused her son to be this sick. Making this resolve somehow gave her a strange comfort. It was a goal to work toward in a world where she and her son had now lost control, and nothing made sense any more.

CHAPTER 2 '…UPON SHOCK'
Later 17th August 1997

When Rob next opened his eyes, he was pleased to see his brother and sister standing next to the bed.

'So, you've decided to throw something at us to keep us on our toes then,' said James, keeping his voice light-hearted. Despite trying to lift the atmosphere in the room, his unruly beard which usually disguised most of his face could not hide the anxiety in the eyes. Outwardly he stood solid and calm.

Rob smiled weakly.

Alice looked drained of all colour and almost as bad as her younger brother. She appeared so thin and vulnerable too. Long dark hair was piled up on her head, her slim figure clad in a black skirt, jacket and white blouse. She had come straight from work. She reached out and took Rob's hand and gave it a squeeze.

'Did you get through to Patrick?' asked Anna quietly out of earshot of Rob.

'I couldn't get an answer on the phone,' said James, 'so I drove round there. He looked pretty surprised to see me and was acting rather furtively. He may have had someone else with him. You know I don't want you to keep in with him mum – not after what he did to you.'

What James did not realise was that it was not the first time such an incident had happened.

'Despite everything,' Anna thought, 'I still love him, unreasonable as it may sound and would really like it to work.'

She knew only too well from her work within the NHS that abusive partners never showed their true colours initially. They usually appeared gentle and attentive at first - possessiveness being mistaken for being protective - and then gradually, oh so gradually, they would wind the hook, line and sinker in. First, they would find ways of isolating their victim from family and friends. Then they would control their partner in subtle ways – "come into my parlour said the spider to the fly."

How could she have not read the signs? She realised now that she probably had not wanted to, love is a powerful drug.

When they had met, there had been an instant attraction from both sides. They shared so much in common, he with his medical background and hers with nursing. He was retired now and had taken early retirement although she never knew the real reason. Patrick would give a variety of explanations ranging from a row at the surgery to ill health.

They also shared a love of walking, writing, exploring, and music and a sense of humour.

He had seemed so perfect, the perfect match. Unfortunately, it turned out to be made in hell not heaven, but by then it was too late. He had woven the spell in such a way she felt she could no longer manage without him despite the sudden mood swings.

She was aware of a movement out of the corner of her eye and looked up. There, framed in the doorway stood Patrick. His tall well-built figure was slightly stooped and thick glasses added to the serious expression on his square face which was accentuated by a high forehead and a receding hairline. He looked shaken and dishevelled as though he had just got out of bed.

They had not seen each other since the 'incident' a few weeks earlier, but they had been in touch by letter and also, he had sent encouraging verbal messages through mutual friends. 'He says he misses you very much,' said one friend, 'and says he will always love you.'

Patrick had promised he would seek professional help with managing his anger, and he vowed they would soon be together again.

Anna had undergone major abdominal surgery earlier that year and Patrick insisted she move in with him or he would 'wash his hands of her' was the expression he used.

From the moment they entered his home on discharge from hospital only six days after the operation, he had become domineering, and was almost looking for an excuse to hit her. The first attack occurred only a couple of days later. He seemed shocked himself afterwards and insisted she have a check-up with the doctors as she felt something had happened inside, perhaps to the stitches, while trying desperately to pull away from him. 'She twisted awkwardly in bed,' he had lied over the phone to the hospital.

A week later, something similar happened again, only it had escalated this time. And finally, a week after that, a further escalation when Anna became so scared that she ran to the phone unsure whether she should ring the police or James for help. She had opted for James because she knew in her heart, if it was brought to the attention of the police it would really be the end of any chance the relationship might have.

Patrick tried apologising as usual, and tried to persuade her to stay, but as soon as James had arrived she rushed to her son's car to escape. Then she attended her own GP surgery so that the fist marks on her body would be entered into her notes. 'What do you want me to do with this information,' asked the doctor. 'Do you want to involve the police?'

'No,' Anna had said. 'I just want it on the notes to remind me that it really did happen, so that I can't let my mind play games with memory later when denial might try to creep in.'

It was then that her doctor had told her emphatically that she must not go back - not only because of danger to herself, but more particularly the danger to Rob. 'Your son could be drawn in to protect you and either get hurt himself, or else get into trouble with the police if he struck your partner.'

It was the thought that Rob might be in danger which finally convinced Anna that she would have to stand firm until Patrick had sorted himself out.

Despite all that had passed during that terrible time, seeing Patrick now on the ward provided comfort and her heart gave a little leap and she longed to rush into his arms, but she noticed with a certain surprise that tears were welling up in his eyes. This was out of character and bearing in mind he had been a doctor it seemed strange that he should not be able to retain his composure in the circumstances.

'Can we have a moment together?' he asked.

Anna felt strangely unnerved. She was loath to leave Rob and was torn, but as James and Alice were keeping their brother company, she agreed to go with Patrick into the ward kitchen where they sat on opposite sides of the plastic table.

A smiling nurse asked if they would like a cup of tea, and they both nodded gratefully.

Even though she had no sugar in her tea, Anna played with

the spoon, stirring it over and over again, as if in a trance. None of this could be happening surely. Soon she would wake up from the nightmare.

Patrick caught sight of the opal and diamond engagement ring she wore.

'You still wear it then,' he said taking her hand in his.

'Of course,' she replied. 'We are still engaged aren't we?'

She had a vivid flashback to the Christmas Eve three years earlier when Patrick had put the ring on her finger as they sat alone in the church of St. Edmund in the village of Corfe Castle in the Purbecks. It had been such a perfect day.

The haw frost was sharp and crisp that morning and made every tiny twig stand out individually on each tree as though they had been sprayed white like delicate Christmas decorations, and later when the sun broke through the mist it made everything sparkle like the diamonds in the ring. Surely that was a good omen.

For a brief moment the happy memory lifted her out of her torment. 'It gives me comfort,' she said twisting the ring around her finger, 'despite… everything.'

'Anna,' said Patrick. 'There's something I have to tell you. If only I had known earlier about Rob, and all this…. then...' his voice tailed off.

A strange chill ran down Anna's spine at the tone. 'What do you mean?' she asked puzzled.

'If only I had known,' he repeated still staring at the ring as he held her hand. 'I would never... I would never have let her move in.'

Anna still could not work out what he was trying to say. Perhaps the shock of Rob's diagnosis had dulled her senses.

'Let who move in – where – what are you talking about?'

'Do you remember that woman we met on the beach a few months ago, the one who was with my friend Paul?' he hesitated before choosing his words carefully 'Just before our argument.'

Anna nodded unable to work out where this conversation was going.

'She was Paul's sister in law and had nowhere to live.'

'Yes, I remember her vaguely,' Anna said, still struggling to work out what he meant.

'Well I let her move in this afternoon, only about three hours ago to be precise.' He could not look Anna in the eye.

Still the full impact of his statement did not dawn on her.

'What as a lodger you mean?' she said. 'Paying for a room.'

Patrick remained silent. Silence can often say far more than words.

'As a friend then…' she persisted.

Again Patrick stayed silent.

'Not in our room – our bed,' she said, and the full horror of what he was trying to say hit home like the aftershock to an earthquake which had already hit once. The man she was looking to for support and who she loved, had betrayed her in the worst possible way, and at the worst possible time.

'You know how I hate being alone,' he said, as though that were a valid excuse. His voice had become defensive, as though it were all her fault.

She stood up suddenly, pushing the chair back hurriedly and snatching her hand away from his. Her stomach churned over and over and she felt another surge of panic.

'I've got to check on Rob,' she said rushing past Patrick and out into the corridor too shocked to cry.

She entered the isolation room and sat on Rob's bed, holding him and fighting back tears, just hoping he could not see. 'Whatever happens he needs me to be strong,' she told herself.

James noticed though. 'Are you OK mum?' he asked quietly and touched her arm.

'Fine,' she murmured. 'It's just the shock of everything. It is for all of us.'

Patrick slipped awkwardly away, making excuses and mumbling that he would call in again next morning in time for the Specialist's round. Anna could not bear to look at him.

That night, after James and Alice had left, and Rob had fallen asleep, she lay fully clothed on the hard couch alongside the hospital bed trying to settle and determined not to leave her son.

Rob slept fitfully. Nurses flitted in and out of the ward, checking all his vital signs at regular intervals. Anna lay awake staring at the ceiling and watched the patterns of light change as dawn broke.

The hours of darkness had been quiet. While the night time had drifted slowly by, memories came flooding back of her childhood experience in an isolation hospital as a frightened four-year-old diagnosed with a combination of polio and diphtheria, and paralysed from the neck down. Parents were not allowed to stay in those days, in fact they were only allowed to visit once a week and had to look at her through glass. She was not allowed to have familiar toys with her because of the danger of cross infection. But when night slipped its mantel over the ward a strange peace would envelop her. The low night lights glowed gently and seemed to take her into another world, and the loud noises of the ward during daylight hours were replaced by a hushed quiet.

As Anna now lay awake alongside Rob, she was once more transported into that strange dream-like world between night and day.

The memory of her own separation all those years ago made her even more determined not to leave Rob's side now. There was no way she was going to let him fight this battle on his own.

CHAPTER 3 'ADJUSTMENTS'
18th August 1997

Morning was heralded by a baby crying somewhere on the ward, and the chinking of the tea trolley as it was wheeled up the corridor.

Rob was awake.

'When's this specialist coming then mum?' he asked.

'I don't know the exact time, they just said he would call in this morning,' said Anna. 'How did you sleep?'

'Well I feel so tired it isn't difficult to drop off, but then I suddenly wake in a cold sweat, at the thought of what lies ahead probably.'

'I know Rob,' said Anna, 'but as I told you last night, you will not be going through it alone. I am not going to leave your side, and you can always count on James and Alice for support.'

Patrick appeared at the doorway again like some silent ghost. Anna was no longer sure whether she wanted him around after the news he had given yesterday; and yet somehow, despite everything, his presence still meant something. Love does not die that quickly or easily. There would be fewer broken hearts in the world if it did.

'I thought it would be good to have someone else with you when the consultant calls,' he explained. 'A second pair of ears is always helpful. It's so easy to miss parts of a consultation or misinterpret what is actually said when you are in shock.'

'That is an understatement,' Anna whispered under her breath. 'There have been so many shocks in the past 24 hours,' and she tried to drive out the thought that he had spent the previous night with the other woman in what he had convinced her was supposed to be their new home. The rest of her thoughts she kept sealed inside. 'Thank heavens I had not moved in permanently with you. You were supposed to be taking care of me as a trial period after my major operation. Well it certainly was a trial anyway and for all the wrong reasons.' she thought with a mixture of anger and sadness.

Anna's clothes were creased and crumpled from where she had tried to sleep in them on the hard bench next to Rob's bed. She had tossed and turned all night.

But somehow, she didn't care. The only thing that mattered to her now was her son's survival.

The Consultant arrived surprisingly early. It was Sunday morning, so no formal ward rounds were expected, but he had come in especially to see Rob.

The doctor was dressed in running shorts and a sweatshirt.

'Just done a couple of circuits of the park,' he explained. 'Have to keep fit you know.'

Rob decided to chance his luck again with the question avoided by the doctors the previous day.

'Does it mean I am going to die?' he asked hesitantly as the Consultant took a look at him.

'Well some we can treat and some we can't,' said the Consultant with brutal honesty.

Anna felt rather than saw Patrick's whole body tense. She knew these were the danger signs when he was about to 'lose it.'

He said quietly so that only Anna could hear 'You don't need to be quite so direct with a fifteen-year-old boy. All he needs to know now is that he can be made to feel better than he does at the moment.'

Anna nodded. 'Everyone needs a thread of hope,' she whispered back.

The consultant continued. 'Well at least we know what sort of leukaemia it is; it's what we call AML or acute myeloid leukaemia. Quite unusual in a lad your age and more common in adults. The problem is we can't treat this type of leukaemia here, and so we will be sending you to the city hospital as soon as possible.'

Anna's heart sank. So, it was to be the hospital thirty miles away and with the likelihood that they would be staying there for six months before any chance of returning home. She felt the chill of fear rising inside once more.

Trying to remain composed she said, 'So can we call home first to collect a few things?'

'I will let you do that so long as you promise you will only stay long enough to pack your bags,' said the Consultant.

'Is it really that urgent?' Patrick asked quietly.

'Afraid so,' said the doctor. 'His white blood count is dangerously high, and the sooner the proper treatment starts the better.'

Then turning to Anna, he said 'My registrar will give you a note to take with you and also a map of directions to the hospital.' Then he added, 'well better get on – good luck.' That last message directed at Rob.

A nurse entered and said, 'I have your eldest son on the ward phone.'

Anna duly followed her. 'Oh, James I'm so pleased to hear you,' she said. 'We've been told we have to go to the city hospital; is there any way you could drive us there this morning, I really feel a bit too shaky to drive myself.'

'Of course, Mum' he said. 'I'll meet you at home. I know Alice will want to come with us too.'

The relief that her eldest son was taking charge in an impossible situation nearly broke Anna's resolve not to give way openly to her emotions.

She went back to the small isolation room. Patrick was standing by Rob who was in a collapsed state on the bed. He was deteriorating rapidly.

'I'll have to get the car,' she said. 'I can collect it from the car park and bring it to the hospital main entrance, so you don't have to walk too far.'

But then looking at her son again she realised he was now even too weak to stand.

'I'll get a wheelchair,' said the nurse disappearing.

Anna made her way to the hospital car park where she had left their car the previous afternoon. Patrick followed her and then kissing her briefly, left with promises that he would come up and see them in the city hospital the next day. He asked her if she could find him somewhere to stay near the hospital. Anna was already under pressure and she felt convinced he could find his own accommodation rather than land her with another job.

However, she agreed, still feeling torn between the yearning when she saw him and the sadness and anger when she thought about the circumstances.

Anna drove her car to the front entrance where Rob was waiting in the wheelchair. She manoeuvred him into the car, aware how painfully thin he was and how much weaker than the previous day.

When they arrived home and opened the front door, they were given a warm welcome by their two ginger cats. 'Animals are so constant,' thought Anna, 'more reliable than humans. At least their affections don't switch at the slightest change in the wind.'

James and Alice arrived while Anna quickly threw clothes into a suitcase for both herself and Rob. She had no idea where she would stay or for how long. And that was the most painful question of all. She would stay for as long as Rob had to, but just how long would that be? Would he indeed ever be coming home again at all? Would he even survive the next week?

She fought back tears and hid them. 'So, we are all ready to go then.'

James packed the case into the boot of his car, and Anna helped Rob into the front seat so that it could be altered to a semi prone position. She would travel in the back with Alice.

'Why don't you and Sandra move in here at the bungalow for a while James?' said his mother. 'It would make sense.' He and his fiancée were in the process of looking for their own flat.

'Thanks mum,' said James 'A good idea. At least we can keep an eye on the cats, and the post and field any phone calls.'

The family left home at 11.30 a.m. and drove across the

high road that followed what was known as 'the roof' of the New Forest.

Alice and Anna gripped each other's hands tightly. Despite James's attempt to keep a bit of banter going to lighten the atmosphere the sense of fear that filled the car was almost palpable.

Gazing out of the window, Anna noticed the purple heather and yellowing bracken of the moors reaching as far as the eye could see. The sun beat down with the intense heat of high summer. In the distance, she could just make out the blue-grey shape of the Isle of Wight and the white chalk cliffs at the end shaped like a polar bear. Soon the road they were travelling dipped into a closely wooded area and they were on the motor way.

The journey went too fast. Anna had an overwhelming feeling that she wanted it to go on for ever and that somehow they could run away from this entire nightmare if only they just kept on driving. Common sense told her this was an impossible scenario; but all the same, it was a tempting thought. That way they could pretend it was not happening. In a way they were all in denial.

In fact, what she really wanted to do was to turn back home, herd all her family indoors, close all the curtains, lock all the doors, keep them all safe together and shut out the world in the hope it would all go away. The urge to do this was all encompassing, egged on by some inner voice.

She remembered the natural history programme shown recently where elephants had surrounded their young in the centre of a circle to protect them and the adults all faced outward to ward off any threat. She had an image of herself,

James and Alice, surrounding Rob in the same way; their backs to him, he in the centre and they ready to fend off the danger that threatened to overtake their lives. They would unite in a strong bond and fight this awful disease all the way until either they won, or the last breath had gone.

She shook herself. 'Enough of this negativity,' she thought. 'We will win through, by the Grace of God, we will win through.'

'Ah God,' she thought. 'I wonder where He is in all this.' She suddenly had a picture where Christ's mother Mary had sat at the foot of the cross, and how she must have felt watching her son suffer.

'Mary would understand how I feel,' she thought, and then remembered the Beatles' song. She heard Paul McCartney's lyrics running around her head 'When I find myself in times of trouble Mother Mary comes to me, bringing words of wisdom – let it be.'

'Yes, please let it be' prayed Anna silently.

The journey was over. James dropped his passengers off at the main entrance of yet another hospital, the third they had visited in two days. He went with Alice to find a parking place. Meanwhile Anna commandeered a wheelchair that was near the door, and Rob collapsed gratefully into it.

His mother looked at him anxiously. 'Can the disease really work this fast?' she worried. Despite training as a nurse before she married, she had never nursed a patient with leukaemia, and certainly not a young patient with any sort of cancer. This was new territory for her, made worse by the fact it was her own son, and she felt helpless.

Alice was the first to find them. 'It's Ok mum,' she said. 'James is explaining things to the parking warden, and they're finding him a place. I'll just phone Brian and let him know what is going on.

Brian was her husband and they had been married very young only two years ago when she was just twenty.

What a wedding that had been. Alice had been the bride looking serene and beautiful on the surface, but all sorts of things were unfolding while she was in cloud cuckoo land. Chris, Anna's ex-husband, the children's father, had just dragged Anna through the courts again only a couple of weeks before trying to find an excuse to stop paying support for Rob. So the last time they had seen each other was across a Courtroom where their solicitors were battling it out. Family courts were not meant to be places of vitriol, but unfortunately Chris had turned it into one. So when they all met up at the wedding, the wounds were still raw.

One thing led to another, and Rob was so nervous at meeting his father he had accepted plenty of red wine supplied by his brother to give him Dutch courage. Chris started to shout at Anna saying she didn't know how to look after the children. James carried Rob semi-conscious up to a private room in the reception hotel and as he came back down again was met with a scene where his fiancée Sandra was putting a protective arm around Anna and calling her future father in law all sorts of things she should not. It was after all their first meeting!

James rushed to get help to diffuse the situation and found his Aunt who filled the doorway looking like an angry wasp in a yellow suit with diagonal navy stripes and hat to match.

Out of the blue she struck Chris across the face knocking his sun glasses askew.

Why he was wearing sunglasses no-one quite knew, but it added to the Mafia effect of his shiny grey suit.

The aunt seemed to warm to the task and struck him several more times. Obviously there was some deep-seated grievance that no-one else knew about and she was giving vent to it.

She was finally hauled off when the Manageress said if she didn't stop she would have to call the police.

Despite the seriousness of the current situation Anna was now in with Rob and his illness, she could not but help supress a smile at the memory.

Of course, she would once again have to come into contact with Chris, and just hoped he would behave himself and not upset everyone as was his nature.

She was thrust back into the present with the challenge of having to face her fear of lifts as her eldest son wheeled Rob in a chair and Alice followed alongside.

Anna hated lifts, but the children's cancer ward was on the sixth floor, and in the current situation she had no choice. She was very claustrophobic and just shut her eyes as the lift doors closed. 'At least they have emergency phones in a hospital lift,' she thought.

As they reached the appropriate floor on the top level, a disembodied woman's voice from inside the lift mechanism announced 'G level.' There was a sort of finality about the way it was said that was very depressing. The tone ended on a down note, unlike all the other floors they had passed where the voice sounded quite upbeat.

This is where the panic began to set in for all of them. They could no longer pretend they were just on a day out as they approached the locked ward door.

James pressed the intercom and announced who they were. The buzzer clicked into action and they were allowed through the double doors. No turning back now. The doors closed behind and Anna had an overwhelming urge to grab her son and say to them all: 'Quick. Run.'

They entered the ward to be faced with bright children's paintings on the walls, and a few toys strewn around a play area.

Rob groaned. He still just had about enough energy to let his feelings be known that he did not appreciate being on a children's ward.

A cheerful nurse approached them. 'Hello,' she said, 'this must be Rob. I'm your dedicated nurse Sophie and you'll be in my care during your stay.'

Sophie did not seem that much older than Rob, and for a brief moment his face lit up. She was very attractive.

'We'll just get you settled in,' continued Sophie, 'and then start you on some treatment to fight your problem as soon as possible. Tomorrow, Jean our Paediatric Oncologist, child cancer specialist if you prefer, will be on duty and then the whole team will look at you and decide on the best course of action. But as today is Sunday, I suggest you just take time to rest. It will get very busy from tomorrow.'

She led the little family group toward a single room which had a fine view of the docks in the distance. It was light and airy. However, it had a blue elephant on the door.

'What is it with me and elephants,' complained Rob. 'There was one over my bed at the last hospital. I keep saying I am not a child.'

'Will it be alright for me to stay overnight in the chair?' Anna asked.

'No need for that,' said Sophie cheerfully, 'we have a bed that folds down from the wall next to Rob, look.' And she pulled out a well sprung bed which was hidden away during the day.

'Just as long as you don't do a James Bond,' said Rob laughing weakly. 'You know where someone folds him up into the wall while he's still on the bed.'

They all laughed at the thought, and then felt strangely guilty. They should not laugh in this situation, should they?

Anna remembered Patrick's request about accommodation. 'Do you know any bed and breakfasts round here at all?' she asked.

'We have a CLIC hostel at the back of the hospital where parents can stay if there's no room for them on the ward.'

Anna explained the situation with Patrick but only said that he was her fiancé. She made no mention of the other things that had happened. However, she did wonder if Patrick could even be considered her partner any more after all he had done.

'I'll get a key for room 3 in the hostel for you to give him,' said Sophie, 'so he can have access when he comes up tomorrow.'

The nurse then settled Rob down and made sure he was

comfortable and started to fill in details on the chart at the end of the bed.

'Right,' she said. 'When I am off duty you will be looked after by Kim. You will probably meet her tomorrow.' Then to Anna she said 'if you follow me I'll show you where the ward kitchen is. You can make your own tea or coffee any time and cook food for you and Rob if you like. Particularly if he can't eat the hospital food, although I have to say it is very good here.' They left the room.

Anna confided in Sophie 'I am afraid to leave him, even to make a tea, just in case he slips away when I am not there,' and she began to cry feeling able to let go at last.

Sophie put her arm around her. 'That won't happen,' she said reassuringly. 'We would know if it had got to that time and would tell you. It is quite alright for you to leave him and make a cup of tea, and even visit the dining room on the lower ground floor. Just let us know where you are going.'

So Anna took time to be shown round the ward unit while James and Alice kept an eye on Rob.

There were a few other single rooms, two specially designed for bone marrow transplant patients. They had an airlock system to keep the rooms isolated from the outside. There was one double room which was known as the 'Teenage Room' and a four bedded ward which was occupied by smaller children. There was a school room which doubled as a play room, and another room which was only for teenagers and which had a television, pool table and a computer for games and a selection of books.

Despite the awful situation and being trapped, somehow it was a safe place to be.

As she re-joined her family again, she heard a burst of raucous laughter from the neighbouring room and felt an inexplicable surge of anger. How could anyone laugh like that in this place, a ward full of critically ill – even dying children? She remembered her own feeling of guilt earlier when they had laughed.

But later she would learn that laughter was in fact very appropriate. It was laughter that kept people going in an impossible situation and laughter that made life bearable in otherwise unbearable circumstances.

Seeing her reaction Sophie said 'don't worry that's only Sister, she has a great sense of humour. I know it is all strange at the moment, but once you know what treatment you are having Rob, and once we have started, you will be on the road to feeling better.'

Anna noticed there was not the promise of 'You will be well again', but then, she knew that Rob's future lay in the balance.

Sophie then explained about the 'Hickman Line' or central line as it was also called. She showed them a diagram. A catheter was posted through the soft flesh on the shoulder and passed under the skin where one end was placed in a main vein entering the heart, and the other end was left outside the body in the chest wall. This outer end of the tube had a sterile plug sealing it off from outside his body.

It was very daunting.

'The reason we use this,' the nurse explained, 'is that some of the chemotherapy drugs are so strong, they can make the peripheral veins collapse. Once the Hickman Line is in place, you won't have to have any injections to put the drugs into your system; and don't worry - the line will be put in position under a general anaesthetic. Usually we do it within a couple of days of arrival, but unfortunately as this is a weekend you may have to wait just a little longer. Everyone is fighting for theatre space.'

Anna looked at Rob's face which remained passive, almost resigned. He seemed to have accepted now that there was no other way to fight this disease but just go with the flow. Anyway, he was too tired to fight any more.

It was time for James and Alice to leave. Anna walked with them to the lift where the depressing disembodied voice announced 'G Level' again as the doors opened. She suddenly rushed forward to hug them both.

'I wish we were coming home with you,' she said her heart pounding. She felt very vulnerable and alone once more. 'If we could all just be together…'

'I know mum,' said James putting his arm around her. 'We have to get back, but we are only forty minutes away. If you need us we can be with you very quickly. Be strong for Rob.'

'Yes of course,' said Anna feeling ashamed of herself. Then she added 'You will take special care driving home won't you.'

'Of course we will,' said Alice giving her mother a kiss.

As the lift doors shut she felt inexplicably as though her whole family was under threat and at risk. What if something happened to them on the way home? It was irrational thinking she knew, but now that one of her children had become so vulnerable, perhaps she would lose them all. Nothing was secure in life any more, not that it ever is of course, but normally she wouldn't have thought like that.

She turned to go back to Rob's room. The nurse had put the television on for him.

'Blasted Telly Tubbies now,' he grumbled. 'Automatically went to that station.'

'We can change it,' said his mother reaching for the controller which was on the window sill.

'It's all written around drugs you know,' said Rob. 'The Telly Tubbies I mean.'

And with that things started falling out of the sky in Telly Tubby land, including the lower-case letter 'e' which La-La caught with glee.

'See I told you,' laughed Rob. 'Why is it that the only letter to fall out of the sky is the lower case letter 'e' – you know that stands for a drug don't you?

Anna was glad he still retained his sense of humour despite everything that was happening to him.

As evening fell, she looked out of the window across the city rooftops to the docks in the distance where large cruise liners were lighting up and the tall cranes had now stopped loading the container ships. She felt like a caged animal.

She felt envious of the people boarding ships for a wonderful holiday. It seemed strange to think that everywhere else, on the other side of the glass, normal life carried on. But here on the ward her son was fighting for his life and about to start on a very different journey.

The moon hung in the sky and she gazed at it for a moment. 'That is the same moon above everyone, but some of us are free and some of us are not.' Again, the regular feeling of panic rose in her chest. 'We are prisoners of Rob's disease.'

She pulled the bed down from the wall and stretched out gratefully on the sprung mattress, very different from the hard couch of last night. And oh… she felt so weary suddenly.

While Rob closed his eyes, she locked herself away with her own thoughts. 'Where has this dreadful illness come from?' Again, the weight of blame and the tyranny of 'ought' consumed her.

'What have I as his mother done? Has he spent too much time in front of the computer, have I given him the wrong food? Cause and effect is after all one of the rules of the Universe so somewhere there is a reason why he has been struck down.'

'I'll ask the specialist tomorrow,' she thought. 'The consultant must have some idea what causes leukaemia and cancer in young children. It is definitely on the increase.'

With her mind in turmoil, she slipped into an uneasy exhausted sleep.

CHAPTER 4 'CHOICES
20th August 1997

D espite being at the point of exhaustion where her brain seemed to make a permanent high pitched electrical sound as though it were tuning in to all the nerve activity in her body, Anna did not rest at all that night. There comes a stage in absolute fatigue where it is impossible to find the sleep one is desperate for. The brain is still working at over load and will not give up to the gentle renewal when it should shut off from the world and recharge.

Although they were very quiet, nurses came in and out to check on Rob at regular intervals, and they had inserted a cannula into the back of his hand so they could administer some intravenous drugs.

The problem was that every time Rob moved his hand, even in his sleep, it would trigger the alarm on the drip which immediately alerted the nurse who could be heard running down the corridor.

'It's usually letting us know that the line has occluded,' said Sophie. 'That means that the line has been squashed, kinked or moved in such a way that the fluid can't get through.'

During the night, each time the alarm went off or one of the nurses entered the room, Anna would sit bolt upright to see what was going on. She felt it would be rude not to acknowledge their presence, and also she wanted to keep an eye on Rob.

She watched her son, his pale face emaciated and his dark

lank hair in contrast as he lay motionless on the bed.

'You OK Rob?' she asked softly.

'Yes mum - just thinking about the science project they're doing at school at the moment. It was actually something I was looking forward to. If I can't do the course work for Science GCSE I'll lose the chance of taking the exam. And I do miss my friends too – we had a lot of plans for the holidays.'

Science was Rob's favourite subject and he hoped to go to University to study some form of it later. His predicted grades were A star in each of the sciences for the GCSE exams next year. He was a hard-working student.

Again, it was hammered home to Anna that Rob was missing out on the years when he should be finding freedom, getting into trouble, trying out the world, planning a future. Instead he was thrown back to being as dependent as a toddler once more.

Later in retrospect, Anna realised her bobbing up and down every time the nurses entered quietly at night, must have driven them mad, but they were very patient and understanding.

The following morning began very early as predicted.

She checked on Rob and helped him wash his face and brush his teeth. 'Always feels a bit better to freshen up,' she said and he smiled faintly back at her.

After a quick shower in the small en suite part of Rob's room she emerged to find Patrick standing beside the bed. He came toward her and put his arm around her shoulder and gave her a fond kiss.

'I've come up by train,' he said. 'My hip is playing up and it's affecting my back again.' And with that, and to Anna's embarrassment, he lay down on the floor. 'It helps to relieve the pain,' he said, but she could not help thinking it was perhaps a way of drawing attention to himself. He always had to be the centre of attention, and Rob was upstaging him now.

She had put her bed back up into the wall and did not offer to bring it down for him to lie on. Cleaners had already started their morning routine, and she had to keep the space as clear as possible for them to do a proper job without giving them extra obstacles. Her suitcase was unpacked and stored away in a cupboard. The Specialist was due any moment.

Then the ward round arrived. A whole team of people suddenly filled the room.

Jane, the Consultant, was a tall, attractive and very pleasant woman with an easy smile and manner. She was accompanied by her Registrar and a very good-looking houseman who would have made an excellent James Bond and was undoubtedly a heart throb amongst the nursing staff. Sophie, Rob's dedicated nurse was there, and they were joined by the Ward Sister and Rob's other special nurse Kim who was shortly to take over duty that day.

Together they all pulled up seats or stood around Rob's bed.

'The first thing I want you to know Rob,' Jane said addressing him directly, 'is that we will include you in all the discussions about the treatment and realise you're not a child and will not talk behind your back.'

Rob relaxed and gave a smile. Although his face was painfully thin and drawn, there were still the traces of the teenager trapped inside. He had many friends and, although a gentle nature, would fight when necessary (as a damaged hand had proved recently when he insisted to his mother that he had caught it in a door. Later she was to discover it should have been described as 'caught on a jaw' when a class bully overstepped the mark one too many times.)

'I think you've already been told that you have AML, which is why you are here rather than at your local hospital, and it will mean that you'll most likely be here continuously as an in-patient for six months,' the consultant continued. 'I won't lie to you, the time ahead is going to be very hard work, for both you and your mum, but we'll start the proper treatment today. I have the results of the type of Acute Myeloid leukaemia it is, so we know which drugs to use and how to attack it.'

The other members of the team were making hasty notes in their books.

'I think Sophie has already explained about the Hickman Line,' said Jane, 'and we will get that set up as soon as possible as it will make your life much easier. It'll mean fewer injections as any drug or treatment you need can then just be added via the one line,' she grinned at Rob. 'I am sure that is an incentive.'

Rob looked relieved – 'No-one likes to be stuck with needles all the time, unless you are an addict of course!' he joked.

'We'll put you on the list for it to be done as soon as possible but with the Bank Holiday looming as well as the weekend, it's not that easy to slot you into a theatre spot so unfortunately we all have to be patient – even the patient.' She smiled.

Her casual manner eased the tension.

'There is one other thing I must mention to you and your mum,' Jane added, 'and that is in this hospital we take part in trials so that we can improve treatment as we go along. How this works is that some people remain on the treatment that was last considered the best for your type of leukaemia, and others try out a new regime of drugs which might or might not be better, and then we compare the results when treatment is over. I know this is a difficult question for you, but would you be prepared to take part in the trial? It is entirely your decision. The names of the patients who are willing to take part are put into a computer, and the computer picks at random who will be on the new trial drug regime and who will be on the tried and tested recent drug regime which has proved most successful so far.'

She glanced toward Anna, who was looking horrified.

'You are asking me to play Russian roulette with my son's life,' Anna said fearfully. 'You want to use him as a guinea pig. I just want you to tell us which you feel will give him the best chance.'

Patrick added sensibly, 'what would you do if it was your child?'

'I realise the predicament you're in,' said the consultant, 'and that it's been sprung on you, and of course we will leave you alone to discuss it, but please don't leave it too long as every minute we delay the treatment, whichever is chosen, it will take longer to be effective and speed is important.'

Her last statement reinforced the urgency of the situation.

The team rose to their feet and left the room, but not before Jane turned to say, 'Believe me I do understand that you're still in shock and this is not an easy decision to make.'

As the medical team left the room and closed the door behind them, there was complete silence for a moment.

'I just want them to take responsibility for what is best for Rob,' said Anna. 'I can't make such a decision. Suppose we chose the wrong path?'

Patrick remained silent.

Then after what seemed an eternity, Rob said, 'Well the way I look at it mum is that if we let a computer decide for us, then if things go wrong we can blame the computer and not ourselves.' Despite the seriousness of the situation he managed a smile.

With the clear thinking of youth and strength that she was proud of, Anna realised that her son truly was on the way to maturity. Surely that was the most sensible reasoning of all.

She rushed out of the room and caught up with the team further down the corridor.

'Rob has decided,' she said, and then told them his exact words.

'Good,' said Jane with a smile. 'Then we'll get started with the trial treatment right away.' She turned and said something to the nurse who nodded and went off to the treatment room.

Anna re-joined Patrick and Rob, and she handed Patrick the key to Room 3 in the hostel. It was a private house in a back road and within sight of the ward, converted to hold up to twenty relatives who may need to stay close to the hospital. Funded by the charity CLIC – Cancer and Leukaemia in Children - it had been set up by Sir Malcolm Sargent the famous orchestral conductor.

'I'll go and investigate,' Patrick said, 'drop my things off and come back'

His "things" were in fact a rather tatty pink and mauve back pack.

Within ten minutes, the nurse had set up a bag full of bright blue fluid and attached it to the drip line.

'It looks like poison,' said Rob.

'Well you could say it is,' said Sophie the nurse, 'but it is a poison that is going to kill off the bad cells. You'll notice that there are two lumens on the cannula.' Then seeing Rob's puzzled expression, she added 'lumens are where the line divides into two tubes so that we can give you a blood transfusion or administer another drug at the same time as the chemotherapy drug.'

Rob laid his head back on the pillow. If it was at all possible to look even paler, he was. All remaining colour had drained from his cheeks.

'There's a funny metal taste in my mouth,' he said, 'and I can feel it really cold as it goes up my arm.'

'That's the drug. Unfortunately, it does change the taste buds. You may find that all the foods that used to be your favourites you can't tolerate any longer and you'll want something totally different. But don't panic this is perfectly normal and you'll get your old appetite back once the drug has left your system.'

What she did not say was that once this drug was finished, there would be another and another and it would be a long time before he really fancied eating anything again at all.

As the day gathered pace, there seemed no time to breathe before the next event.

Rob was weighed and then sent down to have a heart echo. This was an ultra sound in full colour, mainly bright red and blue, which showed how his heart was operating and to make sure the blood flow was correct.

'We have to do this,' explained Sophie, 'because some of the drugs are so toxic they can affect the heart and the liver, and we need to keep a close eye on what's happening and if necessary change the drug.'

In the darkened X-ray room Anna was allowed to stand by her son for this procedure.

He had been wheeled down on his bed as by now he was too weak even for a wheelchair. Anna walked alongside and pushed the drip stand while the porter and a nurse manipulated the bed round corners and out of the ward.

Of course, this trip involved using a lift but it was a much bigger lift used for beds, so she did not feel so closed in. However, as the porter pushed the bed into the lift, the nurse told her to hurry and not be left outside with the drip stand. Apparently not long before someone had not been quick enough, and the lift doors had closed on the line, leaving the patient inside the lift, and the drip stand on the outside with the danger that the line would be trapped in the doors and dragged down as the lift descended. The nurse who was inside with the patient had the temerity to detach the drip immediately as the lift started in motion. This would remain a dread of Anna's over the next few weeks as she wheeled her son around on her own while he was attached to drips.

The radiographer asked Rob to turn on his side and face the wall, and after oiling his chest she then began to roll the head of the ultra sound over his heart.

On the screen Anna could see Rob's heart in every colourful detail. Each valve as it flapped open and closed to let the blood through one way or the other, each contraction of the heart muscle.

She felt a chill of fear. She was looking at the very core of his being, the part of him that kept him alive, and she could not help wondering how long his heart would go on beating and how long would those valves snap open and shut. She fought back tears at the mere thought.

***

Once they had returned to the ward she found that Patrick was waiting.

'Have you eaten anything?' he asked Anna

'I can't remember when I last ate,' she replied. 'I really don't feel hungry.'

'You must keep your strength up,' he said, 'for Rob's sake if not your own. Otherwise you'll never cope.'

'Mind if I take mum down to the canteen for something?' he asked Rob.

'No go ahead,' said Rob. 'I just want to sleep anyway.'

So together Patrick and Anna headed for the lift which would take them to the lower ground floor where the dining room was situated.

As the lift doors closed, Patrick took Anna into his arms. 'I love you,' he said. 'Always have and always will. I am going to ask her to leave,' (meaning the interloper who had in Anna's eyes stolen her place) and with that he kissed her and said, 'I have been waiting to do that ever since I saw you again yesterday.'

His arms around her, and the warmth and familiar smell of him brought Anna a feeling of comfort and security and also a longing that things could be how they had been before, but the hurt was still an open wound.

They jumped apart guiltily as the doors opened.

Walking hand in hand to the dining room Anna said, 'I must ask the consultant what is the cause of leukaemia.'

'It's an illness that remains a mystery as far as I know from my GP experience,' said Patrick.

But Anna thought, even with his medical background, he had been out of the picture for some years now, so would not necessarily be aware of how things had progressed.

Patrick ate heartily, but Anna could only play with her food.

She looked outside the dining room window into the little courtyard with a lone tree in the centre. The leaves were turning to autumn even though summer was still in full flood. Small birds flitted in and out of the branches cheerfully, picking up crumbs from sandwiches where some members of staff sat outside to eat their packed lunch.

'Will life ever be normal again,' she wondered. 'Could it ever be normal after all that has happened? I don't even know what 'normal' is any more.'

CHAPTER 5 'FIRST STEPS'
21st August 1997

A nother broken night passed followed by another early morning start. The alarm attached to the cannula in Rob's hand had summonsed the nurse many times throughout hit fitful restless sleep.

At one stage, the nurse had to change the vein where the cannula was situated.

'The problem is,' she said, 'the drug is so powerful it can cause the peripheral veins to collapse, and this has happened. We will have to keep finding a new site until the Hickman Line is inserted. So sorry Rob, I know this is uncomfortable.'

Anna had already been up and about for an hour before Patrick reappeared at the door.

'You can see the CLIC house from here,' he announced walking over to the window and indicating one of the ordinary looking properties on the road behind the hospital. 'That one with the conservatory extension built on the back, my room is exactly above the point of the conservatory.'

'Did you sleep well?' asked Anna.

'Like a log. It's very comfortable over there,' said Patrick. 'Are you ready for some breakfast then?' he added.

'Still thinking of his stomach first,' thought Anna with some annoyance. 'Hasn't even asked how Rob is feeling.'

Despite having started the treatment, Rob actually looked terrible, but then that was to be expected. They had been warned the drug would make him feel really bad before any good would come of it. Things would get worse before getting better. They had also been told that his hair would start falling out at some stage.

'The best way to cope with that,' Sophie had said 'is to wait until it starts to fall out and then shave it all off. This saves bits of hair getting into your clothes and annoying you. Anyway you are lucky to be a guy; it's really cool to have a shaved head these days.'

What she hadn't warned him at the time was that it would affect the hair all over his body too, even his eyelashes and eyebrows. The harsh drugs attacked all the fast growing cells in the body.

Rob had already started suffering from some of the other side effects. He felt very sick and struggled to keep a simple thing like toast down, even water posed a problem. 'Try flat coca cola,' Sophie had suggested. 'We don't know why, but when all else fails, patients seem to be able to tolerate that as a drink, even more so than water, but you have to let it go flat first.'

They were warned his blood count would soon plummet to naught. This stage was known as neutropaenea. Not only did the drug kill off all the fast growing cancer cells in the body, but also it would kill off the platelets, the clotting agents of the blood, as well as the red blood cells and the good white cells which would mean he would need blood transfusions and platelet transfusions. It was during this neutropaenic phase that he would be at his most vulnerable. No-one would be allowed near him if they had the slightest sign of a cold, and certain foods were off limits from the start of treatment. They included fruit, particularly grapes, as everything needed to be peeled properly. They were given a printed list of forbidden foods.

Rob managed a smile. 'You going to peel my grapes for me then Mum?' he asked.

'You may be lying back there like a Roman Emperor,' Anna joked 'but I draw the line at peeling grapes for you.'

Other surprising bans were black pepper, because it was dried out in the open and could pick up bacteria and fungi and also yoghurt because some had bacteria in them as part of the process when they were made. No microwave foods were allowed.

'Is that because of radiation?' Rob had asked.

'No,' said Sophie, 'but with a microwave it is easy not to heat food evenly so sometimes it is not cooked properly in the centre. You should have freshly cooked food.'

Bit by bit since their admission, they heard more and more of the challenges ahead and the rules of coping with the treatment.

They learnt that the reason his gums had been bleeding, and that he had a rash of small mauve marks on his chest, was because already the platelets had been nearly squashed out of existence by the rapidly dividing rogue white leukemic cells, so his blood was unable to clot. The leukaemia cells had almost destroyed his red blood cells that carried iron and oxygen which was the reason why he was so tired.

Rob was very closely monitored for fevers and any changes, and Anna could see now why it was so important to be in hospital and not at home. The nurses were careful not to overload them with too much information all at once, but just give them a bit at a time on a 'need to know' basis.

Anna made sure that Rob was as comfortable as possible and also notified the nurses that he was being left on his own before reluctantly following Patrick to the lifts.

Once they had reached the lower ground floor they walked hand in hand to the dining room. Patrick piled his plate high with the biggest cooked breakfast possible, and Anna just had a small plate of porridge.

They sat opposite each other at a table by the window.

Patrick suddenly reached across and took her hand.

'As you know I am going to ask Val to leave,' he said, 'but I need you to acknowledge our parting was entirely your fault, otherwise we can't go on. You pushed me too far which is why I hit you.'

Anna started shaking. She needed him so much and could not believe what he had just said. How could he or anyone for that matter, use blackmail in a situation like this? He was blatantly taking advantage of her vulnerable state to extract an admission that was not true. It sounded like a classic 'she made me do it' of the 'Eve made Adam eat the apple' scenario, but to use the dire situation that she and her son faced was despicable.

She was still staring at him in disbelief when thankfully one of the nurses came to join them at the table. Patrick could not put the pressure on while they had company and his manipulation was stopped abruptly.

It had stung Anna as if he had physically slapped her face. This was the man she had loved for five years. She had kept on giving him another chance after each violent 'episode' when with his anger spent, he would burst into tears and beg her forgiveness. Now he was using her weakness with Rob's desperate situation to get her to take the blame?

Still she loved him. Was she mad? She began to think she must be. They say love is a kind of madness. She felt sick to the stomach. He should love her back unconditionally just as she loved him, but it would seem he was incapable of such a thing.

On the way back up to the ward, Patrick announced that he would be leaving for home in half an hour, but would be back again the next day, so he would keep hold of the key to room 3. He even suggested that when he returned she might like to visit the room and see what it was like for herself. 'There's a good bath in the house too,' he said, 'much more relaxing than the shower you are using in Rob's room.'

She walked with him to the bus stop and together they sat on the wall, he with his arm around her shoulders. When it arrived they embraced and kissed, and as the bus left, Patrick held her gaze for as long as possible through the window before the bus was out of sight. She felt a strange loss as if part of her had left too.

With a heavy heart she started back to the ward.

On her way she met Jane the consultant.

'There is something I have been wanting to ask' Anna said 'What really causes leukaemia? You see I keep thinking it must be something I have or haven't done, and I need to know. I keep berating myself that it's all my fault somehow.'

'It's very normal for a mother to blame herself in this situation,' said Jane gently. 'But I can assure you it is nothing either of you have done. No-one knows for sure what it is that causes leukaemia, in fact there can be many causes, but it seems to be a set of unfortunate circumstances that come together to make the patient vulnerable. It may be something in the genetic make-up that causes susceptibility initially, but what we do now believe is that about five months before diagnosis, a virus of some sort is the final trigger.'

'So, some sort of virus lights the 'blue touch paper,' said Anna.

'That's right,' said Jane. 'That is the latest theory.'

They walked together for a while then parted ways. Jane turned to her office and Anna to Rob's room.

Anna's brain wouldn't switch off from the conversation she had just shared with the consultant. 'A virus is the final trigger,' Jane had said.

Anna thought back to the spring of that year, searching desperately for clues. Had Rob suffered any bad flu virus or any other kind of bug? But try as she might there appeared to be nothing … except that is … She stopped walking for a moment. About five months previously Rob and the rest of his class had the usual polio and tetanus booster which all children had at the age of fifteen before they are due to leave school.

Could this possibly have been the trigger? There did not seem to be any other possibility as Rob had been really fit all that year, right up until the last few weeks that is.

The hospital where they now were was a teaching hospital, and so Anna reasoned they would have a good medical library somewhere. She resolved that she would wait until there was a suitable moment to leave Rob, perhaps when he was asleep, and she would go down to the library. Maybe she could find out how the polio and tetanus vaccines were made. Perhaps they were suspended in some solution that could bring on an allergic reaction.

She was no scientist but had a very enquiring mind, and now that the idea had come to her, she was determined to check.

Rob was being sick again when she returned to him. She rushed to help. He looked so pathetic now and was too weak to go to the bathroom so needed her to get a bottle or bedpan, or sick bowl, or anything else for that matter.

Looking at his pathetic shape slumped over a bowl, she found it difficult to remember that only a few weeks ago he had been a strong fifteen-year-old, planning for his future.

Anna herself did not mind doing all these personal things for her son, but she acknowledged that it must be so hard for him to accept that he was thrown back to relying on her for everything again.

Kim, Rob's other designated nurse, had taken over from Sophie for two days.

Like Sophie, she was a kind and cheerful soul too. In fact, all the nurses were hand-picked for this ward, and had received special training. Some had come from Great Ormond Street Children's Hospital in London.

Kim entered the room and said 'We're hoping that we can get Rob down to theatre in a couple of days to have the Hickman Line put in. So, your last day for eating and drinking normally will have to be tomorrow. You will be 'nil by mouth' after tomorrow midnight.'

'I shall just be glad to get rid of this thing,' Rob said indicating the cannula which now had two drugs entering the lumens. 'Every time I move it triggers the alarm on the drip stand.'

'Well hopefully they will operate the day after tomorrow. We haven't been given a definite slot though, so we will have to keep our fingers crossed,' said Kim.

Now that Patrick had left, Anna stayed constantly by Rob's side, where she had really wanted to be all the time.

However, she did visit the ward kitchen for drinks on a regular basis. She might be able to manage without food, but cups of tea were essential. It also gave her a reason to get up and move her legs.

It was in the ward kitchen that she started to make friends with some of the other anxious mothers. They all had children, and some were even just babies, who were being treated for cancer or leukaemia. She soon found that she was not alone in blaming herself for her son's condition. Most of the parents were in a state of bewilderment and feeling it must have been something they had done.

The mother of a thirteen-month-old baby was still reeling from the news that her daughter had the same leukaemia as Rob. 'How can it be?' she kept saying 'What could have happened?'

There was another mother who was particularly kind to Anna. Her name was Kath and her son had been an in-patient on and off for five months for treatment of a rhabdomyosarcoma; a rare muscle cancer.

Kath was a cheerful woman, and happy to help all the other

mothers. But because her own son Matt was only a few months younger than Rob, she understood very well what Anna was going through.

'I know it all seems so new and frightening when you first come in,' she said, 'but you'll soon get used to the routine.'

When Anna next phoned her eldest son James, she asked if he could bring up a computer game and console for Rob, and also her guitar.

As they had a room to themselves, she felt it would be a good idea to have 'things to do' while they were confined as virtual prisoners and had no idea when next they would be home. 'Oh, and also could you bring up my word processor and some paper,' she added. 'I can then write a bit and put my feelings down, as well as send letters to people.'

That afternoon James and Alice turned up carrying an array of items which soon filled the small room. 'We'll have to find spaces in the cupboards for most of this,' said Anna. 'The cleaner is very particular about damp dusting every surface including the floor every day. They are very strict about the hygiene here as the patients are so vulnerable.'

Anna was greatly relieved to have James and Alice with her again, and even Rob perked up a bit.

'When you feel the time is right,' said Alice, 'I will shave your head Rob. I've just bought some new clippers for Brian and they haven't been used yet.'

'Great!' said Rob with mock enthusiasm.

They spent two hours together before her older children had to return home once more. It was such a comfort to have them there, but again Anna felt this tremendous fear and sense of loss as they left her.

Rob was exhausted by their visit and said 'I want to have a sleep Mum and could I have the television off?'

This would be the ideal opportunity for Anna to go exploring to find the medical library and start her research.

'Would you mind if I just wander around for a bit and leave you?' she asked Rob.

'No honestly mum, I will be happy just to close my eyes,' he said

Anna let the nurse on duty know where she was going, and that Rob would be alone for about an hour. Then she made her way down to the ground floor and followed the signs to the medical library.

She enrolled with the library as an ex nurse, and then looked through the rows and rows of medical books, not really sure where to start. 'Perhaps vaccinations would be a good beginning, plus haematology which would show how leukaemia changes the structure of the blood.' Anna thought.

Her mission and the hunt for reasons and explanations had begun. She had no idea where it would take her, but at least it gave her something positive to concentrate on and something to help take her mind off things she had no control over.

And with that thought she selected two large books from the shelves and headed for one of the desks and began to read.

CHAPTER 6 'ENDLESS WAIT'
August 1997

Rob was sweating heavily and getting weaker. Each time he moved his hand, or turned in bed, the familiar sing song alarm of the drip would alert the night staff, and by now both Rob and Anna just longed for a peaceful night.

Anna realised that fifteen is a difficult age for a boy. She knew it would embarrass him but at the same time she loved him so much she just wanted to wrap him up and make all the pain go away.

The best way she could help him was to just be there, both physically and emotionally. That was all any mother could do in the circumstances.

The nurses were marvellous and knew just the right way to treat him, with ultimate care and attention, but also with humour. They managed to joke with him and make him laugh. She remembered her anger when first entering the ward when she had heard loud laughter in the next room, but now she understood that this was an essential part of the healing process. Life should be kept as normal as possible in the face of a very abnormal situation.

There were certain things that Rob found easier to accept from his mother, rather than a pretty nurse just a few years older than he was. Bodily functions were the bane of his life. If it wasn't one end it was the other, and even though he resented having to rely on his mother again as if he were a toddler, it was easier for him if she carried these duties out rather than someone he fancied.

Whilst going on a trip to the kitchen, Anna saw a notice board with pictures of happy people smiling back at her. There was a young man with two small children, a student who had just graduated and a child enjoying herself in Disney World.

Kim came up behind her while she was gazing at these photos.

'That's our rogue's gallery,' said the nurse. 'All those you see there have been where Rob is now, but came through and were able to return to a normal life again. The young man with two children, well he had the same sort of leukaemia as Rob, and one of our ex patients is currently training as a doctor here.'

For the first time since they had been given the diagnosis, Anna felt her spirits lift slightly. So, it didn't have to be a death sentence after all. There is always hope. Miracles do happen.

And then, as Anna went off to make another cup of tea, the Consultant appeared with a smile on her face. 'Good news,' she said. 'Just had the final blood test results.'

For a brief moment Anna's heart leapt. 'They've made a mistake – it isn't leukaemia after all,' she thought. But Jane continued.

'Rob has a translocation of two particular chromosomes that mean instead of him having a 50% chance of recovery, it has gone up to a 70% chance,' said the Consultant.

If Anna had not previously been a nurse in that oh so distant life before she married, she would not have known 'a translocation of chromosomes' meant that by a trick of nature, a bit of one chromosome had 'broken off' and attached itself to another.

'In some types of leukaemia,' continued Jane, 'for a reason we don't understand, people have a better chance of survival when these two chromosomes have been translocated.'

The last ten minutes had lifted Anna out of a position of deep despair to one of hope.

For the first time since her arrival on the ward, she was tempted to buy a sandwich when the lunch trolley came around.

She gave Rob the good news. 'We are going to get out of this you know,' she said, 'even though you are feeling so rough at the moment there is a light at the end of the tunnel.'

Rob grinned 'If you say so mum.' But in reality he was feeling too awful and too weak to respond in a normal way.

And then Patrick materialised at the doorway in the ghostly fashion he seemed to have adopted. It was a new habit of appearing silently as though he was avoiding people. He took stock of the way that Rob was looking.

'How are you feeling old chap?' he enquired.

'Rubbish,' said Rob

'I like the colour of the booze going into your arm,' joked Patrick, 'matches the colour of your eyes.'

Rob smiled politely. He had not trusted Patrick for some time; not since the man had thrown him down the hall when he was eleven for not doing the washing up. It had happened in front of Alice, but both her son and daughter had decided not to tell Anna at the time because they knew how much she loved Patrick. Now Rob knew he had abused their mother as well, he could not look at the man with any feeling of friendship and just went along with it for Anna's sake. Deep inside, he hoped that his mother would not be tempted to return to the relationship.

Turning to Anna, Patrick said, 'How about coming over to look at the room I'm in. You can see what the whole house is like. They have a wonderful sitting room. It's very relaxing over there. Good for you to get out of the hospital atmosphere.'

Anna hesitated, torn once more between her erstwhile lover and her son.

'Its OK mum,' said Rob. 'I will be fine, I need to sleep a bit more. It's one way of ignoring all the side effects of this stuff.' He nodded toward the bag of brightly coloured fluid.

Anna watched as the drug steadily entered the line running into the back of his hand – drip, drip, drip. She couldn't help feeling 'that's poison they're giving him.'

'Go on mum,' urged Rob. 'I will be well looked after, you know that. It will be an excuse for me to get one of the nurses in here,' and he smiled. But inwardly Rob felt a pang of resentment. Patrick had suddenly come back into their lives and was now trying to manipulate his mother once more. He could see that but obviously she could not.

Reluctantly Anna let Patrick lead her by the hand out of the room, down in the lift to the basement, and across a car park. They then entered through a gate in a high wooden fence. Inside there was a garden and then the conservatory. Someone was relaxing in there reading a book, and seeing them approach, jumped up to open the door for them.

Patrick then took her upstairs to his single room. 'Look,' he said. 'You can see Rob's room from here.'

Then Patrick took her in his arms and said 'When I am at

home all I can think about is you and when I am here I never think of her and it is almost as if she doesn't exist. You must believe me.' Then he added, 'Please phone me any time you need to - but don't ring after 4.30pm as she will be back from work.'

Suddenly Anna felt like 'the other woman.' But she was not the usurper, Val was, and he had promised that she would be moving out.

'Isn't she going?' asked Anna 'I thought you said she would be leaving.'

'Well I have to do it gradually,' said Patrick awkwardly. 'After all she has to find somewhere else to live and I can't kick her out on the streets with all her belongings.'

'I don't see why not!' thought Anna.

Patrick led her to the bed and said 'have a lie down on a proper mattress.' Then he took her into his arms once more and before she knew it they were holding each other as if nothing extraordinary had ever happened.

To Anna she felt as if he had never made love to her like that before. He must surely love her truly.

At first there had been feelings of guilt. She should not be indulging herself while her son was suffering. His room was even visible from where they were. But finally she had totally abandoned herself to her lover, and tried to pretend everything was normal again.

'Perhaps it will all be alright in the end,' she thought. 'He could not behave like this with me if he cared anything for Val. Maybe we were meant to be together and so tragedy had drawn us back again.'

They lay in each other's arms for a while, feeling close and complete - even dozing briefly.

As Anna began stirring, Patrick said 'I'll run a bath. You might as well have the luxury of wallowing in water instead of a quick shower in the cramped en suite on the ward.'

She lay with the water and bubbles up to her chin and let the stress wash away from her. Reassured by his love making, and remembering what Jane had said, a flicker of hope for Rob's recovery crept cautiously through her mind.

Finally, she dragged herself out of the warm water and dried, putting back on her simple clothes which she had packed to cope with sitting alongside a patient in hospital.

'I'd better get back to Rob now,' she said.

Patrick seemed put out. 'Aren't you going to wait for me to have my bath?' he asked. 'We can go back to the ward together.'

'I've been away long enough now,' said Anna. 'Much as I would like to stay in this atmosphere where everything else seems like a bad dream, the truth is that my son is the one who needs me most.'

It was clear Patrick did not approve of this. In his world, he should always come first whatever the situation. Nothing had changed that attitude. But he could not compete with her son fighting for his life.

As she turned to leave she said, 'I've started some research into what I think may have triggered Rob's leukaemia.'

'Oh yes,' said Patrick rather grumpily, 'so what's that then?'

'Last evening, I went to in medical library to look up about how polio vaccines are made' she said. 'Rob had a booster just at about the time the consultant reckons he would have had some sort of contact with a virus that triggered the leukaemia. That is what made me think about it.'

'And?' asked Patrick 'go on.'

'Well – have you ever heard of SV40?'

'Never,' said Patrick 'Have you found out what it is?'

'I hoped you might know what it was,' said Anna. 'It's just that I found a reference to the fact that, whatever it is, it contaminated polio vaccines in the 1950s, 60s and early 70s. The thought of any sort of contamination at any time made me wonder… could whatever it is, still be contaminating the vaccines.'

'Well the only way to find out is to go on reading through the medical books,' said Patrick. 'Just keep following your instinct.'

'They do have computers there,' said Anna, 'but you have to book in a time and they are usually only available for the medical students. And anyway, I have no idea how to use a computer.'

Then she turned again and said, 'I'll see you back on the ward soon.'

Patrick lay in the bath mulling over Anna's ideas.

'She could just possibly be onto something' he said to himself.

***

Eventually he re-joined Anna and Rob on the ward.

'I hate having to leave again later today,' he said, 'but I've got to check on the post and things at home. Don't forget to phone, any time during the day - just avoid the evenings as I said.'

'I don't understand why she has such a hold on you if you are asking her to leave,' said Anna.

'Well you know how it is,' he mumbled. 'I hate any sort of trouble.'

Rob gave his mother a certain look as much to say, 'don't trust him mum', but she missed it; or perhaps it was that she did not really want to acknowledge it.

CHAPTER 7 'MORE CONFUSION'
August 1997

Patrick left again later that day. This time he handed the key to room number 3 at the CLIC hostel back to the housekeeper. He had received a rather curt note from her stating that he was not supposed to hang on to it while not using the room. As the housekeeper explained, the rooms were in great demand, and he could not block one when he wasn't at the hospital.

'I'll be up again as soon as I can,' he promised Anna as she accompanied him to the bus stop outside the hospital. He gave her a kiss and a hug. 'Keep going with the research,' he said.

Once more she felt bereft as she returned to Rob's room alone. Although Patrick seemed a strange mixture of moods and promises at the moment, they had been together for five years, so she was sure he meant what he said about loving her, not Val, and that the woman would be leaving. It had been good to have his support, and he had been present at a couple of the ward rounds and been able to join in the discussion about treatment. It helped to have another adult there as he had predicted.

Of course, James had let their father Chris know what was going on, but Chris lived in a very remote part of Lincolnshire now, and he did not seem anxious to come down to see his sick son.

Rob was deteriorating despite the hopeful news earlier in the day. It concerned Anna greatly and upset her to see him suffer. She felt helpless yet again.

He now had ulcers erupting in his mouth which made eating difficult. He was still losing weight at a speed that was frightening.

In the afternoon James and Alice, and Alice's husband Brian, came up to visit. They were visibly shocked at the change in Rob. He could no longer sit up on his own, unless propped up on the pillows.

'Want a game?' asked James indicating the computer console. We could get the James Bond one up on the TV.'

'Okay,' said Rob trying to sound enthusiastic. 'But don't expect any great moves from me at the moment.'

While her sons kept occupied with James Bond, Alice and her mother went to the kitchen to make some tea.

Alice was in tears. 'Mum, I thought this treatment was supposed to make him better.'

Anna said, 'I know,' and she put her arms around her daughter. 'But I believe it is one of those things that make you worse before any good signs appear. Don't forget, the chemotherapy is killing off good cells as well as the bad. His whole digestive system is ulcerated, and he doesn't want much to eat except a bit of toast and even that he can't chew properly because of the ulcers. We just have to trust the medical team that they know what they are doing.'

'How long will it be before he picks up?' asked Alice wiping the tears away. 'He's my little brother.'

'I really don't know, this is his first batch of treatment so it is unknown territory for us. This one will last ten days, then the neutrophil cells in the blood count will plummet down to nought. That will be his most vulnerable time, when the slightest cold or infection could be fatal if not acted on immediately, but it means that the leukaemia cells will hopefully have taken a bashing too. That is when they give blood and platelet transfusions to get him back up. And then it starts all over again.'

'It's so cruel,' sobbed Alice. 'What has he ever done to deserve this?'

By now Anna was crying too and they held on to each other. 'I don't know,' she sobbed, 'it just doesn't make sense.'

They composed themselves and went back to join the brothers who were laughing.

It lifted Anna's heart to see that Rob could still laugh despite everything.

'Can I have a go?' asked Alice

'Ok' said James 'but you won't be any good at it' and unfortunately he was right. Alice could not manage the controls and her attempt at being James Bond ended up with the hero staring at the ground and shooting himself in the foot while walking backwards.

By the end of the game they were all laughing helplessly and ridiculously. It was so much better than crying which was the supressed emotion always just below the surface.

Later after they had gone home, Rob felt quite shattered.

Nurse Kim entered the room. 'Don't forget, no food or drink after midnight tonight and with any luck you will be in theatre tomorrow and the Hickman Line in place. It will give you a bit more peace.' She did not add that it would also give the nurses a bit more peace too. While Rob had been playing the game, the alarm was going off almost continuously as Rob moved his hand, and the nurses had been in and out of his room every few minutes to check it wasn't a real emergency.

But the next day, all their plans were thwarted. Emergencies and staff shortages prevented Rob from having a theatre slot, despite him being fully prepared.

He was getting dehydrated, and very hungry, so when evening came he was allowed a small drink and he managed a bit of bread. Then from midnight again it was nil-by-mouth.

'I am sure you will go to theatre tomorrow,' said Kim hopefully. 'Sophie will be back on duty then.'

Another fretful night followed, and once more the vein where the cannula was situated collapsed, and they had to find yet another site. It was really painful for him. He was skin and bone now, and they had to make several attempts.

Anna found it unbearable to see her son suffer like this. His eyes had become dull and the ulcers in his mouth had become infected. One of his gums was very swollen and giving cause for concern.

'We'll get a maxillofacial specialist to look at that,' said the consultant when she found out. 'It might be an abscess that needs dealing with. We have to keep on top of any infections.' Turning to her registrar she said, 'I think we will put him on a broad spectrum antibiotic to be on the safe side.'

'Yet more tablets,' said Rob. 'I am already beginning to rattle.'

'We'll put it in by drip,' said Jane. 'It will be assimilated by your body quicker.'

The following day, again Rob waited for his theatre slot, but the evening came and still no call for his operation.

Once more he was allowed to eat and drink something small late in the evening, but not after midnight. However, by now, what with the infection in his gum, the ulcers in his mouth and having gone so long without food, he no longer felt like eating anything at all.

The fifth day arrived, and still the same series of events followed.

Anna was getting desperate. She hadn't left Rob's side, and had abandoned her research for the time being.

She phoned Patrick. He was quite chatty to start with and then said 'Shhh – got to go, she's coming up the driveway,' and he put the phone down.

This left Anna feeling very odd and unsettled. Why was he so afraid of this woman?

The sixth day arrived and still no sign of Rob going to theatre. He was getting desperate by now and the medical team were becoming frustrated.

Again Anna rang Patrick for support, but this time she had a terrible shock. Val answered the phone.

For a while Anna was stunned into silence. 'Oh, oh…' she hesitated 'is Patrick there?'

'Yes,' said the syrupy sweet voice. 'Is that Anna? I'll just go and get him.'

Patrick picked up the phone 'Hello?' he said in a hard voice. 'I've actually just phoned James to let him know I will be away for a few days and I asked him to tell you.'

'Well he hasn't phoned yet,' said Anna. 'Why not tell me direct? Where are you going then?'

'We are going to Exeter to stay with my mother and sister for a few days,' said Patrick coldly. 'I had hoped James would tell you so that we would not have this confrontation,' he added.

'We?' said Anna shocked. 'You mean you are taking her to meet your mother and sister? What about this promise she was going to be asked to leave?'

'Look I don't want any trouble,' said Patrick sharply.

'But you promised…' said Anna limply. 'You asked me to let you know what is going on here, and it is dreadful, we need your support. And in fact, you told me you were coming up to see us in a couple of days…' she tailed off.

'Well we are going to Exeter and that is that,' said Patrick and slammed the phone down.

Anna felt sick with fear. The support she was depending on had suddenly and cruelly been taken away again. She stared at the receiver in her hand and listened to the dialling tone on the end of the line. He had cut her off!

The conversation had taken place on the phone in Rob's room, but she had been behind a curtain and talked quietly.

However, he still had heard.

'You OK mum?' he asked weakly

'Oh oh yes fine,' said Anna lying. 'I've just got to go out for minute, won't be long.'

She went quickly from the room, her head ringing with the treachery she had just been subjected to. 'You don't take someone to meet your family if you are really on the point of throwing them out,' she thought desperately and suddenly felt tremendous hatred for this other woman.

But it was then she realised just how manipulative Patrick was. After all, if he could say awful things about the other woman to her, she wondered what he might be saying to the other woman about her in return. He could well be building up some story full of lies about both of them and playing one woman off against the other. Perhaps that was how he got his kicks. Surely, he could not feel as deeply for Val as he did for her… or could he? Maybe his so-called feelings had been a sham all along, right from the beginning of their relationship.

'Hardly surprising he can't bear to be left alone with himself,' she thought. 'He is running away from what he really is. Can a man be that weak and treacherous?'

Anna did not know where she was going. She just had an urge to run up and down the six flights of stairs in an effort to do something, anything, rather than stay in the room stunned where Rob would notice. She again had the feeling she wanted to wrap her son in her arms and run home where everything was secure, and she had trusted family around her.

Her hands were clammy with shock; her heart was pounding with fear. She was alone again and in a very dark place.

She went back to the ward and said to Sophie 'I am just going down to the medical library; can you keep an eye on Rob for me?' she asked. 'I've just had a terrible shock and don't want him to pick up on it. Tell him I am fine and have just gone to the shops in the main entrance and will be back soon.'

'Okay,' said Sophie, studying Anna's frantic expression. 'Are you sure you are alright?' she asked.

'Yes, yes I will be quite OK. I just need a bit of space to quieten down for a moment.'

Anna walked along the corridor to the medical school where the library was situated. She asked for some paper and a pen, and then picking up from where she had previously left off, she continued reading about the vaccine and trying to find out what this SV40 really was. It seemed better to set her mind concentrating on something constructive. Perhaps it would take her mind off Patrick and his lies and deceit.

She found a heavy and detailed book on viruses which explained their construction and effects. Checking in the index she found the word SV40. At last she might find out what this illusive intruder was.

What she then began to read filled her with horror.

SV40, stood for Simian Virus 40, and turned out to be a monkey virus. The reason it was associated with the polio vaccine was because the vaccine itself was made on a culture of monkey kidney cells.

She continued to read that SV40 was cancerous in any mammal other than the monkey itself; that it translocated chromosomes, and even the very ones that identified Rob's type of leukaemia. It was evident in the white cells.

Dodging from book to book she found more damning evidence of possible contamination. Both the inactivated and the live vaccines had been found to be contaminated by SV40 in the 1950s, 1960s and early 1970s. However, it was believed that such contamination had been eliminated by changing from the use of the kidney cells of Macaque monkeys who were known to be carriers, to the use of the wild African Green monkey. But Anna wondered how they could be so sure.

According to other excerpts she read that the wild African Green monkey had proved to be very susceptible to the SV40 virus in laboratory conditions – therefore surely contamination was still possible she reasoned.

There was another thought too which struck her. The polio virus, and therefore vaccine, is absorbed through the gut, and the gut lining is very thin in order to aid digestion. Supposing another virus, such as SV40 or any other monkey virus for that matter, "piggy backed" on the polio vaccine and was absorbed into the bloodstream through the gut. That would be one way in which a rogue virus such as SV40 could gain admission into the body – by the "back door".

The whole idea of vaccines being made on kidney cells from another mammal so close to our own species filled her with disbelief.

And then Anna stopped in her tracks. It could also explain a lot of the other cancers that very young children and babies were getting. After all, doses of the polio vaccine were given at two, then three, and then four months, so there was plenty of opportunity for any contamination to take hold early on in a baby's life.

She remembered being told during her nursing days that the reason they had to give three vaccines in such a short time was because there were three strains of polio. Complete immunity to all strains was not triggered in the first vaccine, but would be activated and completed in the second and third doses.

Frantically she began writing, making notes, taking references. She knew that if any report she wrote was to be taken seriously, it was vital to have it backed up with proper references to text books and articles.

After an hour she felt very tired and realised just how long she had been down there.

'I wish I could discuss this with Patrick,' she thought sadly. 'It's always good to have someone else with medical knowledge to bounce ideas off.' And once more the rawness of the situation hit her.

They would be there in Exeter by now, with his mother and sister whom she had known for many years. Val would be taking her place.

Her feelings were confused. Was he being deliberately cruel? How could he be so duplicit and how could he have made love to her like that in room 3 of the hostel, only to turn his back on her a few days later?

With a heavy heart she made her way back up to the ward. Rob was asleep.

Silently she pulled the bed from the wall and climbed in. But there was no way she would be able to sleep. She just turned to face her son and wept silently. Would he really pull through this terrible ordeal, or was it already too late? He looked so ill.

At the end of the day, no matter how much her heart was breaking over Patrick, it was her son that she loved the most; well all three children equally, but it was Rob she needed to be with at that moment just in case he slipped away silently in the night. Despite what Sophie had told them both when Rob was first admitted, she still had that fear continually lurking just below the surface.

CHAPTER 8 'CHALLENGES'
27th August 1997

A nother day dawned, and yet another hope was dashed. There was still no space on the operating list.

Rob no longer complained he was thirsty or hungry. He had a saline drip attached to one of the lumens from the cannula as he had become so dehydrated. He no longer struggled to get out of bed and did not complain about what was on the television, not even the Telly Tubbies, he was too weak now.

Anna did not leave his side. She felt she was losing him moment by moment, and whereas at first every full day had been a challenge, it had gradually reduced to counting every hour, every half hour and now every five minutes.

When Jane the consultant came around to see how he was getting on, she took one look at him and said 'I am going to insist he goes to theatre tomorrow; whatever their pressures are on their list. This is ridiculous, we have never had to wait this long before.'

So at least now they knew the Hickman Line would definitely be put in place the next day, but it did not prevent another of Rob's veins collapsing with the entry of the next toxic chemotherapy drug, so once again he had to undergo the painful procedure of finding a new vein to re-site the cannula.

Anna deliberately put all thoughts of Patrick out of her mind, although they had a nasty habit of creeping in when she was not concentrating. Every now and then she wondered what he and the other woman would be doing. Would "they" be going on a day out to Exeter Cathedral and having coffee in that little shop with his mother as she herself had done only a few months previously? What would his mother make of it? His mother had once inadvertently introduced Anna as her 'daughter-in-law' to a friend so at least she had assumed the relationship was serious.

The next day, Rob was wheeled down to theatre on his bed in the early afternoon. It had been such a long wait. Anna was allowed to go with him into the anaesthetic room.

As the anaesthetist injected the drug that would put him to sleep, Anna watched Rob slip into unconsciousness. She could no longer hold back the tears and wept uncontrollably.

The nurse put an arm around her and led her out into the corridor again.

'He will be fine with us,' she promised. 'We will keep him here for about an hour and a half, and then he will be back on the ward. Why don't you get a cup of tea?'

But Anna did not want a cup of tea. Although meant kindly, why did everyone think "a cup of tea" was the cure all for stress? Instead she felt the urge to walk and keep walking. She wanted to exhaust herself until she could not think of anything anymore, so she left the hospital and headed off toward the city centre. Something drove her on and it was almost as if her feet had taken possession of her body. Perhaps if she kept active, her brain might switch off she hoped.

Unfortunately, all her thoughts were intermingled, and raced around her brain like cars on a speed track so that she hardly took in her surroundings, unaware of the bright summer day, green trees, flowers and twittering birds of an English summer.

Eventually, she came across a park and sat on a bench watching a game of bowls. It wasn't until she sat down, she realised just how tired her limbs were.

She had barely spent five minutes staring vacantly at the white clad pensioners leisurely rolling the balls across the turf, before she glanced at her watch and realised she must get back to the hospital immediately as Rob would soon be out of theatre. Anna desperately wanted to be there on the ward when he returned.

It was when she finally reached the road behind the hospital that her mind snapped out of its paralysis and she became suddenly aware of a gang of boys aged ten or eleven coming towards her.

They surrounded her, and one approached giggling. 'Want to shake my hand?' he asked and put his hand toward her. She suddenly realised that had she done so, her handbag would have been snatched off her shoulder.

She was overwhelmed by a terrifying anger that she had never felt over anything before.

It frightened her to realise she could have killed this boy quite easily and without any regret, attacking him with her bare fists, fired by pent up fury - anger at the world, anger at the disease, anger at Rob's suffering and anger at Patrick's cruelty. Up until this point, she had kept control over irrational feelings, but now pure hatred manifested itself against this little thug.

'Why is scum like this allowed to roam the streets, when decent children are suffering and dying on a ward within a stone's throw?' Anna thought.

She hurried on, but reported the incident of the boys' intent to snatch her handbag to the porter at the main desk. 'Oh, so they have started that up again have they,' he nodded.

So not only were these boys the scum of the earth, they were obviously known to the authorities already. Why had no-one done anything about it? The parents were obviously as bad as they were.

She ran up the stairs to the ward, as she still avoided using the lifts, and she had found that each time she climbed the steps she could go just that bit further without having to stop and pant for breath. No wonder she was losing weight. She had noticed it when she was standing in front of the mirror in the bathroom at the CLIC house.

Arriving back just in time, she was informed that Rob was being sent back from theatre. 'He'll be here in a minute.'

Anna waited with a heavy heart empty of all feeling except sadness. Would her son really make it through the six months intensive treatment? Would they ever see home together again? Each precious moment could be his last.

When he was wheeled in, he was drowsy, and now a Hickman line with two lumens disappeared into his chest wall.

Suddenly he seemed even more vulnerable than before, if that was possible. Anna looked uncomfortably at the plugs blocking the end of both lumens. 'That line goes straight to his heart' she thought with a certain amount of terror. 'All that separates his heart directly from the world outside are those two plugs.'

Wilf the charge nurse came into the room. He had been a

Lieutenant Commander in the Royal Navy and trained as a nurse. He had joked with Anna that often nurses from the Royal Navy would be required to go to parties, but of course no-one had expected male nurses and he used to enjoy the look on the faces of the hosts when he turned up.

'Tomorrow we are arranging for a heart echo,' he said. 'It's non-invasive; a bit like the sort of ultra sound scan when you check on a baby in the womb. We need to keep a regular report as the drug he is on can affect the heart and liver, and any damage unfortunately cannot be reversed, which is why we monitor it so closely. We'll stop the drug at the first sign of any adverse reaction.'

For a moment Anna felt complete despair. 'So, if the illness doesn't get him, then the treatment will.'

To her surprise, when Rob came around from the anaesthetic shortly afterwards he seemed quite upbeat. 'At last,' he said, 'no more needles, and no more broken nights. I will be able to play the computer game too without sounding off the alarms.'

'You seem to be losing bits of your hair on the pillow,' observed Anna.

'Okay,' said Rob, 'then I reckon it's time to get Alice up with the clippers. I must admit it is beginning to irritate my neck.'

The phone extension in Rob's room gave them easy access to family and friends without having to go into the day room and use the public phone.

She called Alice. 'Next time you come up, can you bring the clippers? Rob is ready for his head to be shaved,' explained

Anna.

'Of course,' said Alice, 'and as James's birthday is in a couple of days, I thought of bringing a cake and some balloons so he can have a family party that includes Rob.'

It wasn't that Anna had forgotten her eldest son's birthday on the 1st of September, but she was not in a position to make cakes, or buy presents for that matter, and it was a relief that Alice was taking charge.

Although they had a phone in their room, there were certain calls that Anna arranged to make and receive using the public phone in the day room. They were the calls when she wanted to be brutally honest about what was going on both with his treatment and other things, such as Patrick's behaviour, when she did not want Rob to overhear.

She had two trusted friends each of whom were wonderful sounding boards, but with very different attitudes.

Ruth had been friends with her since their daughters had been to school together from the age of four. She and Anna had quickly formed a bond of friendship that had grown stronger over the years. They even took up tap dancing together, and when Ruth had a cleaning job in a factory after closing hours, they used to smuggle their tap shoes in and use the factory floor for practice, while their two daughters played within sight on the swings outside.

Ruth of all people understood the quandary with Patrick. She too had once been in love with a physically abusive man and admitted to still being in love with him now, despite having had to divorce him and move on. Her last traumatic beating had involved the police who had intervened as her husband was banging her head on the pavement outside their home.

'Patrick rang me you know,' said Ruth when Anna phoned. 'He says he really loves you still and doesn't know what he was thinking about. He says he will be up as planned next week.'

'But he has taken that woman up to stay with his mother,' said Anna with disgust.

'Well it was only yesterday he phoned me,' said Ruth, 'so maybe things are not going as well as he hoped. Perhaps he will get a grip on his anger too,' she continued. 'Maybe you can be together one day as I always hoped would happen with me and Will.'

But the fact of the matter remained, that although Ruth fully understood Anna's feelings, she had never been able to trust Will again, and despite her longings had never gone back to live with him.

Anna also unburdened herself to Rob's godmother who she had been friends with since schooldays. Laura, which was her nickname and stage name as she was an actress, had a very different idea. 'You should really ditch him now,' she said to Anna. 'He is mentally unstable and addicted to women and sex. If a tree had a hole at the right height he'd have a go at that!' Anna sometimes found her friend's forthright manner difficult to handle particularly if she was in a sensitive frame of mind; although she couldn't help laughing. 'And by the way, I never felt free to tell you before, but he even came on to me when I was staying with you,' continued Laura. 'Get rid of him. After all, if he really loved you, he wouldn't move another woman in with him within 6 weeks of scaring you away having beaten you up. And anyway,' she continued, 'I didn't tell you this before either, although I wrestled with my conscience, because you were so happy. I found out that his wife left him because he beat her up as well and not because of the affair he told you about, although no doubt that contributed. A leopard never changes its spots, only in this case it is a cockroach.'

The problem was that Laura spoke the truth and life exactly as she saw it. Whereas Ruth, because she had been in a similar situation, knew how difficult it was to stop loving someone you loved so deeply, despite the bad treatment. And the worst part was that most other people thought you were mad to stay with an abusive partner, unless of course they had experienced it themselves. It seemed universal behaviour that after an outburst of anger, the partner would be full of remorse and promise it would never happen again. They would return to the gentle person you always thought they were… until the next time that is.

And now, battling through this entire trauma with Rob and without any support from her ex-husband, she seemed to need Patrick all the more. Not the abusive and disloyal Patrick, but the Patrick she had first fallen in love with. Even though she realised that love had blinded her original feelings for him and he was obviously not that person she loved or hoped he was and who probably had never even existed.

Now that Rob was more settled, and the first ten days treatment was coming to an end, Anna felt free to visit the medical library again.

The more she read about the history of SV40 and the polio vaccine, the more she was convinced the polio booster had been the trigger to Rob's leukaemia. And she remembered another thing; at the same time as the polio vaccine was given, a tetanus injection was given. In one of the text books it stated quite plainly that a tetanus injection should never be given at the same time as any other vaccination or immunisation, because it made the immune system vulnerable and susceptible to attacks from other viruses. The polio vaccine was live.

Picking up the trail again, she was struck with another thought. 'I had a polio vaccine when they first came out despite having already had the disease. Supposing, just supposing the vaccination I received was contaminated, and I am a carrier of SV40 in some way, and if so, has the contamination been passed to Rob where it has lain dormant?'

'It's well known that some viruses, such as the herpes family, are capable of remaining dormant in the body until triggered later by something,' she remembered. 'That is why when someone has chicken pox, it can be reactivated later as shingles.'

And then her heart chilled. 'What about that strange virus Rob suffered soon after his admission when his whole body had become covered in tiny red spots. Even the palms of his hands and the soles of his feet were covered with the rash which is unusual. The specialist had never managed to identify it; could it have been a form of SV40? Did anyone know what symptoms SV40 showed in monkeys? Although SV40 only turned cancerous in mammals other than the monkey host, surely it would manifest itself in some way on the original animal?'

She became so engrossed with the ever-increasing pile of books that she had added to her table in the medical library that she lost all sense of time.

Anna was becoming very tired with all the reading and concentration. Before deciding to finish she found one final clue.

One of the reference books referred to the fact that in Africa, it had been discovered that the Epstein Barr virus, the virus that causes glandular fever, was capable of producing lymphomas, particularly when coupled with malaria.

Glandular fever had been going around his class earlier that year and she wondered if perhaps that had triggered his leukaemia. But then she remembered how they had first tested him for glandular fever or its anti-bodies, and there was no sign that he had had it. So, it would appear to rule out that theory.

She made some hasty final notes. As always, she recorded the references and dates of her findings as proof of her research, and then she put the huge pile of books back and took the three sheets of A4 filled with almost illegible scribble and placed them in her handbag.

Around her she was surprised to see that the library had all but emptied, and looking at her watch, she realised just how late it was.

She ran back up the stairs to the ward.

Wilf, the charge nurse, said with a nod 'Have you seen the message on our notice board?' He pointed to the sign and Anna read -

"Missing one mother, late forties, blonde hair, reasonably good looking with the light behind her but completely dotty. If anyone finds her please return her to room number one."

She faced Wilf who was grinning widely. 'You should have seen what he really wanted me to put!' he laughed. 'We had to edit the original as this is a children's ward.'

Rob was glad to see her.

'I am so sorry,' she said. 'You were quite happy when I left for the library and I just lost all sense of time.'

'Its OK mum,' said Rob, 'but I was worried because I know you are upset about Patrick and you have been a very long time.'

'Please don't worry about him any more,' said his mother. 'I'm not giving him another thought,' she lied.

And with that she plugged in the word processor that James had brought up, and she started typing up the report on her findings about SV40 and the polio vaccine.

CHAPTER 9 'BREAKTHROUGH'
End of August / September 1st 1997

Look,' said Anna, pointing out her notes to Kath when they met in the ward kitchen. 'The same chromosomes we now know are the ones that have been affected in Rob's genetic code are also translocated by SV40.'

'Actually,' said Kath, 'Matt had the polio vaccine shortly before he became ill too. I wonder if there is anything in your idea.'

'Well I am certainly going to fire off some letters to the Secretary of State for Health, and a few Cancer Specialists,' said Anna. 'It's too much of a co-incidence and anyway, it could explain why we even have such small babies and toddlers in here too. And a lot of the teenagers who have been admitted are just the right age to have had the booster in the previous spring term.'

Kath, the mother of the other teenager Matt who was currently still on the ward, had been such a support to Anna. She had calmed her down and talked to her when they were first admitted, and also told her, quite rightly, that it would not be long before she would become accustomed to the routines of the ward, and that she would soon learn to trust the staff.'

Kath had also told Anna that she was still being driven mad by people asking her 'what protocol was Matt on' – in other words what sort of treatment package. Well he did not have one. The doctors were taking a rain check as they went along and deciding on the spot what treatment to follow. 'It's so frustrating,' she confided in Anna, 'other people seem to think it's so simple. At least you have a diary and record for Rob's treatment.'

'One of the worst things for us – you and I,' said Anna, 'is that our teenagers who should be out there testing life to its limits have suddenly been shoved back to the toddler years.'

'But you will find it can still change and the teenage Rob is still there,' said Kath helpfully, 'particularly when his friends call.'

And this was true. Rob had received one or two visitors who had persuaded their mothers to bring them up by car. Another had travelled on the train. One school friend had brought a huge card signed by all his class, and a video (which Anna was not allowed to see) with messages from them all! His science teacher had arranged this. Science was Rob's subject and he hoped to get into University eventually and study all three sciences. His science teacher made it very interesting and was rather unusual in his approach. He had started a snake club, where for a small subscription the boys (and girls if they wanted but none were interested) could help keep the snakes. He also made all the other sciences come alive.

On the morning the family were due to come up on James' 25th birthday, the 1st September 1997, Anna got up to make a cup of tea at about 5.00 a.m.

As she made her way to the kitchen she was met by Mildred, an older nurse in her fifties or sixties, running down the corridor sobbing her eyes out. 'Isn't it awful news?' she said wiping her face.

Anna stopped in surprise to see an experienced nurse letting go of her feelings like this. She was sure one of the children on the ward must have died, but it turned out that what Mildred was so upset about was the death of Diana, Princess of Wales.

Yes, it was indeed terrible news and a shock, but it seemed to leave Anna untouched in her current state. And she was sure that Diana of all people would understand, after all, Rob was only a few months older than Diana's eldest son William, and he was fighting for his life. If ever Diana had a passion in life it seemed to be for children and especially those in need or who were suffering. In fact, Mildred seemed to be acting out of all proportion bearing in mind the type of ward she was nursing on, and the number of their young patients who sadly lost their own battles.

Later in the afternoon, Alice, Brian and James turned up with a cake and a variety of decorations which they started to put up around the room. Sandra, James's fiancée, was unable to join them as her grandfather was ill.

Despite a certain amount of grumpiness on the part of James who hated any fuss, they had a fun time, and because the nurses joined in, James did not declare his annoyance about the balloons and banner. The highlight of the party was Alice shaving Rob's head.

It hurt Anna to watch her son's lovely dark hair falling in clumps onto the floor as the electric shave buzzed away and Alice made sweeping tramlines over his head. He looked so different and even thinner when the job was finished.

'Now you are a really cool dude,' announced Alice standing back to admire her handiwork.

And then, as usual, the family gatherings were over all too soon, and Anna was taking the familiar walk back to the lift with her two other children, wishing so hard they could all stay together again.

***

By now Rob and Anna were thoroughly settled into their single room. Each night it was an amazing sight to watch the dusk fall over the docks as the ships lit up one by one like a picture postcard, and it was a comforting scene. At least all seemed well with the outside world, even if it wasn't on their side of the glass.

It never occurred to either of them that they would be asked to move out, and so it was a complete shock when Wilf popped his head around the door and said 'We are going to have to put you in the double room with Matt, the other teenager.'

'Can't we stay here?' asked Anna 'it's become like another home?'

'Afraid not,' said Wilf. 'A new patient is being admitted who has to have a single room.' Later Anna learned that is was a little girl who belonged to a family of Plymouth Brethren who would not allow television, toys and would not allow her to mix with other children who might be allowed such things. She could not help but feel annoyed that they became a priority. Surely if they were truly Christian they would put aside such selfish demands.

Anna realised that the fragile security she and her son were enjoying was linked to the room which they had made their own. As they packed all their belongings onto a trolley for the move to the other end of the unit, she felt very unsafe and vulnerable again. Strange how territorial one could become and so quickly, as though putting roots down was an important part of recovery.

The teenage room was just about big enough to hold two beds. Then there were camp beds for the mothers, but they were narrow and uncomfortable. The room, instead of having a wonderful view of the docks, overlooked a closed courtyard which was used for the rubbish bins from the kitchens. The banging and clattering noises went on relentlessly over twenty-four hours a day, seven days a week.

Although not what they wanted, Rob and Anna discovered there was a good side to their move. That was they both had company and did not have to completely rely on each other. Rob and Matt got on well; Anna and Kath already knew each other from the meetings in the kitchen.

A nurse called in. 'There is a phone call for you on the public phone in the day room,' she said addressing Anna.

Picking up the receiver, Anna sensed the hesitation before Patrick said 'I really want to come up and see you both. I have missed you so much. We went to Exeter cathedral while the choir was singing evensong just as when you and I visited last year, and I suddenly realised what a mistake I've made and all I could think about was coming back to you as soon as possible. I've asked Val to leave.'

Anna was not sure whether to be pleased or not. She had been put in this situation too many times recently and was still raw and trying to recover her feelings. Her stomach turned over and over in a state of constant panic and she was almost dreading seeing him again as it would drag everything up once more. But equally she longed to see him; longed for things to be as they used to be in the beginning; longed for him to take her into his arms and comfort her.

Since that last terrible phone conversation she'd had with

Patrick before he went away, she had been unable to eat.

'Can you get me a room again?' he asked. 'I will be up tomorrow.'

She booked them a double room at the hostel. This would work out well because it was so cramped in the teenage room, and as Kath said to her 'There is just no space for parents as well as the boys to sleep here. I always book myself into the Click hostel.'

But the room she had booked would not be ready till the next day, and she still hesitated about leaving Rob until he was settled.

She needn't have worried though, because very soon Matt and Rob were laughing and joking, comparing notes, and trying to play a computer game. Peer group company seemed to be beneficial to both of them.

'This wasn't such a bad move after all' she thought.

Later that afternoon Anna took a trip to the medical school once more. The library had that familiar smell of libraries everywhere, and this time she found out how to work the photocopier so that she could print off the relevant extracts from books. Which saved her a lot of time trying to scribble out all the references.

The more she read and delved into the disturbing information, the more she became certain that she was on the right track.

'How will I be able to confirm my findings?' she thought, 'that is the problem.'

She decided it would not be right to inform the press at this stage, or even talk to many people about the theory; not until she could prove there was substance to her thoughts. There was no way she wanted to start a scare which would be counterproductive to health, and anyway, she had always believed in the policy of vaccination; at least until now that is.

If her findings were correct though, then it was vital to let the professionals know so that action could be taken. If she was right, then it would be unforgivable not to alert the right people to prevent further suffering.

She had already worked out that the teenagers on the ward had received their polio boosters prior to becoming ill with various cancers, but perhaps she could do some gentle probing when she was chatting to other mothers. 'Otherwise what on earth could suddenly affect a baby as young as the ones on the ward? They had not been in the world for enough time to have been affected by long term effects from the environment or contamination with radiation.'

That night she tossed and turned and could not sleep. The camp bed which had been put up alongside Rob was very uncomfortable compared to the one in the single room, and she had all these thoughts about the cause running around her head. And of course, there was the other problem – Patrick. However, after their last conversation, she dared to hope that maybe, just maybe he had at last come to his senses, and things might work out by some miracle. 'After all,' she reasoned not for the first time, 'sometimes good can come out of bad.'

And so already exhausted, she rose the next day with some trepidation.

CHAPTER 10 'FURTHER BETRAYAL'

September 1997

S he met Patrick at the bus stop situated outside the hospital entrance.

They embraced each other, and Patrick whispered 'I've missed you so much. Can we take a few moments together in the garden?'

The area jokingly known as 'the garden' was in fact a patch of scrubby grass surrounded by bushes where the medical staff went to smoke themselves to death.

There were three ponds, one leading into another, with an oriental-style bridge crossing over the largest one. Carp of varying sizes and colours swam aimlessly around amongst the weed. Some fish were very large indeed and came to the surface as if to follow the couple's movements, which was unnerving.

Patrick and Anna sat on a wooden bench. The bushes behind were full of birds cheeping and begging crumbs from people eating sandwiches nearby. Facing them was the hospital building, square and stark, the light reflected off its not-so-white walls in the warm sun.

'It's you and Rob that I care for most,' said Patrick putting his arm around Anna. 'Nothing and no-one else matters. I want to rush you away to a registry office and get married right away.'

Anna remained silent, not sure what to say. Then cautiously she said, 'We must be careful not to react for the wrong reasons.' Inside she was too raw to feel much except a strong desire for everything to be as it always had been; before Rob's illness, and before the intrusion of this other woman. Patrick seemed to have become an expert in giving out mixed messages.

(Some time later when Anna had relayed this conversation to her outspoken friend Laura, she had been told 'That's when you should have kneed him in the balls and thrown him to the largest carp in the pond.' Laura had a knack for delivering direct statements and was always a good judge of character – or lack of it as the case may be.

As it was, Patrick and Anna sat on the wooden seat, arm in arm, not speaking for a while longer. The afternoon sun hung suspended in the sky, and meanwhile other people laughed, chatted, smoked and walked while the couple stayed trapped in a bubble of time.

Eventually, they dragged themselves away from the fresh air and once more entered the claustrophobic atmosphere of the hospital.

Hospitals had never bothered her before, after all they had been her workplace for many years, but having to stay for a possible six months alongside her son while he was being treated for a life threatening illness, well it was like some sort of prison sentence.

They got in a lift to save the walk up six flights of stairs as Patrick's back was bothering him.

'How's the research going?' he asked.

'I've made quite a few new discoveries' said Anna and went on to explain.

'In all my time as a doctor,' said Patrick 'I never knew that the polio vaccine was made using monkey kidney cells.'

'Well that's the strange thing,' said Anna. 'Not all countries use the vaccine made that way. Europe and Canada and most of America apparently use a culture made on human diploid cells – although I am not too sure what that means.'

'I think it means that they start the culture on human cells, and then use clones from the cell line of the original cells for further vaccinations,' said Patrick.

'That seems a much safer option to me,' said Anna. 'No cross contamination between species.'

'I wonder why they don't use that method in Britain,' mused Patrick.

'Because it is cheaper,' said Anna with disgust. 'That's why. Also, the other countries do not use a live vaccine, they use an inactivated vaccine. That would seem to be much safer too.'

'I wonder how we can find out if the current vaccines are still being contaminated with SV40,' he said.

'Leave it to me,' said Anna. 'I have an idea and am working on it.'

The doors of the lift opened to the recurring depressing disembodied voice telling them they were on G Level.

'I wish they would change that woman,' said Anna emphatically. 'She always sounds as though she is announcing the end of the world.'

Patrick smiled.

'We had to move rooms,' said Anna, leading him to the teenage double room.

'Hello Rob,' said Patrick as he entered 'You Ok?'

'Yes thanks,' said Rob swiftly. It was obvious he was not that pleased to see him after all the angst dished out to his mother.

Patrick looked uncomfortable. 'It's very small,' he said. 'Where are we going to sit? And I shall miss not having that bed to lie on when my back gets bad.'

'There is a camp bed here,' said Anna, 'but it won't be any good for you, it would probably make your back worse.'

Somehow now that they were sharing a room with another family, it seemed to unsettle Patrick.

'Thank heavens for the room at the hostel,' he said.

'We might as well go and get the key now,' said Anna. 'It isn't your usual room.'

They met Wilf in the corridor. 'Ah yes,' he said, 'here you are – key to room 5 – the double as you asked.'

Patrick stiffened. 'We can't share a room,' he said flatly.

'Why ever not?' asked Anna in surprise.

'I can't share with you; she is bound to ask when I get home.' He replied.

Anna froze. 'You have just told me she is definitely leaving,' she said in dismay.

'As soon as possible,' said Patrick sharply. 'That's what I said, as soon as possible.'

Wilf was witnessing this conversation, and his face showed

great distaste for Patrick. It was as if he already knew what double game Anna's partner was playing.

'Well I am sorry we don't have another spare room,' said Wilf in a tone Anna had not heard him use before, 'so you will just have to use the put-you-up bed in the room you have.'

He handed the key to Patrick and cast a sympathetic glance toward Anna who by now was feeling physically sick. Again her stomach started to turn over and over.

'So all this talk of "you can't treat me as just a friend and she will have to go" is all fabricated then,' she said.

'Look I don't want any trouble,' said Patrick. 'I am trying to give you support.'

Anna stared at him in disbelief. This was a man who was supposed to be intelligent, but suddenly all the words of her friends came flooding back. 'Mentally unstable, addicted to women and sex, selfish, cheat, liar…' They had not been said to her all at once of course, but over a matter of years. Her true friends had seen through him, as indeed so had her children, but they knew she loved him and had just hoped she would find out for herself before it was too late and they had married.

She was certainly seeing him in a different light now, but love is such a powerful drug she still hoped that somehow a miracle would happen and he would change back into the person she had thought he was, the person she wanted him to be.

Anna was sensible enough to realise this could be viewed as needy – but then yes – she was 'in need.' She needed love, especially now. She needed the support of a partner who would allow her to bury her head into his shoulder and let all the awful feelings of insecurity out. Her son could well be dying. One of the worst things that can happen to a mother is to face the possible death of their child. Why was Patrick being so selfish that he could not see how she was torn apart? Was she being selfish too, wanting to be held and comforted and be secure in the knowledge that her lover was there for her – just for her?

Patrick said he would go ahead and sort out the room. He said he knew where the sheets were kept, so would make up the extra bed. He told her that when she got to the house later that evening, just to knock on the door of number 5.

Bewildered, Anna re-joined Rob. He was dozing now, and a blood transfusion was dripping slowly into the Hickman line. She sat alongside him and took his hand lightly in hers and gazed sadly at his pale drawn face.

'This is one of the most dangerous periods,' she thought, 'when his immune system is about to plummet and become susceptible to any onslaught. The chemotherapy treatment is doing its work, but at what a terrible price.'

Kath was sitting with her son Matt, but also other family members had come to visit them. Matt's two older brothers were there, and also Kath's husband. They were laughing and joking around the bed.

Then to her great relief, Alice's face suddenly appeared round the door.

'Hi mum,' she said. 'I wondered where you had gone. They told me you were down here. I had to drive this way to visit a client so thought I would drop in and give you a surprise.'

She looked at her brother. 'How's he doing then?' she asked

anxiously.

'Okay I think,' said Anna. 'It's just a case of waiting now until his blood recovers from the chemo and his immune system is up and running again, then they will start another round of treatment. They say that the next lot of treatment will not be as long as the ten days this time. The first is always the worst apparently.'

'Didn't you say Patrick was due up today,' commented Alice.

'He's already here, but not how I expected,' replied her mother

'Oh mum it really is time to let go of him and kick him out you know. He is causing you more stress and not helping at all,' said Alice studying her mother's face.

'I know you are right,' said Anna her eyes brimming with tears, 'but I am afraid of being alone. Somehow the future looks so lonely and I am afraid, afraid that I will lose everything. I can't imagine I will ever find anyone I love as much again.

'I keep having this recurring dream that I am standing on the top of a pile of boxes, all higgledy piggledy with no proper structure and I am trying to keep my balance. They are continually wobbling around, and I am about to fall.'

'You can't know that you will never find anyone else,' said Alice putting her arm around Anna. 'No-one knows the future. It's as if he has some unhealthy hold over you.'

Perhaps Alice was right, but then that is what happens when an abuser sets his sights on his prey. Select victim, isolate, and beat into submission. Anna remembered well during her training learning this was the pattern an abuser uses, so why had she not seen it creep up on her?

She also knew that it had nothing to do with class, creed, or intelligence. The fact that Patrick had been a doctor made it worse really, because it was easier to convince her that it was all her fault. During her nursing training she was taught that doctors were always right. Not like now-a-days when there was a much more grounded approach, and it was acknowledged they could fail just like any other human being.

And then there had been that physiotherapist who had picked up on the problem when Anna was in a post operation class with ten other people. The physiotherapist had recognised the signs and at the end of the class, when everyone else had left, she took Anna aside. 'The worst you know are policemen, clergy and doctors,' she had said, 'and the problem is that because of their position, the victim is always afraid they will not be believed.'

Bringing her thoughts back to the moment, Anna asked 'have you heard from your dad at all?' She was referring to her ex-husband Chris. 'I know he rang the ward to find out how Rob was doing, but I did not speak to him directly.'

Chris was never a physical abuser but had been a mental tormentor throughout their sixteen year marriage. He was in the Navy and had swept Anna off her feet when they met. But almost as soon as the marriage ceremony was over, she realised she could never come up to his impossible standards. He was a perfectionist and one who took no prisoners. He was not popular in the Navy for the same reason, and most of their Navy friends wondered how she had hung on for so long. 'Probably because he often goes off to sea,' Anna had laughed, but really it was not funny.

Something about her obviously attracted domineering men who presented one face to the world, and another inside the home. It must be something about her she reasoned. Therefore it must be all her fault. Even as she thought this, bells rang in her head from the lessons during welfare training 'the victim always thinks it's their fault – that is part of the grooming technique of the abuser.'

Eventually Rob woke up from his light sleep and smiled at his sister. 'Last time I saw you,' he said, 'you were approaching my head with the clippers.'

'How are you getting on in here then?' asked Alice.

'Actually I like having Matt's company. We have quite a laugh and it gives mum more freedom to wander around a bit too,' he said.

It was getting dark now, and Alice said she had better head for home.

Anna was trying to sum up the courage to go across to the house at the back of the hospital where Patrick would be waiting.

'I'll just settle you first,' she said to Rob, 'make sure you have everything. I don't like leaving you. It will be the first night I haven't been on hand, but while I have the offer of a proper bed in the house, it might be a good idea. The nurses have told me there is a direct line from the ward to there, so if you need me at all, just get them to phone.'

'No worries mum,' said Rob 'I'll be fine.'

And in her heart she knew it was probably good for him to have the space.

Kath was heading over to the house too and offered to

show her the way.

'I usually notify the nurses when I am leaving,' she said 'because you have to cross through a very dark car park, and they alert security to watch on cameras, just to be on the safe side.'

Together they went down to the ground floor, through the children's out-patient department, through the neurology unit and out into the darkness.

Anna could see what Kath had meant. It was pitch black out there, except they headed for some subdued lighting surrounding a small outpatient building. They followed the lights around the side wall and then crossed another very dark area until they came to the high fence. Kath opened the gate with her key, and then let them both into the house through the conservatory.

With a heavy heart, Anna made her way up to room 5 and knocked on the door.

Patrick opened it, already dressed for bed.

She noticed the camp bed was made up. 'I think you had better have the double bed,' she said sadly, 'because of your back problem.'

Patrick did not need a second bidding. 'If you are sure then' he said.

But try as she might, Anna could not get comfortable. The bed was really meant for a child as it was too narrow, and she tossed and turned until eventually Patrick said 'Look you'd better come in and join me. Neither of us will get any sleep at this rate. But we'll keep a blanket between us so that we are not literally sleeping together. Otherwise she will know when I get home.'

Anna turned her back on Patrick and watched the shadows on the wall change shape. Through the blind she could just make out Rob's Ward with its lights dimmed to night softness.

She thought about her son, and suddenly realised she wanted to be there with him, not here with this frigid man she obviously did not know.

The blanket rolled up as a barrier between them might just have well been a sheet of cold icy steel. Such close proximity and yet the impossible distance was the most lonely feeling she had ever experienced. This was a far more cruel situation than if he had turned his back on them all together and left them entirely alone in their desperation.

CHAPTER 11 'ANOTHER KINDRED SPIRIT'
September 1997

Patrick had fallen deeply asleep and was snoring as he was on his back. Anna lay awake, unable to find the solace of sleep. There were times she wanted to reach out but did not want to be accused of 'breaking the rules of the barrier.' A simple comforting arm around her would have been enough to breech her isolation, and the warmth of his body would have been enough to release her to slumber.

Suddenly a phone rang in the hallway downstairs, then the sound of someone running.

She sat bolt upright. 'It must be something wrong with Rob,' she thought, but then she heard a light knock on someone else's door. Another poor parent was being summoned to the ward because of their child's deterioration or change in condition.

The phone rang twice more during the night and each time she sat up immediately, tense with anticipation of the worst. Patrick slept through it all.

In the morning, she slipped out of bed silently, dressed and went back to the ward without saying anything to him. After all, what was there to say any more? He had already told her he would return home immediately he got up that day, and although he muttered his reason was to check the post, Anna realised it was because he really wanted to return to the other woman.

When Anna entered the room, she could see that Rob had deteriorated in the night. She sat by his bedside concerned and anxiously holding his hand. To take their mind off things she put the TV on with the sound low.

After a while he asked her for help to go to the bathroom. Anna supported him with one arm, whilst wheeling the drip stand with the other.

As soon as they reached the bathroom all hell broke loose. Rob's nose started to bleed profusely, he was being sick bringing up an unusual bright green fluid. It was too bright for the colour of bile, and he was passing a dark black jelly which she realised were solidified platelets. This meant there was internal bleeding. He shook uncontrollably was covered in another rash and she struggled to keep him balanced on the toilet and to support his head. He was beginning to pass out and she did not think she could hold him any longer.

Unable to leave him, she pulled the red cord just within reach.

Almost immediately she heard the sound of running feet pounding down the corridor and from more than one direction.

The door burst open and Barbara, a lovely Irish nurse who they had got to know, took stock of the situation. Soon she was joined by two other nurses.

'It's alright,' she said to them, 'it's not a cardiac arrest but we do need a doctor's help here right now.'

Anna apologised 'I am sorry I didn't know that emergency cord was for cardiac arrest – I just didn't know what to do.'

'Don't worry my dear,' said Barbara kindly, 'you did the

right thing, he does seem very poorly.'

As she helped clean Rob up and held on to him the other side so they could get him back into bed, she said quietly to Anna.

'Where's your partner?'

'He's gone back home,' said Anna

'Look my dear,' said Barbara, 'in view of this development I think you should have some support.'

'Is it that serious?' asked Anna in horror.

Barbara paused and looked her straight in the eye. 'Just say, if I were in your position I would certainly want that support.'

Anna shivered at the hidden implication. 'The problem is…' she hesitated, 'the problem is… that I am not sure whether we really are partners anymore. He left this morning to return home. I don't want to be accused of making use of the situation to get him back here under false pretences.'

'I wouldn't worry about that,' said Barbara.

'Could you… could you possibly talk to him, medic to medic, and explain the situation?' asked Anna. She was feeling very scared that the end was near for Rob. She remembered what Sophie had told her when they were first admitted 'Don't worry, we would always know if he was in danger, and warn you.' This was definitely a warning from Barbara.

'If you just explain the situation to Patrick on the phone, and leave it up to him to decide, then I am not involved in whatever he does. He cannot accuse me you see' said Anna.

Barbara gave her a look of sympathy. 'I will most certainly do that for you,' she said and after having settled Rob back in bed, and asked another nurse to stay with them, she went off to the phone.

She returned remarkably quickly. 'Patrick says he has only just got home, but he is coming back straight away.'

Anna was left thinking 'What on earth could Barbara have said to him to make him react that quickly? Rob really must be in a life or death situation at the moment.' She felt another surge of panic and despair, and clung on to her son's hand. 'It's Ok Rob,' she said. 'I'm here and not leaving you.'

Despite not wanting to rely on Patrick any more, the thought that she might have to face the worst possible situation on her own left her feeling frail and numb and unable to make decisions any more or cope with anything.

The other mother and son in the ward looked on anxiously. 'Are you OK?' asked Kath.

'I feel bad that this is all going on while Matt has to witness it,' said Anna. 'Must be rather frightening for a teenager.'

'We've had our moments too,' said Kath, 'and quite understand, so don't fret about it.'

Doctors and nurses huddled around Rob for the next hour. They put up another blood transfusion, but this appeared to have air bubbles in it, so they had to withdraw it and set up another. We had been warned to watch for any air bubbles in the blood as it was being transfused as it could be dangerous.

An hour after the phone call, Patrick returned looking concerned.

By now Rob was sitting up and looking very weak.

'Have you still got the key to room 5?' Patrick asked Anna.

'Yes,' she said abruptly.

'Then we can share properly tonight,' he said. 'As soon as I got the call, I knew where my priorities lay. I was such a fool last night.'

'No,' said Anna, 'I won't be leaving Rob's side tonight, and not any more until he is a good deal better than now.'

Patrick looked at her. This was the first time he had not been able to rail road her into whatever he wanted.

Anna realised she was finding a much deeper strength than she ever thought she had. She had nearly lost her son and somehow this empowered her in a way she had never felt before. Perhaps it was the primeval instinct shared by every mother of every species on the planet – to protect her young above all else. That 'collective unconscious' state that Jung the famous Psychologist had talked about. It seemed to her at that moment as though all living beings of every sort were connected at some very deep level by a river of empathy which ran between them all, and particularly the maternal instinct.

'I'll bring you a cup of tea,' said Patrick still stinging from her refusal to bend to his wishes.

Rob smiled weakly at his mother as if to say 'That's the way mum, keep going.'

A nurse entered again, but this time it was not for Rob, but for Matt. 'We're transferring you to another hospital for your radiotherapy today,' she said. 'But don't worry you'll soon be back with us again in about a fortnight I should think.'

The news obviously had unsettled both Kath and Matt. The hospital they were in had become their second home, in just the same way it had for Anna and Rob.

The boys were obviously disappointed to be separated as they had formed a strong bond of friendship during the time they had shared the room. They had even joined forces to avoid being drawn into the clutches of the "on ward" school teacher. 'After all,' Rob had said at the time after they had both hidden beneath the sheets pretending to be asleep, 'the only perks of being in hospital is that we do not have to do school work.' Matt was already a dab hand at avoiding the poor woman whose job it was to educate those in hospital for a long time, and he had given Rob a few tips for the future.

Patrick decided to return home once more as the crisis seemed to be under control, although not over, and this time Anna was relieved. She had never felt that way before.

Later that evening, another teenager, Daniel who was a year older than Rob, was given Matt's bed.

He was obviously newly diagnosed because the extended family crowded round his bed anxiously, and curtains were drawn and doctors flitted in and out.

Eventually, all the visitors went except for his mother Nita who sat by the side of her son looking terrified.

'I do understand what you are going through,' said Anna, 'but they are brilliant on this ward. Once you have got used to the routine it isn't so bad.'

And then, taking over as Kath had done for her, she took Nita to the ward kitchen and made her a cup of tea.

'Will you be staying overnight?' asked Anna

'No, we live locally so I will leave him once he is asleep,' said Nita. 'It was a terrible shock; he was taken ill while we were celebrating my birthday out in a restaurant. Nothing could have prepared us for this.'

Once the neon glare of the daytime ward had changed to the gentle night lights, Anna arranged the camp bed and settled down. Despite the discomfort, she slept sounder than she had done for quite some while. It was as if she had accomplished something she should have done months ago. She had taken control of the situation between Patrick and herself. Although it hurt and she missed both him and that sense of belonging dreadfully, now she could concentrate entirely on her three children who were the most important people to her., Especially the one that needed her most at the time – her son Rob.

CHAPTER 12 'GOOD NEWS AT LAST'

October 1997

Despite the threat to his life the previous day, Rob woke feeling better. The blood transfusion was taking effect. However, the medical staff decided he should have an X-ray of the abdomen because of the profuse loss of platelets during that frightening episode.

'We have to make sure that he does not have any sort of bleeding in the gut,' explained Sophie.

This immediately brought to Anna's mind her findings about the polio vaccine. The fact that it was absorbed through the gut and that the gut had the thinnest cell lining of the body designed especially for the purpose of admitting substances, usually nutrition of course, but it could also be a weak point where other things might enter the blood stream.

In the back of her mind, she was sure there was a link.

It was a shame that Patrick was not there to act as her sounding board anymore for these ideas, but perhaps she would advance more on her own now. She had to prove to herself that she really did not need him any more for anything. She could be strong enough to go it alone.

Laura phoned her later that day. 'How's things?' asked her friend.

Anna filled her in on all the details; of Rob's dramatic fight for life the previous day, and of how she had finally dispensed with Patrick.

'Sorry you and Rob had such a rough time, but well done you,' Laura almost shouted down the phone. 'At long last. I couldn't really tell you before how much I detested the man because I was afraid of losing you as a friend, but everyone else could see how he was playing you. I bet the children will be pleased.'

Although liberated, Anna suddenly felt she was like a boat that had been cut loose from its moorings and was left wallowing around in the rough waters. She and Patrick had been part of each other's lives for five years, and it was as though she had lost a limb. Part of her was missing.

She put on a brave face 'Yes,' she said over the phone, 'I have come to my senses. It is very painful, but suddenly I see very clearly what has been going on over the past years. It had been growing so gradually I hardly noticed. Now I must concentrate on the things that really matter.'

Saying it out loud somehow validated it. She put the phone down.

The new teenager in the room had a great sense of humour despite his predicament, and before long he and Rob were in hysterics.

'What are you two up to then?' asked Nita, the new boy's mother.

'We're comparing mothers,' laughed Rob. 'You are both very similar. I told Daniel that you will talk to anything that stands still long enough, even a parked car.'

Nita and I looked at each other. She was not quite as pale as the previous evening.

'We're waiting for the consultant to see Daniel,' she said. 'I gather he has a different type of leukaemia to Rob's. They've told us he has something called ALL – Acute Lymphoblastic Leukaemia – it attacks different cells to AML.'

Anna found she had a kindred spirit in Nita, who was another mother unable to accept the diagnosis without question. 'I'll give you any help I can with your research,' Nita promised when Anna told her the theory.

Nita confirmed that Daniel too had received a polio vaccine a few months earlier. 'He's a year older than your Rob,' she said, 'but his polio booster was delayed because last year, when all the rest of his class at school received the vaccine, Daniel was off sick and they suggested he waited another year.'

Anna made careful note of yet another teenager who fitted in with her theory.

Daniel had a different consultant to Rob, and so when his team arrived, it seemed appropriate for Anna to take leave of the shared room and give them the privacy they needed to discuss treatment.

Rob was beginning to doze off again, so she explained she was just going to check on something in the library but would not leave it as long as last time.

She slipped away and found the library much easier now she knew the route so well.

This time she did not take quite so many books out of the reference section, but what she did read, made her heart stop momentarily.

She quickly photocopied the extract she had found. In 1961 a female scientist, Dr. Bernice Eddy of the National Institute of Health in America, had been deeply disturbed by the discovery of the contamination of polio vaccines with SV40. She was undertaking extensive trials to prove her research. But when she had tried to go public with her findings, she had been silenced in a rather sinister way. Her laboratory was closed down suddenly by the authorities without warning, and all her research had therefore stopped. The drugs companies had then, and Anna was sure still did have, far reaching powers which were probably motivated by money, and which very likely infiltrated the corridors of power higher up the scale.

It was on reading this that Anna realised if she did go public she would be taking on some powerful adversaries and would not make herself popular.

She resolved to compile a report that was as near professional as possible, reasoning that she could at least set out her hypotheses, her reasons and her conclusions so there would be something to supply if required.

The thoughts that had started her out on the road of her desperate quest to find a cause for her son's illness, had now taken on a much more far reaching need. To tell the truth, and make sure that other people might be saved the same sort of suffering.

However, she realised that having a hypothesis was all very well, but it needed some backing and if possible some tests.

Rob recovered remarkably well during the following two bleak weeks after the scare. He had negotiated the most dangerous period between treatments, the neutropenic phase when his immune system was reduced to nil, and he had received enough blood transfusions and platelet transfusions to be able to leave hospital for a few days. And, of course, he was covered by very strong anti-biotic care.

Then some wonderful news came from Jane the consultant. 'You're allowed home for five days,' she told Rob, 'but your mum will have to monitor your temperature every four hours, and at the slightest sign of it rising, you must come straight back here.'

'Home' – that was a word they had not even hoped to hear for another six months.

However, there were two provisos before he could actually leave. One was that Anna would have to learn how to flush the Hickman line with Hepsal and saline to keep it from clogging up or getting infected. The other was that Rob would have to prove he could eat normally again without the help of the nutrition he was receiving via drip. Currently the only way his body was being fed at all.

The Macmillan nurse called to give Anna instructions on care of the Hickman line. She showed her how to lay out all the necessary ampules and needles on a sterilised cloth and taught her how to steer the needle through the plugs on the end of both lumens. 'You must be careful not to touch the sides at all,' explained the nurse, 'and you have to clean the plugs with a sterilised wipe first.'

She then added, 'you might as well learn how to do it as well Rob. We have to teach you both because not even the district nurses at your local surgery will know this procedure. It is specialised treatment for oncology patients and their care'

Rob had not really eaten anything since prior to the operation to put the Hickman line in place. He had waited so long for surgery and had to go for so many days without eating "just in case there was a space on the operating list", that when he was allowed to eat again, he didn't want to. Part of this was due to the way the chemotherapy drugs had changed his taste buds, but also because his stomach had shrunk, and he no longer had any appetite. And during the first course of treatment his mouth had been so ulcerated that eating anything at all was just too painful.

He had therefore survived on a thick white nutritional supplement fed through the line and which was basically food in liquid form. It contained all the essential vitamins and minerals he needed for his body to keep going but produced problems of its own in that Rob's body was not picking up any ideas of being hungry, because he was receiving nutrition.

'We can't let him go home until he can prove he will start eating again,' said Sophie to Anna.

This seemed to kick start Rob and gave him an incentive.

'I can't stand the smell of hospital food,' he said.

'I'll take you down to the dining room then,' said Anna. 'They do a really good curry there. I'm sure that will tempt you.'

'Well I'll give it a go then,' said Rob without much enthusiasm.

Anna managed to get him into a wheelchair and pushing it with one hand, and wheeling the drip stand with the other, she negotiated their way by lift to the ground floor.

By now Rob had not only lost his hair, but his eyelashes and eyebrows too, giving him a very different look. 'I look like an alien' he said when he first saw himself in the mirror.

On the ward this had not bothered him because many of the patients were in the same state and it seemed normal.

But once out amidst the public gaze he found the 'staring' he was subjected to made him feel like a freak.

Then finally he said to his mother, as yet another person turned to look at him, 'well they're the ones with the problem, not me. Let them stare.'

Once in the dining room, all Rob's resolve to eat went as soon as he saw the food.

The meals were in fact very good, but because he had not eaten for so long, the smell alone put him off.

It was important to start slowly, so Anna suggested she bought just one portion of curry and rice, and they would have two plates and share it between them.

Hiding themselves away in a far corner so they would not attract unwanted attention, Rob began his first tentative moves to passing the test for going home. He had one mouthful and managed to keep it down.

Gradually over the next couple of days, his appetite improved and the drip with the white nutritional fluid that he had been totally dependent on up until that point was withdrawn.

During the period while they were getting his strength back up, he started playing a few pranks with Daniel his roommate who was also feeling a bit better.

Nita and Anna returned from a visit to the shops in the foyer of the hospital one morning to find their sons walking up the corridor making chicken noises and with a surgical glove pulled over each of their bald heads, the fingers pointing upwards like the comb on top of a chicken's head.

The houseman walking down the corridor behind them was

having hysterics.

Then the day before Jane promised Rob would be allowed home, a strange opportunity was presented to Anna in a way she could not possibly have envisaged.

'Rob - how do you feel about having tea at number 10 Downing Street with the Prime Minister?' asked the consultant.

CHAPTER 13 'A BOLT OUT OF THE BLUE'
October 1997

B y now, Rob was getting used to surprises, but usually of the negative kind.

Here he had been suddenly asked if he would like to have tea with the Prime Minister. 'Have I fallen down the rabbit hole in Alice in Wonderland?' he asked, thinking it was some kind of joke.

'It is a real invitation,' said Jane. 'The Scientists working on a cure for leukaemia in children have a laboratory in another part of the hospital. They run a charity so that they can carry on funding the project. They asked the PM a long time ago if they could come up to meet him and explain about their charity and their work – so this tea party has been arranged for some while. But apparently the PM has just contacted them and asked if they could bring up a paediatric patient who is currently being treated.'

'Why me?' asked Rob

'Well you aren't so young that you are likely to wreck 10 Downing Street,' laughed Jane, 'but also you are at a stage of your treatment when it is safe for you to go, and also it is obvious that you are going through chemotherapy.' By this she was inferring to the fact that he had no hair, no eyebrows, and no eye lashes and was as thin as a rake.

'When is this going to happen?' asked Anna feeling like Rob that she had wandered into some parallel universe.

'That's the only problem,' said Jane. 'It is tomorrow, the day you should be going home.'

Rob and Anna looked at each other. 'Well mum,' said Rob, 'it is not the sort of thing that is likely to happen again, unless I get knighted or something, so let's go for it – one more day before we hit home is OK.'

And so it was that Anna started to rummage through her unsuitable wardrobe of clothes crumpled up in a suitcase. 'What on earth am I going to wear?' she muttered.

As luck would have it, she had bought a velvet dress – quite understated – at her retail therapy shop in the entrance of the hospital only two days ago, that would do.

Rob had his school jacket with him for reasons she could not remember – why she had packed it in the first place was a mystery, but it turned out to be a bonus and would do to make him look respectable.

It then occurred to her that this would be the ideal time to take up some copies of the report she was working on. She could hand one to the PM and one to the scientists on the front line.

This was where it was a stroke of luck that she had her word processor with her – it would print off extra copies.

She had never heard back from the Health Secretary, so she could by-pass him and go straight to the top.

The morning dawned, and they got ready for their 'mad hatters tea party' as Rob referred to it.

Unfortunately, it was raining heavily and so Anna, who had no suitable coat available, quickly grabbed the only folding umbrella she had with her as she left the room. It had come free with some offer at Boots the Chemist so was hardly the height of fashion.

Rob was to be a passenger in the car with the scientists, a husband and wife team who had very sadly lost their own son to leukaemia. The irony of this was that they had already been working on a cure for leukaemia before he had become ill, but their son's struggle and loss made their quest for a cure even more driven. In the car with them also was the Charity's public relations officer.

Anna was going to be in the car following on behind and driven by the press reporter from the local Echo. The reporter was a smart and attractive girl who was young enough to have been Anna's daughter, and she was lovely company.

Inevitably Anna told her she was going to give a copy of the report of the research she was doing into the cause of Rob's leukaemia and the reporter wanted to know more so that she could send that to press too.

However, Anna explained she did not want to start a stampede of fear about the current vaccination procedures as she had only her theory and conviction, and no proof with testing etc. 'I don't want to go public,' explained Anna, 'until it has been properly researched by the experts – polio is such a terrible disease – I know I experienced it myself. I don't want to do anything to stop people being comfortable with the vaccination until we are absolutely sure of the dangers I think I've uncovered.'

The young journalist promised to keep quiet until Anna gave her the thumbs up that it was now being taken seriously by the scientific world.

***

The convoy eventually came to a stop at the iron gates leading into 10 Downing Street.

Passes were examined, handbags given a cursory glance, and the cars were waived on to a car park at the back behind the well-known buildings of the street.

The visitors were ushered in through the epic black doors of number 10 – polished brass handle and door knocker reflecting the rain as it fell relentlessly. The journalist was not allowed in and joined a group of photographers and reporters already in place on the pavement opposite.

The band of tea party guests collected inside the hallway and waited to be received.

Rob looked a bit like a scarecrow as he had lost so much weight his school jacket was just hanging from the shoulders.

Anna suddenly realised that the poor reporter was standing in a beautiful red suit outside on the pavement in a deluge of rain, so she asked the doorman if she could just take her umbrella across to her.

He opened the door and Anna without thinking, walked straight out and put her umbrella up. It was only then that she realised it was an unsuitable bright yellow – a defiant Liberal colour and not the colour of the government. She located her reporter and waived the umbrella at her mouthing, 'do you want to borrow this?'

She was immediately blinded by a barrage of flashes from cameras belonging to the photographers standing on the press side of the road. 'Who's that?' she heard one ask. 'No idea,' was the reply. They were obviously trigger happy and ready to snap anyone or anything that entered or exited the famous doorway.

Having established that her reporter friend was okay, Anna withdrew hastily into the door of number 10 again. 'One day in the future,' she reasoned, 'hidden in records stored deep in the recesses of newspaper libraries they will find a photograph of a "nobody" waiving a "Liberal" umbrella outside the "Tory" occupied number 10 and wonder who the hell it was!'

Back inside the warm and dry, where the tea party group were still waiting, they had been joined by another couple – a famous footballer and his wife. The footballer was the President for the charity being represented.

Anna asked if she could use a bathroom.

To her surprise she was escorted upstairs to a roomy and elegant bathroom but left alone inside (for which of course she was glad).

But it did occur to her that had she any bad intentions towards the PM this would have been a loophole in security. She had her usual sized handbag with her – big enough to fit the proverbial kitchen sink in if necessary, as she had learnt to take anything that could possibly be needed around with her. Although it had been studied to a certain extent on the way in, she had not been asked to empty it which she would have thought to be entirely reasonable, as even she had forgotten a lot of the stuff inside.

She returned down the curving staircase toward the hall to re-join her party, just as the Prime Minister's wife arrived and apologised for the hold up. She was friendly and welcoming, although she did drop one awful brick by saying – in front of Rob – that she had a friend whose son had suffered leukaemia but he had died.

There was a shocked silence amongst all those present, as though they were actors being directed for a play which required a unified pause – before conversation awkwardly started up again in an attempt to fill the space left by the gaff. Rob took it very well – he had learnt to deal with people who did not necessarily think of him as being there at all.

This slight error of the unexpected curve ball though gave Anna the chance she had been waiting for. She told the PM's wife of her research and the rebuff from the Health Secretary in that he had not bothered to reply. Anna offered a copy of her report which the Prime Minister's wife took willingly with offers to follow it up, and instructions that if Anna had not heard anything back within the next two weeks, she should ring the wife's office direct.

Anna was also able to hand a copy to the scientists and asked if they could possibly read it sometime and see what they thought.

The Prime Minister then arrived and led them all into a small lounge, where coffee and biscuits waited on a highly polished table at the centre of comfortable seating.

The positioning and seat arrangement for the party, although appearing casual, was carefully choreographed. Rob sat on a sofa next to the Prime Minister, and the official photographer suddenly appeared to take photos of them chatting with each other. This was no doubt a good publicity moment for the benefit of public relations.

The Prime Minister started to ask Rob which football team he supported and other football related questions – which was an embarrassment as Rob had no interest in football at all.

It occurred to Anna that it was strange how every male was

supposed to be a lover of football, when there were quite a few that she knew who found it extremely boring.

Anna was seated next to the famous footballer.

The irony of this was that before Rob had been ill, Anna had attended a Pro-am golf tournament where this footballer had headed one of the teams. It was the sort of Pro-am tournament where one could pay a small fee and wander freely around the vast golf course, watching stars and celebrities alike, head their own teams for a bit of light relief and to raise money for charities.

Now as Anna sat by his side, she was able to tell him the story of how she had been sitting quietly on the ground among the fir trees on the occasion of the golf match, not too near the live action but where the beer tent was situated, so she was enjoying a quiet refreshing beverage, when suddenly out of nowhere a golf ball appeared and ran up her skirt. Once the shock was over she was then presented with the predicament of what to do. Although not a golfer she knew that a golf ball should be left where it fell and played from exactly that spot.

The few other drinkers around had exploded with laughter. Anna stood up and said, 'Well I am not waiting for them to retrieve the golf ball from there!' Moments later, the ball was collected – by the footballer she now sat next to – who was none the wiser as to why people were in stitches.'

So she relayed this story to the sportsman as they sat together on a long sofa in the Prime Minister's lounge at 10 Downing Street and he laughed and said 'just don't tell the wife.'

Once more Anna had a feeling of having slipped into some parallel universe.

There were plenty of publicity photos taken, and all too soon a rather officious PA entered and told the Prime Minister his time was up and he was needed elsewhere.

However, his wife then graciously gave the party a conducted tour of the inside of 10 Downing Street before they reluctantly collected their coats and entered the normal world once more.

The scientist team promised to be in touch once they had had a chance to read Anna's report.

The next day, Rob's photo and story was spread liberally across the newspapers – both local and national – which, at the age of 15 he was not too pleased with. But at least he had had tea at 10 Downing Street with the Prime Minister and his wife, the eminent scientists, and the famous footballer and his wife. A real "pick me up" in the strange world that had engulfed him and his family for the past months – bouncing from one extreme to another.

CHAPTER 14 'BACK HOME'
October 1997

The following day James and Alice came up to collect them.

'Good heavens mum,' said James as he struggled to load a trolley with all their goods, 'you seem to have accumulated a lot more stuff since you've been up here.'

'Well we thought we were not going to be allowed home for six months, that was what we were told when we first got here. The fact that it has only been a matter of weeks is such a bonus.'

Rob was grinning ear to ear as he sat in the wheelchair being pushed by Alice and they reached the main entrance. Fresh air at last. Rob took a deep breath.

Having collected the car from the distant car park, James pulled up in the 'drop off and collect only' zone and it took them some time to pack everything in.

Then miracle of miracles, they were on their way home, through the New Forest once more.

Anna noticed how the scenery had changed completely from their last journey on the way to the hospital. There was definitely an autumnal look now, no sign of summer.

'Even though we're only out of hospital for a few days, it's so good to know that you will be spending your sixteenth birthday back home again,' she said. Inwardly she thought 'particularly as I feared you would never get home again at all or even make it to your next birthday.'

They had even been told that it would be fine to take him out for a meal. So the family had arranged to take him to an upmarket Italian restaurant in Christchurch.

That evening as they sat around the table and were about to eat the meal, a young woman approached them carrying a bunch of red roses.

She held one out to Anna and said 'Would you like to buy a rose for a pound? It's for children with leukaemia and terminal illness.'

There was a sudden hush around the table. Anna felt furious. 'My son has leukaemia,' she said nodding toward Rob, 'that's why he has no hair, you should know that.'

'Oh yes,' said the woman without any apparent embarrassment or understanding, 'but would you like to buy a rose anyway'

Rob could see that Anna was holding back her fury, and it would not take much more for her to swing her handbag at this wretched and insensitive woman.

'Tell you what mum,' he said, 'why don't you give the pound direct to me and we'll cut out the middle man.'

There was a pause, and then the family convulsed in laughter. He had managed to diffuse a very difficult situation, which was about to turn even more difficult with Anna's pent up anger.

The young woman melted away still without any shame and tried her luck at another table.

A few weeks later, it was revealed on television that this

'rose selling' lark was in fact a hoax and a man was arrested for setting up a bogus organisation to cheat people out of money which never went to any charity other than his own pocket.

Rob celebrated his birthday in style and best of all at home.

The family embraced the fact that he was out of hospital and that he had recovered enough after the first intensive batch of treatment to be free, even if for only a few days.

He was on a good deal of medication and Anna found the only way she could cope with this was by writing a chart which she stuck to the kitchen cupboard. The regime was very complicated. Some tablets were four times a day, others twice and another was just once a day. Then the Hickman line had to be flushed out as well. It was hard to juggle all the pills around food at the appropriate time.

Rob's appetite had increased immensely since returning home. There was nothing like good old family cooking.

Anna received a phone call from the scientist she had met at 10 Downing Street.

'I am fascinated by your theory,' he said, 'and would like to do anything I can to help you forge ahead with this theory. One thing I could do is if you can get me the name of the drugs company and the batch number of the vaccine Rob had, I can then ask for a sample and test to see if it is contaminated with SV40. Surprisingly enough it is easy to trace SV40 in this way.

'So can you just do a bit of sleuthing and get those details for me from your Surgery. Let me have them as soon as you can.'

'I am so pleased you've suggested helping in this way,' said

Ann overjoyed. 'At last I feel I am being listened to. I will get that information for you as soon as possible.'

'One thing though,' said the scientist, 'I won't mention to the Company what I need this sample for, but will just say that I have found it helpful in the past. If they get wind of the fact that we are searching for a link with leukaemia, they will clam up.'

Now he was home again, Rob's friends were able to come around and spend plenty of time with him too.

This gave Anna the chance to slip out to the Doctor's surgery one day and ask the receptionist if she could give the information needed by the scientist running the leukaemia research charity at the hospital.

'Could you let me have the name and number of the batch of the polio vaccine that was given to Rob at school earlier this year please?' she asked politely. 'Oh and also the name of the drugs company that made it.'

She seemed to be standing at the waiting room window for a long time.

Eventually the receptionist returned looking puzzled. 'I am really sorry,' she said 'but we cannot find any trace of his vaccination details for that particular booster. We have all the others but not the polio vaccine given in February.'

'What can I do then?' asked Anna.

'Well, when a vaccination takes place at school,' explained the receptionist, 'the records are kept in three different places for security for just such an occasion as this when it seems to be missing in one of the places. You should be able to find out from the school doctor who gave it, and also it will have been kept in the health department records at the local authority. Give one of them a ring and they will be able to tell you and perhaps you could let them know that they do not seem to have notified us as they should.'

When Anna returned home, she rang the school.

Again, after a long pause, the secretary returned to the phone and said 'I am really sorry, but they seem to have gone missing from here also. The only thing you can do now is contact the local health authority.'

This Anna did and to her surprise she was given the same answer.

'How can it be missing in three different places when the whole idea is to be a safety measure so such an event can't happen?' she asked. But all she got in return were mumbled apologies, and 'I really don't know the answer to that, but it is unusual.'

She then rang the scientist in charge of the leukaemia charity. He sounded quite shocked. 'This doesn't seem right at all,' he said. 'I am afraid without those details I can't go any further – unless…' he paused for a moment, 'unless you ask one of Rob's school chums who had the vaccine done at the same time if they could find out the batch number and details from their own doctor. We can probably trace it that way.'

As luck would have it, the mother of one of Rob's friends called to pick her son up after a visit.

Anna explained what was going on 'Do you think you could give a hand and find out for me from your own doctor?' she asked. 'The more I am learning about this vaccination, and the fact that Rob's records for that booster has gone missing in three different places, makes me very suspicious indeed.'

The other mother agreed it was indeed strange. 'I will do my best,' she promised.

Within a day, she had come back with the information that Anna needed, and this was immediately passed on to the scientist at the hospital.

'Leave it with me,' he said, 'I will get onto it right away.'

Then on their final day at home, just before they left to return to the hospital, the phone rang.

It was the scientist.

'Things are getting more suspicious by the minute,' he said sounding intrigued. 'When I contacted the drugs company and asked for a sample of that particular batch, they told me there were no samples left. The reason I find this so strange is that legally they are required to keep a sample from each batch for at least two years after it has been used.'

'What do we do now then?' asked Anna.

'I am afraid there is nothing I can do without the sample,' explained the scientist. 'We are up a creek without a paddle so to speak,' he said, 'but I think the whole thing is very suspicious indeed.'

'Could it be a cover up do you think?' asked Anna

'I think it could be,' said the scientist. 'But don't give up hope. Keep on researching as you have been and we may get somewhere even now.'

So with those thoughts running through her mind, she loaded up her own car and took Rob back the thirty miles back to the hospital for his second stretch of treatment.

She had bought herself a mobile phone for emergency use only, now that she intended to drive herself and Rob back and forth to the hospital over the coming months. If the car broke down, or Rob was suddenly taken ill on the journey, she had a point of contact with the family and the emergency services.

It was not fair to expect James to drive them up and back each time, and now she knew the route and was more confident about Rob's treatment, it seemed the right time to take charge of transport, and for that matter, take charge of their lives.

CHAPTER 15 'REVELATIONS'
October 1997

R ob was given a bed in the teenager room again. As he would be sharing with Daniel who was still an in-patient, they did not mind at all.

The friendship between Nita and Anna grew, as did that between Rob and Daniel.

With the boys settled in each other's company, both mothers felt able to leave them and visit the shopping mall at the entrance to the hospital without any feelings of guilt at all.

It was tempting. There was a small boutique which sold all manner of things, and despite never having an occasion to dress up, Anna found herself splashing out. Mind you, she was already grateful that she had been tempted to buy that velvet dress that went to 10 Downing Street with her. Sometimes she and Nita would sneak parcels in to hide in the wardrobe, but the boys always knew when they had been for some retail therapy and would tease them.

Nita showed interest in coming to the medical library with Anna one day. She was a great reader, although mainly in her case it was fiction, but she had a very astute mind and was keen to read up all the references herself.

Anna told her the latest update – about Rob's medical records for that particular polio booster going missing in three separate places and that this had happened after she had sent her report to the Secretary of State for Health in the first batch of letters posted with her concerns. She also told Nita the latest news from the scientist working within the hospital.

'I will see if I can check on Daniel's vaccine details too' said Nita. 'We could try from a different angle and see if the same thing happens.'

Anna still did not receive a reply from the Heath Secretary so she alerted the Prime Minister's wife as asked. She also started to send copies of her report to the heads of as many cancer charities as possible. They were all medical doctors or scientists so would understand what she was trying to prove.

One day she received a reply from a professor who was in charge of a national leukaemia research charity.

It said:

"Many thanks indeed for taking the trouble to write to me about the polio vaccine and possible link to your son's leukaemia. There is a considerable amount of circumstantial evidence that suggests that there is indeed clustering in leukaemia and that it might be related to viruses. Whether SV40 is involved or not, it is too early to say. The fact of the matter is however, that in a recent study of American volunteers about 8 or 9% of them had SV40 in the blood. Just seeing viruses in their blood or even virus particles in the cancer cell doesn't prove cause. It could be effect because people are immunosuppressed because of the cancer and are more likely to get infections.

The challenge of the re-awoken interest in SV40 is to do new experiments, which are long overdue. I expect it will be another two or three years before we really have the solution and a real answer to this situation.

Thank you for writing to me, if you are interested in

keeping up on this subject I will be happy to write to you with any new evidence coming through."

Anna felt elated when she read this – someone else was taking her theory seriously.

She then decided to write to the Committee for the Safety of Medicine, and somehow from there her report was passed on to the Head Virologist of a World Health Organisation laboratory without her knowledge.

It was therefore a shock when Anna heard from the virologist with an invitation to come and discuss her theory with him, as he said 'I am intrigued that you as a mother of a patient have come to the same conclusion as an eminent American scientist, Janet Butel from Baylor in Texas, and your research is working along the same lines.'

The letter from a second professor meant that surely there must be something in her idea that had some basis of truth.

Meanwhile, Rob was making steady but slow progress with his treatment. He had setbacks though, and it seemed as though he would take two steps forward and one back.

There were occasional problems with the Hickman line. Sometimes it would become clogged up. The worst problem was when a yeast infection managed to get into the line, and this caused him to have a fever and was difficult to clear.

Occasionally he would be sent down to X-Ray to check on the placement of the line because it was feared its position in the main vein that entered the heart might have shifted.

On that particular day he had become very ill with a chest infection, as well as more ulcers in the mouth, and infection around a wisdom tooth and possible problems with his bowel again. He had to be wheeled down on his bed to the various departments for ultra sounds, and heart echoes – he was too weak to sit in a chair.

Each time there was a setback Anna was thrown into a state of panic again. This raw fear always remained there simmering under the surface ready to reappear at the slightest opportunity.

The nurses were caring and cheerful, but also appropriately concerned when necessary.

Whilst staying on the ward and getting to make friends with the other mothers, Anna had managed to carve out some sort of normality. Setting a routine seemed to help. The chaotic situation they had entered when Rob was first admitted, and which initially had seemed so alien and claustrophobic, had soon become a regular and almost comfortable routine. She had learnt to trust the excellent staff totally and knew that Rob was in the best possible hands, with the best possible chance of survival. A cure or remission was a dream she hardly dared to dream.

Mostly though, they took a day at a time and did not dare to look too far into the future. When his health suddenly deteriorated to a particularly vulnerable state, they would set their sights on just getting through the next hour or even next minute. Every moment she shared with her son was a bonus and each minute was precious.

There was no doubt that having other teenagers around him, really helped Rob's spirit. No matter how ill one or other of them at the time was they seemed to manage to laugh and joke. They would flick bits of paper across the ward to wake each other up and be annoying, or just talk or play computer games when they felt well enough. And, of course, there was the regular game of "avoiding the ward tutor at all costs." It was amazing the different ideas they came up with to do this. Rob having been well primed by Matt his other partner in crime, he was happy to pass on the advice to Daniel.

It was his last year of GCSE and because he was trapped in hospital, not even the ward tutor could help him with the fact that he was unable to continue and finish his science course work. Science had been the way he had wanted his career to take off. At the half way mark of the end of the first year, he was predicted to have A and A star in every subject. This would not be possible to achieve now though.

There was the other disappointment too, that having been voted to be Head Boy of the school before he was ill, he was now in no position to take up the duties once the new school year had started.

The headmistress though had been very understanding and said that they would still consider Rob as being Head Boy, even though he could not yet attend. The Head Girl would assume responsibilities for the both of them Rob was told, until he could return. That sent Rob the very positive message that they expected him to recover and go back to school again. Whether they really felt this or not did not matter. After all they were well aware of just how ill he was, but the main message was that they had not "written him off" and this was very important to his psyche.

As Rob and Daniel were admitted and sent home in between treatments, they nearly always found themselves in-patients together, and that included Matt too, even though he was in for a completely different form of cancer. The three of them bonded well.

It came therefore as a terrible shock one day when Nita confided in Anna out of earshot of their sons, that Kath had just told her she had been given the worst possible news. There was nothing more that could be done for Matt. It was now just a question of managing his pain until the inevitable happened.

Anna stood in shock. Matt was part of their family now just as Kath, and Nitan and Daniel were. It was a feeling that they were about to lose another son or brother, and they were helpless.

'I am not going to let Daniel know,' said Nitan. 'I think it is better they don't know.'

'I agree,' said Anna wiping tears away, 'we have to keep them positive.'

And of course that was the other side of the dreadful news, not just that they were going to lose a friend they had come to love, but that it suddenly made their own sons seem so vulnerable again as though they were right back at the beginning when first diagnosed.

Nitan had said to Anna only a few days earlier, 'one word we will never use is "relapse".' Neither mother wanted to face the possibility that this treatment was not going to cure their son permanently.

And then there was poor Kath. When Anna next met her in the ward kitchen, all she could do was put her arms around her and let Kath sob her heart out. It was difficult keeping a brave face on the world when you have been told that your fourteen-year-old son is going to die and there is nothing that can be done about it.

'I am so sorry, so sorry,' is all that Anna could say.

The following day, Rob was allowed home for two nights in between treatments again.

As she drove away from the hospital, all Anna could think about was Kath and Matt.

Rob was particularly fond of a band called 'The Verve' at the time, and he kept playing their album on the car CD player as they set off.

The rain was driving hard against the windscreen, and it was dark and dreary.

The Verve's song played over and over 'The drugs don't work, they just make you worse, but I know I'll see your face again.'

That is when the tears flowed silently down Anna's cheeks. The words were somehow prophetic and tragically appropriate with the news about Matt.

'Thank God it's dark and Rob can't see me,' thought Anna.

But Rob sensed something anyway and just said 'You ok mum?'

'Fine,' lied Anna. 'I am just finding it difficult to see in this awful weather, and my nose is running a bit.' She sniffed and wiped her eyes with a tissue.

Despite the sentiment of the song, she was glad that Rob's attention was taken up with the music, so she was not expected to talk. She was afraid she would give herself away.

After forty-five minutes, she turned the car into the driveway. It was really dark by now, but fortunately the security light that James had set up to switch on when it became dusk had worked, so the home was not in complete darkness.

The two ginger tom cats greeted them enthusiastically.

Helping Rob out of the car, because he was still quite weak after the latest treatment, she managed to get him up the steps to the front door.

As she was about to use the keys, she noticed a small parcel hidden away behind one of the pillars.

'I'll just get you into your room Rob and then I'll see what it is,' she said. 'Probably a present left for you by one of your friends.'

Rob sat heavily on the bed with a sigh of relief, and Anna gave him the remote to the TV.

'Be back in a moment when I've unloaded the cases, then we can have a hot drink' she said.

She was gone for a longer time than Rob had expected, and he started to worry.

'What's up Mum?' he called out, but there was no reply.

He struggled to the door of his room and clung to the handle. 'What's wrong?' he asked when he saw his mother standing stock still with the parcel open in her hand.

'Nothing,' she said hastily 'I think it is someone just playing pranks.'

When she had opened the box, there was one dead red rose, and something which looked quite revolting – as though it was part of the inside of an animal – some sort of offal. She put her hand hurriedly to her nose and felt sick. A note read 'do you really want to keep going?' And then the writing was followed by some numbers.

She felt shaken but was not going to let on to Rob. She

quickly closed the box again and left it outside.

'I'll just let James know we are home again' she called out.

After making Rob a coffee she went into the other room to phone James. Her voice was trembling.

'What's wrong?' asked James when he heard the unusual hesitance in her voice.

'James – was there a parcel when you were last here, waiting for me in the front porch?'

'Not this morning,' said James. 'I would have seen it when I dropped by to feed the cats.'

'Someone's been here during the day and left me a dead rose in a box, but worse than that, there is something quite disgusting – I - I really don't know what it is. She felt a twinge of fear. 'Oh - and also a strange note.'

'I'm coming over now,' said James.

He and Sandra had moved out of the bungalow after the long six-week period of the first treatment. They had now found a flat of their own, so they were no longer living at Anna's home during the week, and James was only calling in to look after the cats, collect the post, and check on any answer phone messages.

When he arrived and looked at the parcel and its contents he said 'I can't think who would put you through this with all that's going on – but I think I know what that disgusting object is. It looks like a kidney – from a small animal.' At one time James had considered becoming a vet, so he had undertaken a few vivisections. That was what had finished him off and changed his career choice.

'Could it be a monkey's kidney?' asked Anna horrified.

'Could be – never saw one specifically. Why don't you take box up to the professor you know in charge of the leukaemia charity – see what he makes of it. You are due back at the hospital the day after tomorrow.'

'If I can bear to keep it that long,' said Anna feeling sick again.

'I'll wrap the box up in several plastic bags and leave it in the porch out in the cold – it will be fine till then,' said James. 'Just try not to think about it until it is time to go back – then you can hand it over and be rid of it.'

'What do you think those numbers are?' asked Anna 'Is it a phone number, or some sort of code.'

'Let's wait until we hand it over to the professor' he replied.

'You don't think it could be Patrick, playing some sort of spiteful joke do you?' she asked.

'We could all see through him mum,' said James. 'That was what was worrying us when you were under his spell. He is a nasty piece of work, but I can't see any reason for him doing this – even though you have at last given him his marching orders. And anyway, don't let him intimidate you. You can't go through life looking over your shoulder as if he is about to jump out at you.'

But deep inside Anna felt that terrible fear again when she had run from Patrick's house after he had hit her over and over again. It seemed as though he were some sort of Jekyll and Hyde character. One moment he was the most loving partner you could wish for, then for no apparent reason he would suddenly flip. It hadn't happened until a year after they had met. During the first twelve months if he could not get his own way, he would suddenly throw a strop and storm out, and often she would not know the reason. He had taken his time before the relationship had become physically abusive. It was as if he had measured the strength of her feelings for him and had deliberately waited until she was dependent on his love. Except that of course it was not love from his side, but a selfish passion to control and manipulate. She had finally come to realise with great sadness that he was not capable of love as she knew it.

'Will you be OK tonight Mum?' asked James anxiously. 'Sandra and I could move back in if it would help.'

'No dear – I shall be fine. Rob will get wind that something is wrong, and he has enough on his plate at the moment. There's been a bit of bad news about one of his friends on the ward too, but I haven't told him yet – just want to keep him as calm and positive as possible.'

Anna usually slept well when they were in their own home, but this time she lay awake wondering who could have sent such a message in such a menacing way, and what it could mean. Was she perhaps getting a little too close to the truth?

CHAPTER 16 'THE PLOT THICKENS'
November 1997

When dawn broke the next day, the sun was shining, and the rain and wind had died away.

Somehow things did not seem so bad, and she dismissed the strange packet from her mind. 'Can't do anymore about it till we go back to hospital tomorrow,' she reasoned.

Her life had been turned upside down over the past few months in ways she could never have previously imagined.

Nothing could have prepared her for the fact that Rob's life would be threatened, or that Patrick would turn out to be such a violent psychopath addicted to women despite his promises that he would never hit her "because she was not the same personality as his ex-wife", and nothing could have prepared her for the terrifying realisation that the medical profession everyone relies upon, not only get it wrong sometimes, but lets the drugs companies rule by wielding the wallet.

It was becoming ever more shocking to her with each new discovery, that public health had nothing to do with caring for the individual, but was just for the benefit of the 'herd' – in other words the majority – rather than taking into account the disasters that could take place in any one individual as a result of bad judgement. It may well be that the monkey kidney cell route to the making of the polio vaccine did not affect the majority. But for those whose lives were being dramatically changed by the introduction of another mammal's DNA, infected by a virus which could molecularly change the human cells into something cancerous, well that was just callous rejection of all things ethical. It was obvious that using monkey cells rather than diploid human cells was a much cheaper method of producing the vaccine, and basically Britain was saving money. The drugs companies were laughing all the way to the bank. After all what do they care about the individual child or young person fighting for their lives against a disease caused by their ill thought out methods?

It occurred to Anna that she was changing. Her whole personality was shifting, and she wasn't sure whether she liked it or not, or whether it would do any good. But the fact was since Rob's diagnosis, she felt a deep anger toward injustice burning within her. It was this anger that had given her the strength to finally send Patrick on his way, and for her to see him for what he really was. Why on earth had she never seen it before? 'Because I was always the victim before,' she thought. 'Now I am taking control of my life and not just for my sake but for my family. We have never been in such a precarious position as this before.'

She thought of her daughter Alice and her other son James. 'They are suffering on the side-lines of helplessness too. They love their younger brother and deep down are frightened for him just as much as I am.'

Alice was juggling both marriage and full-time job, and she did her best to call in either at hospital or home wherever they might be and whenever possible.

'I'm thinking of running a dinner dance or holding some sort of event to raise funds for the children's ward,' she said. 'It will be a positive goal to work towards, and do some good at the same time.'

Anna could not but help admire Alice. She too was hurting so much inside, but she always held a steady and brave face for her mother and younger brother. And both she and James always retained their sense of humour which lifted Rob. This was one of the true gifts left to the family by Anna's father who had always retained a wonderful wit and feeling for fun no matter what predicament he found himself in. Somehow this had been genetically handed down so that Anna and her children could change a deep dark situation into a peel of laughter just by one simple word or observation of the ridiculous. It was a lifeline that they would use many times over during the coming weeks.

The uncomfortable part of Anna's new insight with her ongoing change of personality and view on life, was that she could now see how much suffering Patrick had caused her children during their stormy relationship.

Each time Patrick had thrown a tantrum, or let Anna down, or been seen with another woman on their brief breaks, her children would rally round to comfort their mother and even against their better judgement would try to heal the rift because they knew how much she loved this man. They were prepared to do that despite their hatred of him for all he had done. They hid the fact that he had got James by the collar one day and pushed him against a cupboard and waved a fist in his face because of some minor disagreement. Later James admitted that he had wanted to floor the man but had held back for the sake of his mother.

Although Patrick had never shown any level of direct violence toward Alice, her then fiancé Brian had been literally thrown out of the home on one occasion and left with a bleeding nose and with his hand being shut in the door. Anna had physically stood between them to break up the fight, although the only violence had been precipitated by Patrick.

This event had led Alice to leave home, which left Anna heartbroken. And yet still, she was trapped, mesmerized even, by the controlling power of this man that made her think he was some sort of hero she needed.

The brain and body so closely linked are powerful tools and although they seem two separate issues, they are completely entwined. However, the mind, which is in essence not the same as the organ of the brain, can ignore the things that should be noticed when the hormones and heart need something else than the brain is detecting – common sense can be shut down. Does the heart rule the head, or the head rule the heart or is it all down to hormones in the end and chemical reactions and synaptic snaps that have nothing to do with free will at all?

Anna had managed to blank out the bits of the relationship she did not really want to address, and this had been quite successful, up to that point where he had beaten her three times within a month of her major surgery. And that last time, when she had looked into his face and realised he had almost been taken over by someone else, someone she certainly did not know or recognise, and that is when fear coursed through her veins. Despite being in a weakened state after surgery, she had found the strength to push him off her and run for help.

Looking at the situation now in the cold light of day, she could see that it was at that stage when their relationship changed and there could be no turning back. Although she had continued hoping he would get anger management and alter his behaviour, realistically there could be no "happy ever after" solution, even though she tried to trick herself into thinking it might still be possible. It had been then that the abandonment and freedom of their love affair had come to an abrupt end. He would always be on guard now, and he could not live with someone who had any sort of power over him. In the world of Patrick, he always had to have the power and control, and with that gone, he would always be on the lookout for another victim to take her place.

As soon as Patrick had learned the G.P. had her injuries on record, and even though she had not opted to take it to the police as suggested, as a doctor himself he knew that he would now be watched, and if ever such an event happened again, that last episode would be brought into account.

This is why at her most vulnerable time, when she had just learnt of Rob's diagnosis, that Patrick had quite despicably and deliberately tried to get her to admit it had all been her fault so that once more he would regain the power and control.

'Perhaps he can't live with himself,' thought Anna 'or rather that he cannot live with the demon which resides somewhere deep inside, ready to take over at the slightest chance.' And suddenly she realised that was probably the whole problem. Patrick had no control over himself or his alter ego which was ever ready lurking just beneath the surface, ready to turn him into a monster that the outside world would not believe, and that his partner could not accept existed.

Her mind turned again to the strange and disgusting packet on the doorstep. It couldn't be anything to do with Patrick could it? Whoever had left it was within reach as it had not come by post or special delivery.

Once more she found herself making excuses, because the truth was too unpleasant to contemplate.

Today was the day when she would have to touch the package again. They were going back to the hospital for Rob's third treatment session. She intended to take the box to the professor as soon as possible – apart from anything else, she wanted to get rid of it.

Later after they had driven the 30 miles through the New Forest, and Rob had been settled back on the ward, she took the box wrapped well in the plastic bags and searched out the professor in the part of the hospital housing his lab.

After explaining how it had mysteriously arrived, she handed him the package and asked him if he had any ideas about it at all.

The professor opened the box and for a moment looked horrified. 'It is not so much what it is that disturbs me,' he said, 'but the manner in which you received it, and that you received it at all. It is definitely a monkey kidney. As for the dead rose, well I have no idea of that significance. The note... I just can't make out whether that is a kind of threat, or an encouragement to keep going with your research. As for the numbers, just give me a bit of time to think things out, and I hope I will have some ideas for you. In the meantime, try not to worry about it, but if anything else happens, perhaps you had better inform the police.' As he turned to go he added, 'Oh and I will be testing it for SV40 in case you are wondering. Someone seems to know something!'

Anna left feeling unsettled. The fact that the professor took it so seriously made it seem even more threatening.

Later in the day she had a phone call through to the ward asking her to go to the professor's laboratory again.

He looked serious. 'As you know I just thought I would test

the kidney for SV40 and it would appear it is infected,' he said, 'and as for the number, well it could be a batch number the sort you have on vaccines, but I can't be sure at this stage. I suggest you just leave the whole thing with me and go back to look after Rob. Try not to worry about this even though it is difficult. It is probably a one off and you won't have any more trouble.'

***

Rob's third lot of treatment reached the last day, and Anna decided she should go to the medical library before they returned home again. She had not been there for a while.

Once amongst the musty smell of books, and in the quiet amidst students and fully trained medical staff alike who were all studying, she found her mind ticking away again and wondering what path she could follow.

She had no idea where the thought came from, but she suddenly remembered a news report once that had stated in a place in Cornwall, a rural community, there had been an inexplicable cluster of three cases of leukaemia amongst young teenagers, and that sadly one had proved fatal. At the time it had been blamed on a spill of chemicals into the water supply, but subsequent extensive studies had proved that the cluster had not been caused by contamination of the water supply after all.

However, it did turn out that all of the teenagers were pupils at the same school and they were all fourteen. She found herself wondering if they had received a polio booster at the same time and therefore from the same batch as each other.

Working from a different angle, she looked up other press reports and found that there had been clusters in quite a widespread range of rural communities over Britain. Despite research into magnetic fields and radioactivity, nothing ever proved to be a cause.

'But,' she thought, 'in a rural community it would be reasonable to assume that there was only one GP surgery, and therefore that surgery would have one batch of polio vaccine. It only needed one batch of contaminated vaccine to spread the chance of mutation of cells into cancer cells.

She decided to write of her concerns to the Lancet and the British Medical Journal, enclosing a copy of her report and her more recent findings.

The Editor of the Lancet wrote:

'We are interested to read what you have to say, but I am afraid that we can take no action at this stage.'

They had addressed her as 'Dr.' and so had taken her to be a qualified medic, but the wording of their reply left her with an uneasy feeling. It was as if she were being warned off in some way. Another sign that maybe she was treading on dangerous ground and getting too close to a guarded secret.

CHAPTER 17 'MYSTERIES'
December 1997

R ob's fourth treatment was due to start in the first week of December.

This time the ward was so full, he had to be put in the four bedded ward with three much younger children.

He missed the company of Daniel, or indeed Matt, who he knew was being looked after in one of the isolation rooms used for bone marrow transplant patients, but he didn't know the reason why.

With a television at the end of each bed, the sound level was very disturbing. Mostly it was the Teletubbies again, while Rob was trying to listen to modern music.

'I can't cope with this,' he confided in his mother. 'I'm not even attached to a drip for this lot of treatment. I could go home and come up every four hours.'

Even as he said it, he realised it was not a sensible solution, but at least Sophie his nurse understood what he was going through.

'I think I have an idea,' she said. 'We could book you and your mum into the CLIC hostel at the back of the hospital, and then you could spend most of your time there and just come across when you need the injection and tablets. How does that grab you?'

Rob's face lit up. 'Just to get out of this four-bedded room with all the young kids around me would be wonderful,' he said.

So Sophie got the key to room number 5 and sent them across on the strict understanding that they would return to the ward at the appointed times for the treatment.

It was such a relief to Anna too, because sitting alongside Rob in such a crowded space with the noise of the youngsters around them was sending her brain waves off the scale and into the outer hemisphere. She did not feel it fair to leave him alone and go off to the medical library again whilst he was trapped in such an environment.

Staying in the house, Anna met another parent, a father called Daryl. His fifteen-month-old son had the same type of leukaemia as Rob.

'Can you tell me what effect each drug has on you?' he would ask Rob. 'Peter is too young to tell me himself and it'll help me to understand what he is going through.'

Daryl was a lot of fun, but he admitted that his coping mechanism in this traumatic situation took the form of copious cans of lager.

Everyone had to have some sort of coping mechanism, whether it was family support, faith, drinking or smoking. It was not the sort of situation where you could just "manage".

Daryl used to track Rob down in whichever room he was staying on the ward, and always came for a joke and a laugh. 'Just checking on you,' he would say. 'What colour drug have you got today, and what is it doing to you?'

One day he used the toilet in the ensuite bathroom of the teenage room on the ward which Rob and Daniel were sharing. He had been drinking quite heavily. There was a crash, and he came out holding the detached toilet seat up so that it framed his face and he was peering through it grinning. 'It just came off in me hand,' he said and hiccoughed. Everyone, including the nurse who was adjusting Rob's drip, doubled up with laughter. That was the best coping mechanism of all – laughter.

Before each new treatment session was started, Rob always had a heart echo and a lumbar puncture. This was done under light anaesthetic and was carried out to check if any of the leukemic cells had strayed into the spinal fluid.

He and Daniel were lying side by side on trolleys before they both went in for the examination, and again when they came out and recovered from the anaesthetic.

'I'm being allowed across to the house as the ward is so crowded,' said Rob.

'I'm actually being treated as an out-patient at the moment as my home is close to the hospital' said Daniel.

While the boys chatted, Nita and Anna had the chance to speak out of earshot.

'Any more news of Matt?' asked Anna

'He's become resistant to morphine as a painkiller,' said Nitan, 'and it was changing the way he behaved. I saw Kath the other day and she said Matt had taken to having everything lined up in height order on his bed table and wouldn't let anyone touch them or re-arrange them, and he was getting a bit short tempered which is so unlike him. They are trying to sort out some new cocktail of drugs that will give him pain relief instead of the morphine.'

'Poor Kath – poor Matt,' said Anna. 'She must be in the worst kind of hell anyone could imagine.'

'Have you done any more of your research yet?' asked

Nitan

'Not really had the chance,' said Anna, 'but I am getting response from various professors of medicine, and virologists and such. In fact, I have been invited to meet the virologist of a WHO laboratory when I can get there. What I am finding out though is truly worrying and I wonder if our Government knows what it is insisting we shove into our children. There comes a point where the risks of vaccination outweigh the benefits it would seem.'

'Have you heard about the guy who is making a fuss about the MMR?' asked Nitan.

'No,' said Anna, 'I haven't seen the news lately.'

'Well he is a Paediatric Consultant in a London hospital, and he reckons that the MMR is responsible for causing autism in children. There are lots of mothers now refusing to have their children vaccinated with it.'

'That's good and bad news for my theory about the polio vaccine then,' said Anna, 'because it will now look as though I am climbing on the band wagon and trying to gain some sort of credibility from his ideas. But I knew nothing of his venture when I started out. And anyway, my aim is certainly not to start a panic. I just want it properly investigated, but I somehow doubt it will be with the Drugs Companies breathing down the Governments neck!'

'Well you have enough proof down on paper and the fact that you sent it off to various renowned medical sources on dated documents, means that they cannot accuse you of stealing his thesis. It will be obvious you had your ideas before he had gone public.'

However, the backlash against the MMR showed Anna how important it was to make sure of her facts before going public. She did not want to go public to the press for fear of starting a panic, but she did want her idea validated and properly researched. If what she suspected was true, then many more children and young adults would be subjected to unnecessary cancers and leukaemias.

That week of treatment went quite fast. Rob and Anna enjoyed their stay at the hostel at the back of the hospital, only venturing over to the ward when it was necessary, and it gave them peace and quiet. Although it was not as relaxing as being at home, it was a very good second best.

The hostel was run very efficiently, and there was a friendly atmosphere amongst the residents who were all parents of the patients on the children's ward, apart from Rob who was himself a patient.

Even so, it meant that a lot of the time during the day they had the place to themselves because the parents were on the ward with their children.

There was now a whole lounge where they could watch television, read or play a computer game whenever Rob wanted. The conservatory was light and airy, and although the winter had set in and the garden was too cold to sit outside, they found just relaxing in the sunlight indoors was healing to both of them.

The organised kitchen had a cupboard marked with the number of each room, so that each occupant could store their own favourite foods and cereals in their own space.

Rob was even managing the short walk between the house and the hospital, and the fresh air and exercise seemed to be doing him good. Things were looking up at last.

One evening after they had gone to bed, there was a knock at the door.

'Hello,' said one of the other parents, 'sorry to disturb you but there is someone on the phone for you.'

Anna slipped on her dressing gown and went downstairs to the public phone in the hallway. She felt apprehensive. It was late at night to receive a call, and she wondered if her other children were alright.

She picked up the receiver 'hello?' she said, half expecting James or Alice to answer. There was a long pause. 'Hello,' she said again 'who is it?' But there was just a silence. She could hear slight movement in the background. 'Is that you James – or Alice?' she persisted. But again there was no response. 'Can anyone hear me' she shouted thinking that perhaps it was a bad line. Another long pause and then the receiver at the other end clicked with a finality that sent shivers down her spine.

'Was it Patrick playing silly devils, or is something else going on?' she thought as she slowly climbed back up the stairs feeling unnerved. Memories of the disturbing package came to the fore of her mind once more.

As she entered the room Rob said 'Who was that mum?'

'Just a wrong number,' said Anna.

'Don't give me that old chestnut,' said Rob. 'They asked for you by name, otherwise we would not have had a knock at the door.'

'Well the truth is Rob I don't know; they just hung up on me. I think it might be Patrick.'

'Oh - that creep,' said Rob. 'Mum don't let him worry you. It is the first time you have stood up to him and he won't like it -wouldn't surprise me in the least if he doesn't try to make you anxious. He probably wants you running back to him for protection and is trying to set up some fictitious threat.'

'Well I'm not going to let it get to me,' lied Anna, and inwardly she thought 'Rob has a wise head on young shoulders; he could well be right.'

It was on the last day of Rob's treatment. They were due to go home that evening, when something else happened.

James visited out of the blue in the afternoon.

'We're due home tonight,' said Anna, 'you could have saved yourself a journey – mind you we are pleased to see you any time as you know.'

'Well I wasn't too far away,' said James. I had to see a client and I thought I'd give you this letter as it looked kind of official.'

Anna opened the letter cautiously wondering if it was some sort of bad news, but in the end it proved to be the contrary.

The letter was yet another response from a professor from a different cancer charity. In it he admitted that they were finding SV40 in several types of solid tumours now when doing biopsies. These included brain tumours, lung tumours, testicular cancer, prostate cancer and they were expecting to identify it in some lymphomas too.

The scientist admitted that they could not fathom out where this virus contamination was coming from, but it was disturbing that it was showing up in these types of tumours.

She held the letter out to James. 'You see,' she said, 'there must be something in all of this after all. Even the highest medical professors are now baffled how a monkey virus can be isolated in cancerous tumours, but it is all out there. Polio vaccines have been known to be contaminated in the past with the virus SV40 and they are now finding it in current biopsies.'

'I thought you said that the type of monkey they use has been changed and that it's supposed to be eradicated now,' said James.

'You have hit the word on the head,' said Anna excitedly. 'You said "supposed" but that does not mean they have succeeded in getting rid of it altogether. It only needs a few batches to be contaminated. After all, the different type of monkey they are now using, the African Green monkey, has been proved to be "susceptible" to contamination by SV40 in laboratory conditions. The professor in charge of the leukaemia charity here told me that.'

'Can we have a word on our own for a moment,' said James quietly. Rob was engrossed in some sort of battle game on the computer.

'Just going to make us a cup of tea,' called out Anna, 'we'll be in the kitchen.'

As soon as they had left the lounge where Rob was sitting, Anna told James about the odd phone call with no-one on the end of the line.

He went strangely silent for a while and then said 'Do you think you might be getting a bit out of your depths mum? You are up against some pretty big players. Drugs companies do not take it lightly when their moral code and ethics are challenged and particularly when it might end up affecting their financial status. Nor will the government look on you in a kindly light either if you throw a spanner in the works and wreck their vaccination programme.'

'What are you suggesting James?' asked Anna.

'Well these rather random things that have been going on,' said James, 'it may not necessarily be Patrick you know; it could be you have stirred up a hornet's nest or as they say – opened Pandora's Box.'

'So far it's only been some ghastly joke with a monkey kidney sample and a dead rose – and there still might be a reason for them,' said Anna defensively, 'and that phone call last night that could have just been a mistake.' She didn't dare let her imagination get too carried away or she would be terrified into silence.

'Mum there is something else I should tell you, and it's the real reason I am here today so near to the time you are going home. I'm afraid there's been a break in back at the bungalow.'

Anna froze in a state of shock. 'What do you mean – a 'break in' – what's been stolen?'

'That's the odd thing,' continued James, 'I can't find anything gone at all. Our technical stuff is still there, and they don't seem to have gone for your jewellery. It's as if they are just trying to ruffle your feathers a bit; perhaps put the wind up you.'

'Did you tell the police?' asked Anna feeling the sudden need to sit down.

'Of course mum. I discovered it last night when I went in to feed the cats. I didn't want to tell you then because the night time is not a good time if you know what I mean. Mind you, no time is really a good time to tell someone they've been broken into.'

'How did they get in?' asked Anna still in shock.

'They seem to have jemmied a window in the sitting room. The glass pane isn't broken, just lifted out. The police can't find any finger prints anywhere and they've been over it with a fine-tooth comb. They are just as baffled as we are. The only suggestion they can come up with is that I somehow surprised the burglar when I came in to see the cats and deal with the post, and the intruders just left in a hurry; through the woods at the back.'

'Oh – James,' is all that Anna could utter. 'As if we haven't enough troubles at the moment.'

'Look mum, try not to worry. Sandra and I have decided to move back home for longer than two days this time. You need some support. The police say that burglars never come back to the house they have just broken into as they know people will be vigilant and there will be a lot of police activity.' What James did not tell his mother was that the police had added 'at the moment.' It was not unheard of for a burglar to come back much later on when all the panic had died down to take things they had seen.

'Didn't we leave security lights on?' asked Anna.

'Yes – oh yes, I made sure of that – and the radio was on,' said James. 'Try not to panic mum, but the police think we may have been deliberately targeted, by someone who knows our movements or who has been watching us.'

'James,' Anna shuddered as she clutched the side of her chair, 'that's awful. Why would anyone want to target us?' Then she added 'it must be that wretch Patrick, he is trying to get his own back on me; tip me over the edge so that I beg him to come back.'

James paused. 'Well of course that is a possibility. But let's face it mum, he is not that clever or as intelligent as he tries to make out, and if we're to believe all the stories about his bad back injury, he wouldn't be agile enough to get through a window either.'

'That is if we really do believe the story about his bad back,' said Anna bitterly. 'I am beginning to wonder if I fell in love with a complete fake. Over the past few months it would seem I fell in love with a mirage and not a real person at all.'

James sighed. 'We tried to warn and protect you mum but as they say "love is..."' Before he had a chance to finish Anna said 'I know – blind.'

'But even if we take into account all Patrick's paranoia and mental instability,' continued James, 'he may have been responsible for the parcel, and even the phone call. But not the break in; I can't see that happening.'

'It's all too much of a co-incidence,' said Anna 'somehow it must be all linked and who other than Patrick would be targeting me?'

'Come on mum how could he get hold of a monkey's kidney? It's not exactly something you can get hold of, unless you work in a laboratory or a zoo. What I am trying to say,' said James, 'is you've been sending your report to a lot of people, and word is getting around. I know you are keeping it from the press, but people in high places know what you are thinking, and also that you are keeping proper research reports.'

'I am only trying to do what is right. People have a right to know, and at least I am doing it in a responsible way and not blurting it out publicly,' said Anna getting upset.

'The main thing at the moment,' said James, 'is to keep calm and know that you and Rob will not be on your own at home, and that Sandra and I will be there looking after things when you next have to come up to hospital. I think we should try and keep it from Rob if at all possible. Stress will not be good for him.'

'But then I shall worry about the both of you,' said Anna, 'if we are indeed being targeted, that will mean I have put the whole family in danger.'

'We'll just sit tight and remain alert,' said James. 'If it is all somehow tied up then whoever it is will be bound to make another move. If it was all just a coincidence, then I doubt we will have any more bother.'

Then he added 'as I said before, I don't think Rob should be bothered with all this. He has the biggest battle of his life on his hands as it is, and he seems to be fighting through. By the way the window has already been replaced and made secure.'

'Thanks James. What would I do without you?' said Anna.

So that evening, James drove ahead with Anna and Rob following on behind.

When they reached the welcome sight of home, Sandra was waiting for them.

'Hope you don't mind us staying again Rob,' she said, 'our new flat is in such a state of turmoil your mum said we could use the old room until it is ready for us.'

'No I'm pleased,' said Rob, unaware of the tension.

And indeed Anna was very pleased and relieved too.

CHAPTER 18 'A SAD GOODBYE'
17th December 1997

It had been a difficult home coming after the break-in. The feeling of safety and security that Anna had always felt in the bungalow had been blown apart.

'Well at least the new window looks very clean,' said Alice.

'Yes,' laughed her mother, 'problem is it shows up all the others now.'

Anna had looked around to see if anything was missing, but all she could see was that her filing cabinet drawer was slightly open where she kept all her information, letters and reports about the research.

Had she left it like that before? She really couldn't remember, it wasn't the sort of thing that she would have taken notice of. After all, there were so many more important things on her mind. Housework and general tidiness had been thrown to the wind. As long as the bills were paid and Rob's room and the bathroom were kept clean, and the kitchen surfaces of course, nothing else really mattered in the great scheme of things.

Although on edge and watching and waiting for the next "happening", she eventually began to relax again, particularly with James and Sandra living with them and keeping an eye on things when they had to go up to the hospital thirty miles away.

Rob was returning to the hospital daily for blood transfusions and separate platelet transfusions on the lead up to Christmas. This meant that Anna was able to attend the ward Nativity play with a confusing mixture of sadness and joy. It was heart rending because there were two Angels in wheelchairs, "Mary" was hooked up to a drip and "Joseph" had lost his hair and eyebrows and looked very thin, but they all sang and performed beautifully.

The only cloud was that the Television company technician who had been sent down to film the Nativity play for use in a documentary, failed to turn up. He had apparently imbibed too much in the local hostelry and been given the sack – however, it was a great disappointment to the children who had all prepared so carefully.

The fact that Anna was up at the hospital daily also meant she was able to attend the carol service held in the chapel.

She noticed Kath hidden away in a corner accompanied by one of the nurses from the ward. It was obvious that she did not want any other company.

Anna had not seen much of her at all since Matt's deterioration. His mother spent all her time in the isolation room with him and they were protected by a sign on the door which said 'Please ask at the Nurses Station before entering this room.'

However, on one occasion Anna was asked to take a message into Kath.

As she pushed the door open she found the television was on, but Matt was too weak to watch. He was almost unrecognisable since Anna had last seen him; so much thinner, gaunt face and eyes that were not seeing very much at all. He grunted in acknowledgement of her.

She looked at Kath with great sympathy and saw the

desperation in her friend's eyes.

'He's not too good today,' said Kath, 'the morphine really is taking its toll.'

As soon as she left the room and closed the door behind her, Anna felt a great sadness and the sheer pain of the other mother. Only a month before Matt had been fooling around with Rob and Daniel. He had gone downhill so fast.

It was ward policy to get as many children and teenagers home to their own environment for Christmas Eve, Christmas Day and Boxing Day so that they could be amongst their families, therefore Rob was not due for another inpatient treatment until the week after Christmas.

When his blood count returned to normal again after all the transfusions, he was told to go home and enjoy Christmas.

But one of the things that they had both learnt since the beginning of the nightmare - nature has a habit of throwing the unexpected at you - and on the 16th of December, Rob suddenly developed a fever and infection whilst he was at home.

As the rules demanded, Anna phoned the ward and told them.

'Take his temperature again in half an hour,' said Sophie, 'and if it's no lower, then you must come in so we can get the infection under control. Ring us first though so we can get a bed ready.'

The temperature in fact went up, so Anna did not hesitate to ring, and with Rob grumbling, they headed back on the forty five minute journey to the hospital.

At least with James and Sandra now staying back at home,

she felt a bit more secure about leaving the place. She was still very shaken up by the break in.

'Thank heavens I invested in a mobile phone,' she thought. It was still quite unusual in 1997, not many people had them. But it meant that as they were racing their way through the dark and along unlit roads through the forest, she would at least be able to call for help if the car broke down.

When they arrived on the ward, they found that the only other patient there was Matt.

Rob was put back in the single room he had first occupied on that initial admission way back in August.

It was not long before they heard Matt calling out in pain.

The registrar came in. 'They can't seem to get his pain control right, so a specialist is coming up to sort him out.' She could see how distressed Rob was, even though he did not know just how seriously ill his friend was.

Anna put the television on partly to distract Rob, and partly to drown out the cries of his friend down the corridor.

She then went to the kitchen to make a cup of tea. This was opposite to Matt's room and the door was slightly ajar. Inside she could see the Consultant and the Pain Specialist as well as Matt's medical team, but the part of the scene that stuck most in her mind was the sight of the young Houseman who was striding up and down ringing his hands behind his back clearly not knowing what to do. He was obviously very distressed at seeing his young patient in such pain and must have felt completely helpless.

The rest of the ward was eerily silent. Normally there would have been a lot of noise from young children and babies crying, or televisions competing with each other or at least staff busy in and out of rooms. Some of the young patients would even use their drip stands as scooters and rush up and down the corridor unaware of just how ill they were.

It was easier for the youngest ones to cope with the situation. All they knew was how they were feeling at the time, either ill or getting better. They were not aware that their condition was life threatening or even what that meant.

This was what was so hard for the teenagers. They were at an age when they had enough knowledge to understand that they may not make it through the treatment. Bleakly aware that just as their life was starting, and their independence was within their grasp, it could be taken away from them at any moment. It took a very special strength for a young person to face this possibility.

With a heavy heart Anna returned to Rob in his room and sat quietly by his side. 'That could so easily be us,' she thought imagining what Kath must be going through at this minute.

Eventually, Anna noticed that Matt's cries of pain had subsided. She ventured out into the corridor and met the Houseman. 'Thank God,' he said, 'at last they have found the right mix of drugs to take away his pain and give him some peace.'

There was a special charity that granted the children's wishes on the Paediatric Cancer Ward. Rob could not think of anything he particularly wanted despite being asked several times. He was not a boy who expected a great deal from life and was happy that he had a computer at home already. Had it not been so, this would have been his wish.

Matt however, had asked for a snow board and all the gear

that went with it and his wish had been granted by the charity. It waited for him at home. He had once confided in Rob that when he was better he would be off abroad to try it all out on the slopes of Austria.

On the morning of the 17th of December, Anna woke to the most beautiful sight outside. It was snowing, and as always when snow first falls, the thoughts about the inconvenience it might cause later were always driven out by the beauty of the pure snow resting on roofs and trees and roads before people started to make their marks with footprint or car.

Kim, Rob's other designated nurse put her head around the door. 'Want a cup of tea?' she whispered so as not to wake Rob.

'Yes please,' said Anna.

But before Kim disappeared she said, 'He seems a little less feverish and more settled now we have the antibiotics up in the drip.'

'A great relief,' said Anna 'I was really worried about him.'

'I think you will definitely make it home in time for Christmas,' and she smiled at Anna.

'How is Matt this morning?' she asked.

Kim looked rather downcast. 'Not too good I'm afraid, but at least he is not suffering from the pain any more,' and with that she disappeared to make the welcome cup of tea.

With Matt's cancer of three solid tumours in different muscles being so different from the Leukaemia which had hit Rob and Daniel, it was difficult to understand the pain he was now going through, but Anna had gathered it had now migrated to the bones. As always and once again she was hit by the unfairness that decent young people were struck down with such terrible battles, when criminal youths seem to bounce through life without facing anything like it.

Instead of turning the television on to hear the news as she normally did, she went across to the window and watched the silent wonder happening outside. It was a world, fresh and new and magical and it brought back memories of happier times. So very silent. 'If only it was like a fresh page waiting to be written on,' thought Anna 'I would use a pen and re-write our story.'

She supposed it was because the snow muffled other sounds, but it always seemed as though a great hush descended over the world when it fell.

Behind her Rob stirred and opened his eyes. 'Hey,' he said, 'why is the room so bright?'

'It's the reflection of the snow,' said Anna.

'Good, old Matt might get to use his snow board after all then,' said Rob, still unaware of the prognosis and the fact that Matt would never actually get home or even leave the hospital again.

Anna's heart chilled. 'I can't tell him,' she thought, 'it is too cruel to think that one of his friends will not make it through. Not only would it sadden him greatly, but it might also remind him that his fate is not secure yet either.'

That day seemed to go so slowly.

By lunch time, both Rob and Anna had decided everything was far too quiet, so they played a computer game together, not that she was any good at it, but at least it gave Rob a sparring partner. Just as Alice had done once before, Anna made a mess of the controls and her character started running backwards. Rob's character was a German soldier and goose stepped everywhere which meant that when he made it run it looked hilarious.

They both laughed.

Rob suddenly became very tired and was just about to drop off to sleep when there was a light knock on the door and the Registrar put her head round into the room.

'Have you got a minute?' she asked Anna and indicated that she should follow her out into the corridor.

Anna was surprised to see that the doctor had tears running down her cheeks.

'Matt has just died,' she said. 'I am not sure if you want Rob to know or not which is why I called you out.'

Anna could feel her own eyes filling with tears too 'Poor Kathy' was all she could utter.

She slipped quietly back into the room, but instead of Rob being asleep he was waiting for her.

'What was all that about mum?' he asked 'is there some bad news about my tests?'

'No no,' said Anna composing herself. 'It was nothing to do with you honestly.'

'It seems strange that the Registrar called you out if it is nothing to do with me,' he said.

'No honestly Rob, everything with you is fine, I wouldn't lie, and as you remember they promised you would always be kept in the picture and they would hide nothing from you.'

'Then its Matt isn't it?' he said fixing her with a gaze. 'Not good news for him. He's died hasn't he?'

'How did you know that?' she asked.

'I'm not daft,' he replied. 'I realised he must be very ill as he was in so much pain and calling out, and now it's unnaturally quiet. Please tell me.'

Anna hesitated. 'Yes you're right,' she said sadly. 'I have known for a couple of weeks that he wasn't going to make it, but Nitan did not want Daniel to know, and we agreed it was probably better for you both not to know the truth. I had no idea that you would be the only other person on the ward when it happened.'

'I'm not a child mum,' said Rob, 'you should have told me. I am sure that Daniel would want to know too.'

'No,' said Anna quickly, 'you mustn't tell him. Nitan was adamant that she did not want him to know. She only wants him to be surrounded by positive events.'

'Well if I were him,' said Rob, 'and found my mother had hidden such a thing from me, I would be annoyed.'

He looked very sad. 'Poor old Matt, he didn't deserve that'

'No he didn't,' agreed Anna 'and neither does his mother.'

'Ironic isn't it,' said Rob, 'that the day Matt dies is the day he could have used all his snowboarding gear.'

It was indeed ironic and cruel, but Anna fleetingly imagined that maybe his spirit was free to snowboard now – anywhere he wanted to.

Later that afternoon, Kath came to say goodbye. She was very brave. What could they say to her; there was nothing anyone could say so Anna just gave her a long and meaningful hug. Kath turned to Rob and said, 'Good luck with everything,' and then she was gone.

As darkness fell, Anna went to the ward kitchen.

If the ward had been quiet before, it was now unbearably silent. She had never thought that she would be uncomfortable with silence as the ward was usually too noisy.

She waited for the kettle to boil, and two porters arrived on the ward and entered the room opposite pushing a covered metal box on a trolley.

A few minutes later they came out again and wheeled Matt's body away. Not even the porters spoke a word. 'To have to take a boy to the mortuary must be a dreadful experience,' she thought, 'even if they didn't know him.'

She suddenly felt a terrible emptiness and sadness. Silence was accentuated by the white covering of snow outside. It was as if the whole world mourned the loss of such a lovely youngster.

Sensing the effect that Matt's death had had on both Rob and Anna, the nurses said that they would make sure they were discharged again the next morning. 'Now the fever has disappeared, and we are on top of the infection,' said Kim, 'there is no point in being alone on the ward; much better to be at home.'

And so it was with great relief that the boy and his mother drove home again the following day. They were resolved to put the sadness of the last twenty-four hours behind them, and to look toward Christmas with the family and make the most of every minute of every day; so very precious.

But from then on, each year on the 17th of December,

Anna would secretly remember Kath and Matt, and send up special prayers for them and their family. They had met for only a brief time in their lives, but the impact would remain for ever.

CHAPTER 19 'SURVEILLANCE'
December 1997

A nna's investment in the mobile phone paid dividends. It was very basic but at least the old "bricks" that were the first models had now been replaced by ones small enough to carry in a handbag – even though they were still quite heavy and took up considerable space.

It gave her the freedom to go shopping, knowing that if Rob was in trouble at all, he could get in contact with her.

And of course, there was a lot of shopping to catch up with for the Christmas weekend.

Thankfully a thaw had set in the day after it had fallen, and most of the snow had disappeared, just leaving the odd patch of ice around.

This made it even more poignant that the day Matt had died, was the only day the snow had fallen.

As she came back in the late afternoon having run the gauntlet of Sainsbury's and Asda she became unnerved by a helmeted figure sitting stock still on a motorbike in the driveway next door.

She was unloading the boot of her car and talking to one of the cats as it came up to greet her, when the hairs started to tingle on the back of her neck with a premonition that she was being watched.

What made her look over the fence she could not say. Her neighbour's house was in darkness except for a light in the hallway and she knew they were away, so the motionless figure came as a shock.

The motorbike was parked partly hidden by the pile of chopped logs that her neighbour kept ready for their wood burning stove. The figure was in a black leather suit and solid black helmet and visor giving the impression it was a robot rather than human, and particularly as it was so still.

Although her neighbour was always generous with the parking space in front of his property, and on occasion he let a friend park their car there, this was something completely different. Had it just been the motorbike without the rider, she would not have worried, but why was a man, or presumably a man, sitting astride it not making a move?

She hurried indoors and found Rob.

'Had any visitors at all?' she enquired.

'No,' said Rob, 'apart from a load of Christmas post, everything has been quiet.'

'Have you heard a motorbike at all?' continued his mother.

Rob looked at her as though she had gone mad. 'Why are you hoping to hitch a ride on a Harley Davidson then mum?' he laughed. 'I know you've always had a fantasy about men in black leathers.'

To lighten her mood of anxiety, Anna laughed too. 'Not any more. It's just that, well there is a motorbike rider sitting astride his machine dressed all in black, face and head hidden with a helmet, and staying absolutely still. He was only just the other side of the fence when I was getting the shopping out.'

'Well come to think of it,' said Rob, 'I did hear something that sounded a bit like a motor bike about two hours ago, but I thought it might be the police helicopter doing their usual tour of the area. They have a habit of hovering over the wood behind as you know.'

'So,' thought Anna, 'he's been there for at least two hours. Why on earth would he do that, unless – unless…' and she shuddered, 'unless they are keeping some sort of surveillance, and in which case who are they watching and why?'

Thankfully James arrived home from work soon afterwards, so she was able to off load her anxiety. She obviously had not troubled Rob with her thoughts. They had even managed to keep the "break in" a secret as the window pane had been replaced before their return home.

'It's difficult mum,' James said. 'If we alert the police and there is no hard evidence that it is you they are watching, then we will only be noted down as "nutters" and they won't take notice of anything else we might have to tell them. They know you are anxious since the break in, and I did tell them too about the parcel and the telephone call, but they did not seem to take those episodes seriously. If you look at it from their point of view you can understand why. We probably do look a bit paranoid.'

'Did you notice him on your way in?' Anna asked.

'No – but then if he was dressed in all black, and staying stock still in a darkened driveway, I wouldn't necessarily. I'll go out and have a look now.' But even as he said it, they heard the throaty roar of a motorbike as it set off down the road.

'It couldn't be Patrick,' said Anna, 'with all the fuss he makes about his back problem, there is no way he could ride a motor bike; although come to think of it he can still play golf and ride an ordinary bike.'

'Don't be daft mum,' said James, 'he wouldn't have a clue how to ride one. Mind you it doesn't mean to say he hasn't got someone else to do it for him. But why would he go to those lengths.'

'Because as we have said, he is mentally unstable and is obviously very annoyed with me for finally saying "no",' said Anna. 'He does not seem able to manage without a woman – it is like a baby with a security blanket.'

'It could have been the police themselves,' suggested James. 'After all they did use our driveway for some sort of surveillance once didn't they? Because we are on a bend in the road they have a good view both ways. I remember a car being parked up with two police inside for two afternoons running.'

Yes of course that was true. Anna felt she must be getting over anxious.

That was until she picked up the phone to ring Alice and let her know they were home again. She noticed that when she spoke there was a strange hollow echoing sound.

'There must be something wrong with our answer phone,' she said. 'Everything sounds as though we are making the phone call in the bathroom.'

'Probably the weather,' said James. 'Maybe there is still snow on some of the lines.'

Still Anna felt uneasy. She really must get a grip on herself or her crazy thoughts would take over their lives. Even the break-in was the sort of thing any household could be subjected to at this time of year. Thieves were on the lookout for presents, and ready packed ones at that.

She opened the mound of post that had arrived that

morning. Most were welcome Christmas cards from friends that usually only wrote once a year. It was good to keep in touch even if so spasmodically.

Then there was also a letter from the Virologist from the World Health Organisation Laboratory north of London, suggesting a definite date for her to travel up and meet him to discuss her findings and her theory. This had perhaps been the most unexpected contact of all, because she had not written to him, but he had heard of her research possibly through the Health Secretary or one of the other sources.

It gave her heart that he said he was intrigued that she as a mother had come to the same conclusion as an eminent American scientist.

'Bring the batch number with you and also the make of the vaccine that was used on your son when you come up to see me. I know you said the other scientist was unable to get a sample, but let me try,' he wrote.

Anna put the date in her diary – January 13th. She would have to hope that Rob was perhaps in hospital that day as she could then leave him without any worries.

Christmas Eve arrived. It was a day that Anna used to look forward to. A milestone of when she and Patrick got engaged in the Isle of Purbeck, but now it only held sad memories for her of a love she thought was there but in fact she now realised never existed.

She looked down at her lovely opal ring, and to her horror noticed that the third opal was missing.

'How appropriate,' she thought, 'today would have been our third anniversary of the engagement.'

Anna tried to think back to when she had last seen all three opals, and she distinctly remembered admiring them as she opened the front door that morning. 'It must have dropped out in the porch somewhere' she thought.

She was on her hands and knees rummaging around under the doormat, when she was aware of someone standing over her.

It was Patrick.

She got to her feet hastily. 'What do you want?' she asked in a hostile manner.

'It's no good I can't live without you,' said Patrick. 'It would have been the anniversary of our engagement today and I can't stop thinking about you.'

'That means that the latest woman has kicked you out then,' said Anna, sounding strong, but inside she was shaking. This man still had some sort of power over her after all.

'Can I come in to talk for a minute?' he asked.

Despite all her misgivings Anna was about to say 'yes' when James came up behind her.

'No' he said firmly 'you can't'

'But this is your mother's house not yours,' said Patrick glaring at him.

'We are protecting her,' said James. 'If I had known you were being violent to her you would have been thrown out long ago.'

The truth was that when Patrick and Anna got together, James was still in his late teens, but now he had enough experience of life to know how to handle such a situation.

Patrick turned to go. 'Just remember though Anna, I still love you deeply and I don't let go that easily.'

As he disappeared down the driveway she turned to her son 'Was that some sort of threat?' she asked.

'I don't know. Maybe he just doesn't know how to express his feelings properly. He's a very screwed up personality. But at least you have a witness to what he said.'

'I wanted to ask him about the box with the disgusting contents left on the doorstep and the phone calls,' said Anna. 'I don't think that motorcyclist was anything to do with him; that must just be a co-incidence.'

'Don't you mean "phone call" not "phone calls"?' said James.

'Well I didn't tell you before,' Anna owned up, 'but I actually had three of them while staying in the accommodation behind the hospital. I suppose I didn't want to acknowledge it had happened.'

'I'm glad we're staying here and it's good he knows it too,' said James. 'Probably won't try any more funny stuff if it is him at the back of it all.'

The truth was that Anna having seen him again unsettled her greatly. It was easier to hate him while he remained the ogre in her imagination but being face to face with him – well it unleashed all her old feelings.

With the chaos of Christmas now upon the household though, there was no time to dwell on other matters.

Despite everything they managed to have a relaxed and happy time and Alice and husband Brian joined them. The whole family was together in the tight bond they had formed, and this brought comfort to both Rob and Anna.

CHAPTER 20 'MEETING OF MINDS'
January 1998

B efore they knew what had happened, Christmas and New Year were over, and Rob was admitted for his fourth treatment.

As hoped, it coincided with the date when Anna was going up to see the virologist at the WHO laboratory. This meant she could leave her son in capable hands and not be worried about what might be going on at home while she was away.

The journey was arduous for Anna. She did not like driving long distances, and certainly not to completely new places that involved negotiating motor ways and in particular the M25 which she had never had to face before.

Therefore, she allowed plenty of time for the journey.

It was not until she had started out on the M3 that she became aware of a motorcyclist keeping pace with her not far behind.

He was wearing the dark leathers and closed-in helmet of the person she thought had been watching their property, but then she thought 'This is ridiculous, the motorcyclist behind me is dressed just like seventy five percent of all motorcyclists.'

She turned on the radio to listen to some soothing music on Classic FM and with all the traffic gathering in density and speed around her, she forgot all about the "stalker" - until that is, she decided to take a quieter route before joining the M25.

Now she was off the motorway, other drivers became more noticeable to her - and it was then she noticed the motorcyclist who was still keeping pace. But was it the same one or just another clone?

She had to force herself to look forward as she was driving, and not concentrate for too long on the rear driving mirror.

It occurred to her that particularly on the major roads, it seemed strange for a motor bike not to overtake a driver doing just 40 miles an hour. She didn't like travelling fast and always kept in the slow lane.

But then her attention was taken away from her wild imaginings to concentrate on the road signs ahead.

She also began to think again about her theory. She had all the papers on the seat next to her, but her mind still went on searching for more evidence. In fact, would it ever stop?

Anna thought of her brother John, and a sudden realisation hit her like a bolt of lightning.

'About six months before John became ill, he had to go to Nigeria where he'd been asked to be the architect for a university project planned in the wilds outside Lagos,' thought Anna. 'Therefore he would have to have had an update and booster of vaccinations, including polio as Nigeria was particularly susceptible to outbreaks.'

In fact, Anna remembered John saying quite a lot about that particular contract. They had flown him in a small plane over the area to be used. He looked down on many huts with conical shaped rooves made of matted leaves, and thought 'Poor devils, I bet no-one has told them they will be homeless as soon as the University is built.' John was a man of conscience and this had bothered him.

But now suddenly everything clicked into place in Anna's head. If he had received a polio booster about six months before the first signs of the brain tumour, then that would make sense, both timewise and opportunity for the virus to strike. If he had received a contaminated batch, then it fitted in with the picture that the Professor of the Cancer Charity had told her; that they had found SV40 in brain tumours.

Finally, after four and a half hours of driving, she turned into the Laboratory complex.

Instinctively she looked behind her. Good - no sign of any motorbikes.

She was met at the door by a Security Guard. He checked a list for her name and she produced her photo id driving licence as proof she was who she was supposed to be.

Waiting in the large entrance area, she was approached by a thoughtful looking man in his fifties. He was about 5ft 10 inches tall, with dark hair and thick rimmed glasses and he had a gentle face and non-confrontational manner. He neither looked like a mad professor, nor did he have the arrogant air of many medical consultants. In fact, he looked just like "Mr. Normal" who one could easily pass in the street without a second glance. This belied his extreme intellect, intelligence and ability in the field of virology which had claimed for him his top position within the WHO Laboratory.

'Anna,' he said grasping her hand warmly. 'Good to meet you at last. Your report and letters have been circulating around so many scientific circles, that I feel I know you already. Do come in,' he gestured for her to go ahead of him into an office and indicated for her to take the comfortable chair on the opposite side of the desk to him.

Nervously Anna clutched a copy of her report, along with the various letters she had received over the past few weeks relating to leukaemia, SV40 and the polio vaccine.

The virologist looked serious. 'I fully appreciate your research, and as I have said before, it is amazing that you are working along the same lines as Janet Butel in America, but as one of the officers responsible to the government for the safety of vaccines, I have to be very careful in what I say or do. It would not be a good idea to start a panic about the polio vaccine.'

'That's exactly why I have not gone to the press,' said Anna. 'I want to be sure of my facts before any of this gets out into the public domain.'

'A very sensible and responsible idea,' nodded the scientist. 'Just because I don't necessarily agree wholeheartedly with your idea myself,' he continued, 'does not mean that I condemn it out of hand. We are all on the side of protecting the public and in particular children and young people.'

'I've brought the details of Rob's vaccination for you,' said Anna holding out a sheet of paper giving the batch number, name of the drugs company who made it, and date it was given.

'Good,' said the virologist. 'I will see if I can get a sample and test it for SV40. I agree with the scientist at the hospital who is conducting research on a cure for leukaemia that it seems strange the drugs company told him there were no samples left since they are supposed to keep a sample of each batch by law. It might be they were worried when they saw what research he was conducting – smelt a rat as it were.' He smiled at Anna, 'as opposed to a monkey that is!'

'What worries me in particular,' said Anna, 'is that although I know it has been stated that SV40 is filtered out by the gut and therefore should not pass through with the live oral polio vaccine that is used at the moment, I think this is flawed for two reasons.'

'Go on,' said the virologist.

'For the polio vaccine to work, the virus in the vaccine has to infiltrate the gut to stimulate the immune system. Do you think it might be possible for the Simian Virus 40 to be opportunistic and combine in some way with the polio vaccine – sort of piggy back its way into the blood stream?'

'It could be worth consideration,' said the scientist.

'Or,' continued Anna, 'maybe SV40 acts like the HIV virus and takes advantage of a breakdown in the system and invades the blood through cuts, cracks or ulcers within the digestive system.'

'I see what you are getting at,' said the virologist, 'but am still not convinced.'

'I worked out a possible mechanism by which the SV40 Virus causes white cells to become leukeamic – can I tell you?'

'By all means,' he said. 'I am really interested to know how you came to your conclusions.'

Anna took a deep breath. 'Well,' she said, 'while trawling through all the medical books I could find, these are the facts I discovered. Leukaemia cells are immature white blood cells that reproduce too early and out of control. SV40 has a T-antigen which interferes with the cell cycle.

She paused. 'Then secondly – Leukaemia cells often have translocated chromosomes. SV40 has a T-antigen which translocates chromosomes.'

And finally, she concluded, 'Natural killer cells in the blood have been turned off which is what allows the cancer to develop. SV40 turns off the defensive mechanism in the natural killer cells.'

There was a moment of silence. 'I can see you have delved quite deeply into your theory,' said the scientist.

'I know that there are polio vaccines available that do not use monkey kidney cells, but the other scientist at the hospital – even though he could not obtain a sample of the batch used on Rob - was able to ascertain that the company concerned, and the batch concerned, had definitely come from supplies using monkey kidney cells.' She paused. 'And I have to say that I have read a report from the World Health Organisation that states that using vaccines produced on monkey kidney cells is in fact the most risky form of vaccination. And although it does not say so, I would assume it is also the cheapest way to produce it, which is why we are probably the only country in the western world to still use it.'

Again, the scientist remained quiet for a few moments. 'I understand what you are trying to prove,' he said, 'but you see by the time the vaccine is prepared, there are no complete cells from the monkey remaining within it; they have all been broken down for want of a better explanation.'

Anna thought for a while and then said 'That may be, but you are introducing cell protein from another mammal into the human blood stream which could well elicit a response in the immune system – one that is not good.' Then she continued

'You see I have also learnt while reading up about all this that we as humans carry benign viruses in our systems called BK and JC viruses which don't cause us any trouble, but suppose they only remain benign as long as they detect they are in the human body – rather like SV40 does in the monkey – but if they then should discover monkey protein perhaps this tips them over too.'

She realised the more she went on that it must sound like the mad prattling of some wild woman who no doubt could be evicted from the building at a moment's notice.

'There are all sorts of theories out there about the possible cause of Leukaemia,' said the virologist, 'from nuclear contamination, to environmental contamination, but I know that the latest theory is that a virus is the final trigger.'

'What I don't understand,' said Anna, 'is why they cannot definitely track down the specific virus.'

'Virology is a very intense and complicated subject,' said the scientist, 'but I understand your frustrations. When I read your initial letter in which you explained how leukaemia had affected your son and his young life, I was very moved. I have children of my own, and I think any parent reading your letter would have been upset.'

'Thank you,' said Anna appreciating the sympathetic approach. 'But that does bring me on to the other part of my research, which shows that leukaemia and cancers in babies and young children are on the increase, and let's face it, we are now bombarding their immune systems with all sorts of vaccines as soon as they draw breath.'

The virologist laughed. 'Yes, but when you think of all the slobber and muck they come into daily contact with, which is filled with viruses, I don't believe the theory that we are damaging our children's immune systems with too many viruses.'

Anna paused. 'But many of the viruses they would come into contact with naturally are not as devastating as the ones introduced through vaccinations.

'I noticed too,' she continued, 'there are often "clusters" of leukaemia that appear in rural areas, or perhaps confined areas within a town. I was thinking, that this could mean that the patients all belonged to the same doctor's surgery, and therefore received the same batch of vaccine.' She paused again and consulted her notes. 'And the other unusual thing is that sometimes these clusters may not always be in the same part of town, but the patients all go to the same school. In those cases, they are usually in the 14-15-year-old classes which would mean they would all receive the same batch of vaccine in a school booster prior to leaving.'

The virologist was very patient, and not at all dismissive. After all, he had taken the trouble to get Anna to come up and talk to him about her report.

'I know that in the past it was both the inactivated as well as the later live vaccine that was found to be contaminated with SV40,' she said, 'back in the 50s, 60s and 70s, and I know that the contamination is supposed to have been eradicated now. But bearing in mind we are introducing a live vaccine, what if it were somehow being contaminated again, despite all the precautions? I truly believe that we should stop using monkey kidney cells to produce the vaccines.'

'I am in a difficult position to agree with you there,' said the scientist carefully.

Anna continued. 'I believe that when contamination takes place, the virus could remain dormant for a while just like the herpes virus does with chicken pox, and it waits for an opportune moment to strike – perhaps when the immune system is low.'

There was another pause before she continued. 'I have read that when the SV40 virus was isolated originally as a contaminant of the monkey kidney cell cultures used for the polio vaccine, it was found to be capable of transforming human cells, and that they can clone themselves to continue surviving. It was also found that the polio virus and the SV40 virus can persist in human cells by invading the human genome. This surely means they can change the DNA – which is what I am on about. I think of it as a "stealth virus" – that is a term used by Dr. W. James Martin in America I believe. I am not sure if I use the term in the same way he meant, but I believe it hijacks its way into the human body and waits until the time is right to strike.'

The gentle argument went back and forth for another half an hour, with Anna being adamant about her findings, and the virologist treating her with respect, but not admitting that she was right. He was obviously in a difficult position.

Eventually their interview came to an end.

As the scientist showed Anna out he said, 'I will do my utmost to get a sample of the batch you have given me and will contact you as soon as I know.'

Anna left the Laboratory compound feeling drained and exhausted but also strangely elated – at last she was getting somewhere.

She got into her car and drove out of the security-controlled gates to start the return journey to the city hospital and to Rob.

It was after she joined the M3 again, that she glanced in the rear-view mirror and thought she noticed a motorbike tailing her.

'It must be my imagination,' she thought and deliberately tuned into a play on Radio 4 to take her mind off it.

As she got closer to her destination she began to relax. The windows were steaming up a bit, so she lowered the front passenger seat window slightly to get rid of the mist on the windscreen. Then looking at her petrol gauge she decided she ought to stop at the next petrol station to fill up.

She drew into the Rowland's Service Station shortly before her turn off the main road to the hospital.

By now she was so tired all she could think about was getting safely back to Rob on the ward. Not far now.

She let her guard down momentarily when she went to pay. Usually she was very security conscious and made sure she locked the car – and indeed she had – but she had forgotten the passenger window was open.

After paying for her petrol, and as she put the receipt into her bag she looked up just in time to see a motor cyclist draw up alongside her car on the passenger side. He reached in through the open window in an attempt to grab the file on the seat where all her documents about the research was being stored.

'Hey!' she shouted. 'Stop thief!' and she started to run toward her car.

This outburst fortunately caught the attention of other

drivers who were filling up with petrol, and one man made a lunge at the motorcyclist, who immediately revved up and drove off erratically – swerving and slipping on a wet spillage.

The file dropped onto the petrol stained floor of the garage, releasing the documents to the mercy of the wind, but she managed to grab it before the papers blew away.

Shaking she stood for a moment and realised how stupid she had been.

'I was right then about that motor cyclist all the time,' she thought as the adrenaline coursed around her veins putting her into fight or flight mode. 'It must have been the same motor cyclist following me all day – not my imagination.'

After thanking the motorist who had intervened, she stuffed all the papers back into the file – out of order now - but put it on the floor this time. She also firmly closed the passenger window and locked herself in.

Her immediate reaction was one of anger - 'how dare he?' - But soon fear set in and she started to shake uncontrollably.

It had become obvious that someone was after her and her research. The papers were not only important to her, but also she felt responsible for all the scientists who had put themselves in the firing line by trying to help her. She was particularly concerned for the Head Virologist who had made himself so vulnerable in some of his correspondence.

She resolved to take photocopies of all the documents as soon as she got back to the Hospital. 'In fact, I'm going to take two copies of everything,' she thought. 'I'll give one to Alice and one to James to keep separately. It's obvious I am on to something that someone doesn't wish to be out in the public domain.'

Reaching the hospital car park, she sat still for a moment and checked around her before opening the door. No sign of a motorcycle or rider – she would wait until someone else was walking from the car park to the hospital and would follow them so as not to be alone.

She did not relax until she was once more back on the ward with Rob.

CHAPTER 21 'LIGHT AT THE END OF THE TUNNEL'
February 1998

R ob and Anna settled into the routine of the last block of treatment.

The hard work promised by the Consultant all those months ago was still continuing, and for a while Anna had to put behind her all thoughts of research, and indeed all thoughts of being "watched". At least she felt safe within the walls of the hospital and particularly on the ward with its high security protection of locked and coded doors for entry.

Although each drug combination was different, and therefore had different side effects, Rob was used to his body reacting in various unpleasant ways and just accepted the situation and got on with whatever was thrown at him.

He was back in the teenage room again, sharing with Daniel, and so there was a lot of laughter once more.

Rob had been told by his special nurse that the health experts were now considering making cannabis legal for people going through treatment such as he was, and that it could be used safely for certain medical conditions.

Not long after, one of Rob's older friends came in to visit him and brought him a box of home-made brownie cakes explaining that his granny had made them especially.

'Am I allowed one?' asked Anna.

The friend hesitated 'yes of course,' but Anna noticed he

glanced at Rob first before answering.

She took a mouthful. 'This is the most delicious chocolate cake I've ever had,' she said. 'It's so moist and there's a special taste about it. Can you get the recipe from your granny?'

Again, Rob and the young man exchanged glances.

'I'll ask her,' answered the friend with a slight smile aimed at Rob.

'Why don't you offer one to Daniel?' asked Anna.

'No mum,' said Rob hurriedly. 'He won't want one.'

This attitude struck Anna as odd at the time. Usually her son was so generous. But she thought no more about it and took another cake for herself anyway and left him to his visitor.

Suddenly she seemed to see a much brighter side to life and found herself giggling for no apparent reason. Still she had not guessed that there was a secret ingredient which gave the brownies that extra something.

Rob had fallen asleep when she returned, but when he woke he was mortified to find she had given one of the cakes to Daniel and another to his mother Nitan.

'Mum they are mine,' he whispered to her. 'You can't go giving them out.' And inwardly he was thinking, 'God - my mother is high on chocolate brownies made with cannabis and has been giving them out to everyone on the ward. I just hope she hasn't given one to the doctor; apart from anything else – what a waste!'

The truth was that the special brownies were not only helping Rob with his physical pain, but also with the emotional pain that seemed to consume him.

He was fighting sadness about the loss of Matt which was still so raw but couldn't share it with Daniel as Nitan had asked specifically that her son would not be told the news of their friend's death.

'I don't want him to hear anything negative,' she said to Anna. 'Remember we agreed we would never use the word "relapse" – it's the same sort of thing. No negative input.'

Rob still felt that Daniel, who was a year older, would prefer to know.

From a mother's point of view however, Anna understood the way Nitan was feeling. Matt was one of their close circle of friends who they had all looked on as a member of their own family, like a brother in arms, and now he had lost his battle against cancer. It brought to the fore the reality that nothing was secure, and nothing was certain and that no matter how much they laughed, Rob's own vulnerability seemed very fragile again, awakening the feelings of fear when he had received the diagnosis in the first place. 'Was he going to die?'

Matt's death spurred Anna on even more with her search for the cause of these teenage cancers. There must be a common denominator somewhere. Children did not seem to have suffered from cancer when she was a child, or even in her grandparents' generation, so something had changed in the current generation, and it was not just simply that medical knowledge had grown. After all, cancer had been identified in Egyptian mummies thousands of years before.

It would seem that cancer had been around as far back as when the human race began. Neither did it have anything to do with the fact that a previous generation might have been prone to other illnesses, such as consumption, heart failure or TB instead whereby deaths from cancer may have been masked.

No, something had definitely changed either in the environment, or the way food was made, or the way it was cooked… or… and here she returned to her research, a likely reason was that it was a combination of effects finally triggered by an opportunist virus entering the system through vaccination.

Not that she was in any way against vaccination. Quite the contrary, she was very much for immunisation and vaccination to protect against any serious disease. But certainly, the way some of the vaccines were made must be suspect – particularly in the light of what she had discovered about the polio vaccine. 'You cannot mix the DNA of other animals with humans, and in particular close relatives like apes and get away with it,' she thought, 'and there is no excuse when other safer methods are available.'

Anna found she was tormenting herself and wondering if she could have received a contaminated batch when she was given the polio vaccine in the 1950s as one of the first children, and whether somehow she had harboured the virus in her system where it had lain hidden. After all, that is the way the herpes virus lies dormant until triggered, and perhaps she had passed it on to Rob when he was a foetus. This thought was too much to bear. If she was responsible for his illness she would never forgive herself even if the fault was not hers.

But when she thought about it rationally, it could not be her fault. She was given the vaccine as a child when it had first become available. Her friend's father who was in charge of Paediatric Health for the local health authority at the time, had said that even though she had already had the disease itself when she was four, it was still worth her having the vaccine as an extra protection. It was he who had given the injection – since they were inactivated vaccines at the time - and it was not until a few years later when it was changed to a live vaccine and given in drop form on a sugar knob, that injections were no longer given.

Rob's fourth treatment ended, and they were sent home once more. It was now February 1998.

'Only one more session Rob, and apart from the blood transfusions before your blood count stabilizes, you will be able to return to some sort of normal life. You'll even be able to return to school and take some of the GCSE exams that don't require course work. As long as you can get grade C or above in six of them, it'll be possible to get to the Grammar School and then you will be back on track for University.'

Suddenly, it seemed as though he had a future after all. They had been afraid to look too far ahead before.

***

On their return home, there was the same problem with the phone line. Anna had noticed since the 'break-in' that the telephone had sounded odd. It always had an echo, and there were clicks every now and then. She wondered if perhaps they were being bugged, but who on earth would want to do that and why. Perhaps she had read too many John Le Carre novels or watched too many Hercule Poirot dramas on TV.

One time they had returned from a stay in hospital they found that the outgoing message on their answer phone had been completely scrambled.

James had said it was perfectly fine in the morning when he had left for work, so could not explain at all what might have happened to it while he was out.

'We haven't been broken into again,' he said, 'so any interference with the phone line would have taken place outside.'

They did not have any secrets to give away, or anything of great importance at all to say on a phone – at least not unless they counted the research. Could it be possible that the drugs company had wind of what Anna was doing, and were they trying to keep tabs on her? She was intimidated by the fact that drugs companies were powerful and well financed so would be able to arrange most things they wished; including the bugging of someone's land line telephone.

The days passed by quickly while they were at home, but then they had a double blow.

James had not told Anna that he had developed a lump under one arm pit. He had seen the doctor who had immediately referred him to a specialist and it was arranged that he would go in for a biopsy at the local hospital. They were concerned in case it was a lymphoma, and the test would be carried out the following day.

However, at the same time, Rob developed an infection and high temperature, which meant he had to be admitted straight away to the hospital thirty miles away.

Now Anna was torn in two. She was due to take James to hospital locally and stay with him until he came back from theatre, but at the same time, she was told she had to get Rob back to hospital all those miles away as soon as possible. By the time it was obvious that Rob's temperature was not reducing it was already eleven thirty p.m. and that would mean driving through the New Forest at midnight.

Just when they had thought they were getting through one nightmare, they were swamped with two at the same time.

The doctors wanted to move fast with James because of his brother's condition and in case he shared the same genetic traits. He would have to be taken into hospital at seven in the morning for the operation at 9:00 a.m.

Anna drove through the forest at dead of night with Rob feeling very ill and complaining of a blinding headache. This did not bode well at all.

By the time they arrived at the Ward, it was one o'clock in the morning, and Rob had almost passed out.

The Houseman came to Anna and put his arms around her shoulder. 'I just can't believe what's happening to your family,' he said. 'We don't have room on the usual ward for Rob this time, so have given him a temporary bed in another children's ward.'

This would make it much more difficult for Anna to leave him whilst he was so poorly and in different surroundings, but she had to get back for James.

She lay awake on a camp bed next to Rob, but at 5.00 a.m. she got up and dressed quickly and left for the forty-five minute drive home again.

Anna took James into the local hospital and waited until he went to theatre. She didn't know what to do with herself as she now had two sons thirty miles apart, both ill in hospitals and both of whom needed her.

Eventually James was wheeled back into his ward after the operation, and the wait for the result started.

It took two more hours. As the doctor approached, they

both tensed, but then the doctor smiled and said, 'It was a deep seated abscess not a lymphoma, but it was just as well we dealt with it because it would not have resolved on its own.'

With a sigh of relief, Anna took James home and left him in the capable hands of Sandra before returning once more through the New Forest and back to join Rob. She was utterly exhausted both mentally and physically.

By the time she reached him, the new round of antibiotics had taken effect and Rob was looking much better and after one more day, they were discharged home again.

***

At last, it was time for his final dose of chemotherapy. This was the trial one where he was being used as a guinea pig.

He had the usual lumbar puncture, and heart echo and liver function test before the treatment started. But halfway through the week-long trial period, Rob suddenly deteriorated.

The medical team arranged for him to have another heart echo, and it was discovered that his heart had been damaged by the drug. Certain drugs were known to damage the muscle tissue and performance of the heart which is why such careful attention was paid to the reaction and why the patient was checked so regularly. It was a great blow to find that this last treatment had affected his heart, and Rob was told that his heart would never be able to fully recover and they had to stop the treatment immediately to prevent further damage.

'The computer got it wrong then,' said Rob, referring to when he first agreed to take part in the trial on the understanding the computer chose whether he was one of those patients receiving the new treatment, or was on the 'blind' list where he would not receive it.

And so they were discharged home before the whole trial was complete, and were left feeling let down. Not by the medical staff, but by the throw of the dice chosen by the computer that had meant he had pushed his body just that bit too far.

This information would mean of course that the current trial would be abandoned which would help other patients, but not Rob.

***

Before leaving the hospital, Sophie warned them that once the medical team had restored Rob's blood to normal again with transfusions, and they were finally discharged with only monthly, then three monthly follow-up appointments, they would go through a strange period of feeling insecure because they would no longer have the reassurance of regular visits to the hospital each week. The responsibility would be theirs.

Had anyone told Anna this at the beginning when first diagnosed, she would not have believed them. To be at home and without having to go back and forth to the hospital would be heaven. But Sophie was right. They had become institutionalised, and dependent on the medical staff for reassurance in a way they had not anticipated. It was as if a crutch on which they had relied, had been suddenly swept away.

Anna remembered vividly that nightmare she had at the beginning of it all – where she was teetering around on top of a pile of unstable cardboard boxes – ready to fall any minute. That is now exactly what it felt like.

But once home, Rob soon felt well enough to return to school and his old chums. He could also take up his responsibilities as Head Boy.

Of course, returning to school had its own problems. Rob still had lost a lot of weight, had no hair, no eyebrows, no eyelashes; he attracted stares, particularly from the younger pupils, but he had got used to this.

Once when he went across to the local shop to buy some sweets, the shop owner had not recognised him and had watched him with suspicion as though he were about to steal something. His appearance gave him the look of a hardened skin head.

When he was in touch with Daniel, he found he had suffered a similar experience when going into a store in the city centre. There he had been followed round the entire shop by a security man!

Together the boys were able to laugh about it all, but it was yet another challenge.

By the time Rob was back in school, Anna had received a letter from the virologist she had visited at the WHO laboratory.

He told her that he had managed to obtain a sample of the batch used in Rob's vaccination without a problem. Despite the drugs company's protestation to the Leukamia Charity professor that they had none of that batch left, they had sent it without delay – therefore they had been lying before. But then the request for a sample this time had come from a completely different source which had nothing to do with cancer of any sort, so no doubt the drugs company had dropped its guard on this occasion. However, the virologist said that although it was confirmed it was a batch made by using monkey kidney cells, he had been unable to trace signs of SV40. 'Mind you,' he had said, 'it was a rather poor sample.'

Anna was now convinced that her research was being blocked. After all, why was it that one scientist working for Leukaemia research had been told quite definitely that there was none of that batch left, while another scientist in a totally unrelated position had been able to obtain a sample without a problem?

Rather than reassuring her, this latest news made her more convinced that she was right.

Summer 1998

At last life returned to some sort of normality.

Rob took six GCSE exams and was able to get two A grades, three B grades and one C grade. This meant he would leave his current school and start in the sixth form at the local Grammar School in the autumn term.

It was now nearly exactly a year since their nightmare had started.

CHAPTER 22 'SOME SORT OF NORMALITY'
1998/1999

They were home again permanently, and each was trying to regain some of their former routine, but now Anna found that she was missing Patrick much more than she had realised.

While all her concentration had been on getting Rob better and back home and on with his life, she managed to push all thoughts of Patrick to the back of her mind. He had become a complication she could do well without; but now - now she missed his company. There had been good times in between the bad, and it was the memories of those good times that surfaced most to haunt her. She was lonely.

James and Sandra had moved back to their flat soon after the fourth treatment session, so they were well established in their new place and it left Rob and her on their own.

Of course, now she was home again on a more permanent basis, she was able to contact all the friends like Laura and Ruth who she had lost touch with apart from phone calls. They now met up for coffee, or shopping. On one occasion she went to town with Laura when there was a German market and carousel. After downing a couple of glasses of strong mulled wine enhanced by brandy, they climbed aboard, choosing the names of their individual horses carefully. 'I've just kicked the one called Patrick for you,' said Laura. 'It was a bit harder than I meant and I seem to have taken a chunk out of his rear end. It should have been the real Patrick, that's what should happen to him.' Yes, Anna was recovering her slightly mad and abandoned view of the world once more thanks to her friends.

Rob's hair had grown back, his face had filled out and he was living the normal life of any teenager, working hard and playing hard. His check-ups at the hospital had lengthened from regular monthly to three monthly gaps. He was officially "in remission".

This did not mean though that Anna had completely relaxed. She would still wake up in the night feeling a fear and dread in the pit of her stomach, afraid that they would suddenly be plunged back into the nightmare, but gradually these bad nights spread further apart, and she began to feel like her old self.

With this normality came a shift in her priorities. Even the blazing enthusiasm for her research project began to dim, and she gradually let go of the intense work involved. As she became less involved, she noticed too that the strange sounds on the phone stopped, and no longer did she believe she saw people sitting in cars on the road outside, or motor cyclists following her. It must all have been in her imagination she told herself. 'Stress can play all sorts of tricks on the mind' she reasoned.

***

1998 quickly blended into 1999.

Rob was now doing his first year of 'A' levels at the Grammar School.

Alice and husband Brian took him on a special holiday treat in the Easter holidays. They had promised him this break when he was first diagnosed to give him something positive to look forward to, even though no-one had known at that stage whether he would make it through or not.

They went to New York and then on to Toronto.

When they returned home, Brian presented Rob with a strange kind of trophy; it was a framed photograph of a pigeon.

'What's all that about then?' Anna had asked.

Alice laughed. 'It's just Brian's sense of humour. Rob hardly ate anything while we were there. He said he felt sick a lot of the time.'

Warning signs began to flag up in Anna's mind.

Rob was now "off the radar" from regular hospital check-ups and had been deemed to be in "permanent remission" which was as close to a cure as one could hope for.

However, he seemed to be acting normally over the next few months until one day he complained of bad back ache around the waist area. But being Rob, and having been used to far worse things, he just got on with life. Out with his mates at the weekend and working hard for his A levels at school.

Anna noticed that he was beginning to stand and move in an awkward way.

'Is your back still bothering you?' she asked.

'It's my stomach as well,' he said. 'Seems to be getting worse.'

'You'd better go along and see the G.P. then,' said Anna. 'Maybe all the chemotherapy you've had has upset your stomach.'

Inwardly though she was worried. It was too long after treatment for this to be affecting him now - or at least, not in such a dramatic way and with increasing effect.

Rob came back from the doctor with some anti-acid medicine for upset stomachs. But the pain did not go away - it just kept on getting worse.

He went back and saw a different doctor, who said he would put him on a waiting list for an endoscopy – the tube that is passed down to the stomach to see if there are any ulcers. 'Sounds like a stomach ulcer to me,' said the doctor, 'but I am afraid the wait for such a test is about four months.'

A week later, Rob was in even more pain so he saw yet another doctor at the surgery who decided it was a kidney infection and gave him antibiotics.

Then the family had some wonderful news. Alice was pregnant. She and Brian had been longing for a baby, and now it was on the way. For a while this lifted everyone's spirits.

By the time of Rob's 18th birthday at the end of October he was in real trouble.

He was in his second year of A levels and was trying to take his mock exams.

Anna noticed he walked bending over to the right all the time. The pain on his left side had spread round from his back to the front of his stomach. The only way he could get any sort of pain relief was by soaking in a hot bath.

On the evening of his 18th birthday, the family celebrated in a local restaurant, but Rob, unable to finish the meal and in too great a pain to sit any longer, said he would get a taxi home so that everyone else could finish the meal.

James said quietly to Anna, 'Mum I think he needs to go to hospital. If you take him to A&E I will sort out the rest of the family and the bill.'

Feelings of dread rose within Anna and brought back bad memories of his previous diagnosis. She was overwhelmed by familiar fear as she drove her son to A&E.

An out of hours G.P saw them and said he needed a scan, and to return as early as possible the next morning to get it done as the Radiography staff had gone home.

This they did but there seemed to be a lack of communication between the doctor seen the previous night, and the one they saw now in A&E.

'It just says X-ray and ultra sound,' said the doctor reading the notes. 'Nothing about a scan, but we will admit him to our temporary ward while we sort it out.'

So once again, Rob was subjected to waiting despite being in a great deal of pain and unable to eat.

The ultra sound was inconclusive.

'There seems to be something like a cloud of gas in the intestines which is blocking a clear view,' said the radiologist. 'It's probably just wind, but we will do X-rays as well.'

An hour later, a gastro-intestinal registrar visited Rob and looked at the X-rays on a screen. 'I think you are just constipated,' announced the registrar emphatically.

'But look at that constriction in the gut,' said Anna pointing to where the X-rays were still clearly visible on the screen. 'It looks as though something is pressing in on it. It is much narrower there – see?

The doctor regarded her with disdain, as if she was ignorant. But of course, although her nursing experience had been so long ago, she knew enough to realise something was not right with the X-ray.

'I'll give you some mild laxative,' said the doctor, I am quite sure that's what's wrong.

'But I'm not constipated,' said Rob.

Again, the doctor looked disapprovingly at them for challenging his judgement. 'It is possible with severe constipation which has caused a blockage that – how shall I put it simply – the more watery contents can get round the side - sort of bypass the solid block. That is all it is, constipation!'

And with a dismissive attitude and arrogant air he was gone, and Rob's discharge papers signed despite Anna having given full details of his recent medical history.

Over the next week, his conditioned deteriorated quickly. He was in the middle of some exams, and although the school was a mere five-minute walk away up a hill, Anna had to drive him there as he was in too much pain to walk.

On the following Saturday as he lay on the sofa, Anna looked at him with concern and was convinced that whatever they said, the leukaemia had returned. The doctor had taken blood samples and proclaimed that his blood was clear of leukaemia, but Anna was judging his condition by other signs. He was deathly white, could not eat, wanted to sleep all the time and could not get rid of the intense pain.

She was at the end of her tether. What could she do?

Anna picked up the phone and dialled the Paediatric ward where Rob had spent all those months fighting leukaemia before.

Wilf the charge nurse answered the phone.

'He's dying before my very eyes,' said Anna in tears. 'I don't care what all these so-called doctors and specialists are saying down here – I know what I am witnessing.'

There was a pause, and then Wilf said, 'Anna we have known you for two years, and I have never heard you sound like this before. Bring him up straight away and we'll get the Consultant to have a look at him.'

Rob felt too ill to move, but Anna managed to get him into the car, and they drove the thirty miles once more to the hospital. It brought back bad memories, but at least she was comforted by the fact they would be seen by someone who knew Rob, someone they trusted and who would take his condition seriously.

Wilf greeted them like the old friends they were. 'Right now, Rob – what are you up to this time.'

Rob managed a weak smile. 'Not exactly sure, but we hope you can all help find out.'

Soon Jane the Consultant joined them and sent Rob down to the ultra sound unit where the Consultant Radiologist took over.

'I'll give you a shout when we have seen the whole picture,' he said to Jane. She had officially started a week's holiday that afternoon but had come in especially to see Rob. 'Not actually leaving home until tomorrow,' she explained. She looked at Rob, and Anna noticed a flicker of concern cross her face, although she always kept a professional matter of fact approach.

What was worrying Anna most was that the area where Rob was getting increasing pain was the area of the pancreas, and she knew this was a cancer with a very poor prognosis.

She could not see the screen as the Consultant rolled the head of the ultra sound across Rob's stomach, but she could read his face, and the signs were not good.

The Radiologist asked a nurse to call Jane and get her to come back.

He kept a fairly robust manner and smiled and chatted to Rob to put him at his ease.

Jane arrived, and the two consultants went into a huddle.

Then Jane announced 'You will need a proper CT scan Rob, so we can see exactly what is going on. As I am going away I shall hand you over to my partner. You know the Consultant that usually deals with Daniel. He will take good care of you. Meanwhile, after you have the CT scan I suggest you go back home and wait for the results.'

It was an awkward journey home. Both Rob and Anna felt as though they had been thrown back into the nightmare of two years ago when he was first diagnosed. Rob played his favourite CDs on the car system again. The Verve once more sang 'the drugs don't work, they just make you worse, but I know I'll see your face again.' It broke Anna's heart.

As soon as they got home, Rob asked if he could be dropped round to one of his friends to play computer games.

There seemed no harm in taking him there. After all, if the medical team had been really worried they would have kept him in as an in-patient wouldn't they? So instead of taking Rob home first, she dropped him over to his friend's before returning to the bungalow herself.

The answer phone was flashing indicating there was a message.

It was the other Paediatric Consultant who would be looking after Rob until Jane's return. His message said 'Anna, please ring me on my private home number as soon as you get this,' and he recited his phone number. 'We have been trying to contact you urgently.' He sounded annoyed – as though she should be there waiting for him on the end of the phone.

In a state of dread and panic, Anna rang him knowing full well that he would not normally give a patient his home number.

Martin the Consultant said 'Where have you been? We have been trying to get you. You need to ring the ward as soon as possible. Rob needs to come back in right away.'

He did not give any further information, so Anna immediately rang the ward.

The nurse who answered was one of the staff who had taken regular care of Rob during his in-patient stage.

'Hello Julie,' said Anna recognising the voice. 'We've only just got back, but I found a message to ring Martin and he told me to ring the ward. I gather Rob needs to come in.'

Julie did not sound her usual cheerful self. 'Oh yes Anna,' she said 'can you bring him back first thing tomorrow morning?'

'He's not here at the moment, and I don't know how to tell him he's got to come back.' Then she paused 'Julie it's not cancer is it?'

There was a sound of sobbing on the end of the phone – so unusual and uncharacteristic of any of the nurses - and then Julie said, 'I shouldn't really tell you, but yes, it is.'

Numbed with shock Anna replaced the receiver and sat stock still for a moment. She could not cope. Her youngest son was back in danger again. She decided to ring James.

'I don't know what to do,' said Anna crying down the phone. 'I just don't know how to tell him he has to go back in.'

'Would you like me to tell him mum?' asked James.

'Please – I don't know what to say to him,' she replied.

'I'll phone him at his friends and pick you up. We'll collect him together,' said James calmly.

Anna wondered where she would be without her eldest son's support.

Twenty minutes later James let himself in. 'Are you ready mum?' he asked. 'Rob says as soon as he sees the car he will come out.'

And so the two of them drove off to Rob's friend's house and waited outside.

In the dark a bent figure walked slowly toward them, eyes fixed on the ground. He looked so pathetic and dejected that Anna had trouble fighting back the tears. What he must be going through she could only imagine.

As usual James tried to be up-beat about things. 'Well you are still trying to throw things at them then,' he said to his younger brother.

But Rob just grunted, and then asked, 'did they say what it is mum?'

'No,' lied Anna. 'I really don't know any more than we have told you'

The journey back home was silent. James unlocked the front door and said 'Let me know how you get on tomorrow. I'll tell Alice.'

Rob shut himself in his room as soon as they got home. He played a recently bought CD. It was a revival of John Lennon's 'Imagine.' He played it over and over again 'Imagine there's no heaven; it's easy if you try; no earth below us; above us only sky…'

Anna lent against the door post outside his room and slid down to the floor. She silently cried her eyes out.

***

That night she stayed on the floor in Rob's room. He didn't seem to mind. He was so weak, and he was afraid, but did not want to say. Having someone else there helped.

She did not want to leave him. He was now so thin she could actually see and feel a bulge where he said the pain was. A soft and palpable mass - why hadn't any of the doctors picked it up?

She did not sleep at all, wondering if this was perhaps the last night Rob would have at home, and whether this time the disease would overwhelm him.

CHAPTER 23 'A NIGHTMARE RETURNS'
November 1999

The dark early morning in November did nothing to help her spirits. There was a thick fog outside which would mean difficulty in driving, particularly through the forest.

Half of her did not want to leave home at all, and she felt the old urge to just draw all the curtains and shut all the doors and keep the world out. But the other half wanted to get them back to the hospital as soon as possible so they could find out what it was, and if it was treatable.

Rob was not only weak but reluctant to leave home too. He stroked the cats and said, 'Here we go again then.'

The journey back to the hospital was difficult, but now they had left home Anna just wanted to get on with it, and she had trouble keeping her speed down.

When they got back on the ward they were surprised to see Daniel and Nitan there. Because Daniel had a different kind of leukaemia – Acute Lymphoblastic Leukaemia - his less intense course of chemotherapy stretched over two years, and not the six months constant barrage of harsher chemotherapy that Rob had received.

Nitan's face lit up. 'What are you two doing back here?' she said glad to see them, and not realising the implications. She thought that perhaps they had just come for a routine check-up.

Anna said, 'Oh Nitan, you know that dreadful word that we were never going to mention, the word 'relapse' – well it seems to have happened.'

Nitan's face dropped, and she looked horrified and shocked. 'Oh no' she said and put her arms around her friend.

'We are waiting for the consultant now. I'm really not sure what is going on,' said Anna.

'Well we're just in for the day,' said Nitan. 'Daniel's having a blood transfusion. Let me know as soon as you can.'

Anna went back into the single room where Rob was waiting and resting on the bed. It was the same room they had first occupied two years before.

Soon Martin the consultant came in with the medical team. 'We're not sure what is going on,' he said, 'but it appears to be a tumour surrounding the bowel. It could possibly be a lymphoma, but this would be very unusual as a lymphoma is usually associated with Acute Lymphoblastic Leukaemia, not Acute Myeloid Leukaemia, and it is unlikely that Rob would develop both sorts. We plan to start you on some chemotherapy Rob, but we're going to get you down to have a biopsy done first.'

Anna asked quietly, 'will this be done under a general anaesthetic?'

'We can't wait that long for a space in theatre,' said Martin, 'we'll get a result much quicker if we just use a local anaesthetic and morphine.'

And so half an hour later, after having been given morphine as a sedative, Rob was wheeled down on a trolley to wait in a corridor until the special procedure room was free and the previous case had left. Together Anna and a nurse who had come down from the ward waited with him.

The morphine which had been given to him before leaving the ward began to wear off.

'Can you tell them that he will need some more?' Anna asked the nurse.

'I can ask, but I can't promise they will give him more,' said the nurse.

Eventually after half an hour, Rob was wheeled into the small operating theatre and Anna waited outside feeling her son's agony.

He had been in the sterilised minor ops room for nearly an hour, having to lie on his stomach so they could probe the mass from the back with biopsy needles.

The nurse came out very distressed. 'They couldn't get a proper sample until about the sixth attempt. It was very painful for him, not just the biopsy itself but lying on his stomach gave him a great deal of pain.'

'He hasn't been able to lie on his stomach for weeks because of the pain,' said Anna.

Once Rob was back on the ward, it took a few hours to get the results.

'We're still not too sure what is going on,' said Martin the consultant. 'It appears that the tumour is filled with Acute Myeloid Leukaemia cells and this is most unusual. We're sending him to theatre tomorrow morning for them to open him up to see more clearly. He will obviously be under a general anaesthetic for that. The mass is so large that each time we thought we had a sample for the biopsy it appeared the extracts were already dead tissue so not identifiable. That is what took so long.'

The following day was Saturday and the surgeon had agreed to come in especially on his day off to do the operation as the medical team were aware there was no time to waste.

Anna went down to theatre with Rob and left when he was finally wheeled into the theatre. She didn't know what to do with herself for the hour they estimated it would take before he was returned to the ward.

She spent the time in the hospital chapel praying - praying with all her might that he would survive. But inside she was sure that they would come back to her and say, 'There is nothing we can do, it's too advanced' or 'it has spread to other parts.'

She wandered back to the ward and sat on the bed behind drawn curtains. Suddenly the surgeon appeared before her still dressed in his theatre greens.

Anna looked at him hopelessly. 'Is there anything you can do, or is it too late?'

'I think the tumour will respond to chemotherapy in the same way that his leukaemia did,' he said.

Anna had to restrain herself from throwing her arms around his neck. 'So he still has a chance?' she asked unbelievingly.

'Yes, there is still hope' said the surgeon. 'I took away all I could, but it is a massive tumour surrounding the bowel. It is what is known as a chloroma. The fact that it is filled with acute myeloid leukaemia cells gives it a green appearance and sheen, which is another way we were able to identify it; very unusual. If you had not acted when you did he would have been dead within twenty-four hours as it is so large it is about to cut off the bowel altogether.'

He then left as Richard was wheeled back on a trolley and lifted across to the bed. He was still very drowsy.

'So much for mild constipation then,' thought Anna bitterly. 'That gastroenterologist we saw in A&E ought to be struck off.'

Almost immediately he was transferred to one of the isolation rooms reserved for bone marrow transplant patients. Here his bed was raised, and he had a camera trained on him continuously which relayed his every move to the nurses' station.

One of the nurses explained 'In the first twenty-four hours when we hit the tumour with as much chemotherapy as possible it is always a very dangerous time' she said 'There is a possibility of 'tumour lysis'; that is because as the tumour is broken down so quickly it is possible for the waste tissue to overwhelm the kidneys and liver too suddenly and his body could go into organ failure. To be honest, it's the time when Rob could possibly lose his battle and that is why we are monitoring him so closely.' These words were said out of earshot of Rob.

Anna bit her lip. She never thought they would find themselves in this awful nightmare again. Why oh why, when he had seemed to recover once, had he relapsed in such a seemingly different and unusual way?

'My throat is very sore where they put the anaesthetic tube down,' croaked Rob 'can I have a drink of water?'

'I am afraid not Rob,' said the nurse, 'you won't be allowed to even swallow water for twenty four hours until the bowel has settled down again. We have to stop all the movement in your digestive system – you know, peristalsis – because of the surgery.'

Rob looked crest fallen 'Oh God I'm so thirsty,' he said. Although he had a saline drip giving him fluids, it did not help with the dry and painful throat.

After a few hours, the nurse relented saying he could hold an ice cube in his mouth as long as he did not swallow. This was not easy to comply with but at least it relieved his dry mouth.

Anna sat alongside, and because the bed was elevated, she was much lower than Rob.

They were watching television but not really concentrating on the programme.

Rob suddenly looked down on Anna, and it nearly broke her heart. It seemed as though he were saying 'goodbye' and 'I love you mum.' There was a sad but compassionate look about his face. She feared he had given up the battle and now just released himself to acceptance of whatever lay ahead.

She smiled in what she hoped was a reassuring way.

Anna could not forget the nurse's warning that the next twenty-four hours were highly critical, and it was possible that Rob may not survive.

But the next day, he was still hanging on, and was allowed to have some sips of water.

By now, Jane the consultant was back from her long weekend away.

'We 're going to treat it with the same sort of chemotherapy treatment that he had before,' she said, 'but we cannot use any more Daunorubicin because that is the drug that damaged his heart. We will have to work out some other cocktail.'

Then she added, 'I think it would be a good idea to get Rob's father down to see him if you can.'

Anna's heart chilled. This was not a good sign.

Then Jane said 'Where would you rather be treated Rob – here or at your local hospital? Now you are officially an adult, we could transfer you nearer your home.'

Without hesitation Rob said 'I would rather be treated here on this ward. I know everyone so well and I trust you all.'

Anna agreed with him; they knew all the medical staff so well and the routine of the ward, and it would mean they could still keep in touch with some of the teenage patients who had become Rob's friends and support.

That day Rob's father turned up. He had travelled a long way and although shocked to see the state of his son, he obviously had no idea of the severity of the situation.

Anna left them alone so that they could spend time together without any awkwardness; although in truth, Rob did not wish to be left alone with his father who had never understood children and always expected them to respond to military discipline.

She sat in the day room of the ward and looked out toward the docks. Just as she had done on their very first admission two years before, she imagined all the people who would be boarding the ships for adventures abroad while once more they were locked in a prison. It was not so much a prison of the building any more, but the prison of the disease; living with permanent fear and anticipation that each hour could be Rob's last. She never expected to be thrown back to that state again.

Her thoughts returned once more to the research that she had neglected since Rob had been told he was in remission.

She had never really followed up some of the replies she had received from eminent scientists and medical consultants. In a strange way, as Rob had gone into remission, the urgency to keep occupied and challenge the cause slowly slipped away from her. She had just wanted everything to return to normal as soon as possible and to put the awful first diagnosis behind them.

But as she sat there, she remembered that one of the professors had told her that they were identifying SV40 in solid tumours and they didn't know where it was coming from. In a "light bulb" moment, she reasoned that if she was able to obtain a sample of the biopsy that had just been taken from the rare tumour, then it might just be possible to isolate the virus.

While she waited for Rob's father to leave, she wrote a letter to the virologist who had been so helpful to her, asking him if he could test a sample of the biopsy if she was able to get hold of one.

When she eventually went back into the room, her ex-husband, Rob's father was leaving, and Jane entered looking a little flustered.

'Tomorrow,' she said, 'we are arranging for you to be transferred to your local hospital for treatment.'

Rob looked concerned. 'But you promised we could make

the choice,' he said. 'you gave us the choice, and I said I would rather stay here.'

'Yes I know I am sorry,' said Jane. 'But – well I suppose you could call it politics – I am so sorry but we cannot keep you here.'

Anna glanced at Rob who looked rather scared for the first time. 'They are writing me off,' said Rob, 'and don't want it on their records.'

'It might be to do with finance,' I said, 'as you are now eighteen and count as an adult.'

'But think of those other boys. Remember Luke he was nineteen, and Gary was twenty and we were told they were allowed to stay on the ward because they had been treated there when younger. Surely I would qualify that way too.'

Anna agreed. 'But there is nothing we can do to fight it Rob.'

'I feel betrayed,' said Rob, more strongly than she had heard him before. In fact, he had never complained about anything before.

Anna confided in the nurse that this was how they felt. 'We both feel abandoned to be honest – it is as if we are being passed on because there is no chance and he should be near his family.'

'We shall miss you both,' said the nurse looking sad. 'We too would like to keep him here.'

CHAPTER 24 'DEJAS VU'
November/December 1999

The next day dawned, and neither Rob nor his mother had slept well at all. They were told that transport had been ordered to collect them just after lunch.

James and Alice had both come up to help.

Anna asked the ward sister if she could perhaps take Rob in her own car for the journey but was told - no he had to go by ambulance because he had to lie flat after the operation.

So James said he would drive her car with her in it, as she was so shaky, and Alice would travel in the ambulance to keep Rob company. After all, it was bound to be one of those comfortable ambulances that had special suspension to avoid any sudden movements. It was only two days after Rob's major surgery, and that was why Anna could not take him in her car.

One o'clock arrived, then two o'clock.

'I wish they'd hurry up,' said Rob. 'I want to get the journey over with as quickly as possible. I still feel betrayed as though here they are turning their back on us.'

Jane the Consultant turned up. 'I've heard you feel as though we are giving up on you,' she said, 'but I can assure you that is not the case. The Haematologist I am transferring you to has immense experience. I trained with him and know him well and can assure you I would never send you on to someone I did not trust implicitly.'

And then as Anna went with her to the corridor, she turned and said 'This is a very unusual tumour, and we are not sure how to deal with it. Rob will have the best chance with the doctor I am sending him to – and also…' and here she paused, 'it will mean that he will have more chance to be at home and see his friends.'

Anna was suddenly chilled. What Jane was saying was that she was not sure how long Rob would have, and it was better for him to be at home. She knew it was a policy to get any patient home if at all possible in time before they died.

Feeling sick, Anna returned to Rob's side and found him more cheerful with his brother and sister there.

Their wait for the ambulance went on endlessly, and it was becoming unbearable.

Eventually five hours late, at 6.00 p.m. an ambulance driver turned up – with a chair, not a stretcher.

Anna said 'No sorry – the consultant has said he must travel flat – he's had abdominal surgery only two days ago.'

The nurse came in to confirm this. 'We requested a stretcher,' she said somewhat annoyed.

Grumbling the ambulance driver left and it took him forty minutes to return. And when he did eventually arrive, he had a stretcher that looked as though it was left over from World War 2 – canvas and more like a camp bed.

The nurse accompanied them down to the entrance where the ambulance waited, and was visibly shocked – as they all were.

Instead of the comfortable emergency ambulance they were all expecting, there stood an old ford transit van converted to carry wheelchairs or a stretcher on one side. It had the county transport service on the outside, but clearly the men were no more than delivery men with little or no ambulance or medical experience at all. There must have been some mix-up when transport had been ordered.

It was too late to make a fuss now – Rob was all wrapped up and strapped to the stretcher, and they were now well overdue for the medical team at the other end.

The ambulance driver and James arranged to keep in touch with each other by mobile phone, and the idea was that they would follow the ambulance as closely as possible, through the back routes of the New Forest as apparently there was some hold up on the main route which is what had caused transport to be so late reaching them in the first place.

It was with considerable trepidation that Anna watched the doors being slammed on Rob on the stretcher, and Alice sitting uncomfortably on a bench alongside.

If it hadn't been for the restrictions of insurance, it would have been better for Anna to go in the ambulance with Rob, and Alice to be in the more comfortable car in view of her pregnancy – however, there was no chance to change things at this late stage.

***

After a harrowing and bumpy ride through the back roads of the New Forest, they eventually arrived together in convoy at the local hospital fifty minutes later.

Rob was in a great deal of pain, and Alice looked pale and ill. 'It was a terrible ride mum,' she said. 'Rob felt every slight bump, and I feel sick.'

Anna was now worrying about both of them and the baby.

They arrived on the ward in the cancer unit and were met

with the news that the Haematologist had held on for as long as possible, but in the end had had to give up. He would see Rob first thing in the morning.

Looking at her watch Anna saw that it was 7.30 p.m. They had originally been due at this hospital at 3.00 p.m.

The nurse came and handed her a note. She just said 'A gentleman came in earlier and gave me this for you as soon as you arrived.'

Anna opened it. 'Thinking of you and so sorry at the news. If you need me I will be there for you. Love Patrick.'

Anna froze. How did he know what had happened and where she would be? No-one in the family had informed him, and most of her friends knew she had split up at long last and wanted no more to do with him.

But for now, she could not think about Patrick. All she wanted was for there to be a cure for Rob.

James and Alice left them, and the nurses settled Rob down for the night. Anna was allowed to stay in his room, and she made up a "put-you-up" bed alongside.

Another fretful night followed. Rob was still only being allowed sips of water, and he was in a great deal of pain.

The next morning the Haematologist came in very early.

'So sorry I couldn't wait long enough for you last night,' he apologised, 'when it got to 7.00 p.m. and there was no way of telling how far you were on the journey, I decided it was best to leave it till today. Jane has sent all the relevant details and X-rays and scans down with the ambulance, so I have managed to get the measure of your case.'

Rob and Anna waited with anticipation.

'There have only been four other known cases of a chloroma such as yours in the abdomen in the western world before, so we are working in the dark – it is particularly unusual to be surrounding the bowel. We will have to work on intuition and feel our way through for the right treatment. However, because we have established the tumour is full of acute myeloid leukaemic cells, I have decided to treat it in the same way I would an aggressive case of AML, and so your treatment of chemotherapy will start right away Rob. I see that the surgeon who operated on you also put in a Hickman line, but unfortunately it is a single lumen, so we will have to invent ways of extending it until I can replace it with a double lumen.'

'Can he have something for the pain?' asked Anna 'he is in agony particularly after the journey.'

'Of course,' replied the doctor, 'I will write him up for morphine. The other thing I wanted to say was that Rob's best chance is to have a bone marrow transplant, and I understand that his sister is an exact match.'

'Yes, they established that when he was struck down with leukaemia the first time' said Anna. 'but Alice has just discovered she is pregnant – will you still be able to take the bone marrow from her?'

There was a silence. 'Now that could be problem,' said the consultant, 'we will not be able to do anything at all until after the baby is born. When is it due?'

'At the beginning of July,' said Anna. 'It is still early on in the pregnancy.'

The consultant looked thoughtful. 'Well the good thing is

that he has a match ready and willing – we will just have to try to keep the illness at bay for the next seven months.'

He left the room, and Anna followed.

'What are his chances?' she asked anxiously 'Last time he had leukaemia he was told it was 50% - what would you say they are this time?

The doctor looked her squarely in the face. 'I don't believe in giving percentages,' he said. 'After all you never know which side it will fall.'

'I know,' persisted Anna, 'but please give me some idea.'

'20% is about as close as I can get,' he said.

Anna's face fell. 'Oh no – surely not that low.'

'Don't forget what I have just said,' the doctor replied. 'I don't believe in percentages, and what we must do is take a day at a time. All I can promise is that I will do my very best for him.'

Feeling the familiar rise of panic in her throat she took time to compose herself before she re-entered Rob's room.

There was a very different atmosphere on an adult cancer ward – even though most of the rooms were single. The noise of the children on the paediatric ward when Rob was first diagnosed two years previously, and which they found annoying at the time, was now sorely missed.

It did not help that the cancer unit was based on the lower ground floor, and although they noticed the next morning that there was a small garden area outside it still felt dark and vaguely depressing. It was very different from the children's ward in the city hospital where they could look out over the rooftops to the docks in the distance.

Therefore television became an even more important escape. And that was another blow. They found that whereas on the paediatric ward television viewing was free, here you had to pay for it, even as a long-term cancer patient.

When Anna went to the office to arrange payment and for the access to be switched on, she was met with a totally unsympathetic and money-orientated business. She remembered when she had last nursed – in this very hospital – that patients were allowed to bring in their own television sets, or the WRVS used to provide them free of charge. Those days of caring and empathy of the true NHS were disappearing fast it would seem. The NHS was now run like a business, and various parts of it had been farmed out to private industry – such as allowing patients to have televisions – and in some hospitals she knew that even the meals were run by an outside concern. Fortunately, this hospital still had its own kitchens, and a good catering officer.

The next day Rob was still in a great deal of pain. Although the surgeon had taken as much of the tumour and the dead tissue as possible away, what was left was still constricting the bowel and of course he had also had open surgery and it was now up to the chemotherapy to do its job and shrink the tumour.

While she sat by his bedside, Anna found herself thinking of her research again. She was still waiting for the reply from the virologist about whether he could perhaps identify SV40 in a sample of the biopsy.

An idea suddenly hit her – one that was so obvious that she could not understand why it had not occurred to her before.

One of the reasons the doctors had been so slow to pick up this relapse was because the leukemic cells were contained within the tumour, they had not yet escaped into the peripheral blood, so it had not been picked up in routine blood tests.

Supposing, just supposing, that this tumour had been there right from the start, and that he had never really gone into remission at all. Maybe the harsh chemotherapy regime of the first lot of treatment had just knocked it back, and the rogue cells had retreated into the tumour again but would not be visible in his blood. This would explain his loss of appetite over a long period too. And one thing that was never explained was why he had suddenly become intolerant to ice cream and 'shop bought' milk shakes. Perhaps it was the type of fat content which could not be dealt with by the glands around the intestines. It was those glands that were responsible for assimilating the fat into the body and that was the area where the tumour was.

And the other rather radical thought that hit her was – as the gut absorbs most things into the body via those glands, it was more proof that SV40 could have 'piggy backed' its way with the polio vaccine through the intestinal wall and triggered the response.

'Yes, that could be it,' she thought. 'Rob never really went into remission at all.'

Then as her mind rushed on 'maybe SV40 has a 'hit and run' mechanism – allowing it to cause changes to the chromosomes which affects the natural blood cells, but it doesn't leave any trace it has been there in the first place - a true "stealth virus". While in stealth mode it is like a submarine on silent running – disguising its very existence.'

Hastily she wrote another note to the virologist setting out her latest ideas and asked one of the nurses if she could kindly post it for her.

As she handed it over, the nurse said 'There is someone here to see you – he doesn't want to come into the room and disturb Rob – he's waiting in the sitting room.'

Anna's head was so full of her recent theory, that she did not think who it might be other than perhaps one of Rob's friends.

However, when she opened the door of the sitting room she had a shock. Patrick stood up.

'I heard about what was happening with Rob,' said Patrick, not saying exactly how he knew. Anna felt she was being stalked – how could he have possibly known – it certainly would not have been from the family and it had happened so suddenly too they themselves were only just coming to terms with it.

She summoned up her courage. 'Patrick, I don't want to see you any more – you are just making things worse by muddling my head all the time with mixed messages – please leave us alone.'

Anna turned toward the door and was ready to leave.

Patrick placed a hand on her arm. 'Please let me help,' he pleaded. 'I know I let you down, but you mean so much to me. Give me another chance.'

Anna paused for a moment, fighting with something deep inside.

'Look,' said Patrick, 'all I will say is that you can ring me any time, night or day, and I shall be by your side if you need support.'

Anna, still without saying anything, turned back to the door and left.

CHAPTER 25 'LEOPARDS AND SPOTS'

December 1999/January 2000

After that brief meeting Patrick started to send messages via the nurses, either by letter or by word, saying he wanted to meet up.

Each communication was more affectionate than the last.

In the end, and much to her shame, Anna gave in and arranged to meet Patrick in the park opposite the hospital.

She did not let Rob know – it would be one more thing for him to worry about if he found out.

Anna had become used to taking a daily walk to the middle of the town and back, just to get a change of perspective and to give Rob a bit of freedom. Although she didn't really want to leave his side, she realised it was unhealthy to be there all the time watching over him – this in itself would make him anxious and feel a bit claustrophobic.

Therefore she did not tell him that this time she was not going to town but to the park.

Patrick's controlling behaviour still had an effect on her. She hated herself for giving in this one last time – but that is all it would be – one time only.

She was getting no help from her ex-husband. He didn't seem to grasp just how serious things were. He had even been trying to take her to court over the fact that Rob had missed more than two terms of school and therefore according to him the maintenance agreement had been breached and he was no longer responsible for supporting him. What kind of man does that to a dying son? But then, that was the sort of behaviour that had made her leave him in the first place.

'I don't seem very good at choosing men,' she thought as she walked toward the park 'I seem to go for the flawed ones – or is it that something I do attracts them?'

Sure enough, as she approached the seat by the lake, she saw Patrick hunched over and sitting awkwardly on the bench.

Although it was winter, the fresh air was a welcome change from the stuffy atmosphere of the overheated hospital.

Christmas was approaching – and not just Christmas, but the new millennium. Neither Rob nor she had foreseen the possibility of spending both in hospital again.

As she drew near the bench, Patrick stood up. He went to kiss her on the cheek, but she drew away, afraid that if she made physical contact with him again her resolve to be strong would disappear.

'I've brought you a present – for Christmas,' he said holding out a small parcel.

She took it uncertainly. 'Before I open this,' she said, 'I need to ask you if you ever left a parcel on our doorstep after our break up.'

Patrick looked puzzled. 'No – why?'

Anna hesitated not sure whether to go on. 'It's just that – months ago I had a parcel left which had something – well something rather unpleasant in it – along with a note which said "keep going." It was to do with my research – that is all I can think. But try as we might, we could not find out who had left it.' She went on to explain exactly what had been in the parcel.

'Certainly not me,' said Patrick emphatically. 'Why would I leave something like that?'

'I thought you might have done it to worry me?' Anna looked up into his face.

'I may be unreliable in some ways,' said Patrick, 'but I would never do anything like that. And where on earth would I find a monkey kidney – sounds revolting.'

'It's remained an unanswered question in my mind, and it also unsettled me – I was not sure if it was a friendly nudge to keep going with my train of thought with the research, or if it was some sort of threat.'

'Did you report it to the police?' asked Patrick

'No – but I did take it up to the Professor at the city hospital to ask him if he knew what it was. That is how I found out it was a monkey kidney.'

'Well I can assure you this is not another one,' said Patrick with a slight smile.

Anna took the gift-wrapped box and opened it. A silver necklace with a red rose pendant almost fell out as she fumbled with the box.

'Thank you, Patrick,' she said 'It is beautiful, but I am not sure that I can accept it because I don't know what it means anymore.'

'The red rose means I still love you,' he said. 'I know we will have to take things very slowly for you to trust me again, but I am prepared to wait. As I said before, please phone me whatever the time – night or day if you need me.'

They parted still without any physical contact. Anna's feelings were very confused and in many ways she wished she had not agreed to meet him.

As she walked back to the hospital, she felt a sudden chill, remembering the other part of the parcel that had been left on her doorstep all those months previously. A dead red rose – and now Patrick had given her a red rose on a silver chain. Could there be a connection after all?'

That evening Rob took a dramatic turn for the worse, and Anna rushed to the ward phone to call Patrick. There was no reply. Neither were there any replies throughout that evening whenever she phoned or even late into the night. She began to panic. 'Perhaps he has turned his phone off – but why would he do that when he told me to phone anytime.'

Although Rob improved slightly through the night, she phoned Patrick again early on the morning of Christmas Eve – the anniversary of their engagement all those years previously.

To her great relief he answered. 'Oh thank heavens I've got you,' said Anna, and then she gave a slight laugh. 'I thought you must be with another woman.'

She was not ready for what happened next.

There was a pause then Patrick said 'I was – I am really sorry Anna – I was going to tell you. She lives not far from the hospital – I didn't know how to break it to you.'

Anna stood shocked for a moment – then slammed the phone down on him. She decided she had been so foolish to start believing him again, and that any man who could be so false in such circumstances was despicable. Over and over in her mind she could hear his betrayal 'you are the most important thing in my life … it is you I have missed… I can't manage without you.' She wondered at all the lies he had told so glibly.

She grabbed her coat and said to Rob 'I'm just going out for a breath of fresh air.'

'In this weather mum?' he asked. 'Are you mad?'

The rain was slashing down with a biting easterly wind, and the lake in the middle of the park looked as though it was writhing in a force nine gale.

With her hood up, but still getting soaked, she kept driving her feet onwards and onwards as though she were trying to wash Patrick out of her very soul. As the few cars out and about passed, the occupants looked at her in disbelief – she was the only pedestrian to be seen in such weather.

Finally, when she had neared exhaustion battling the weather, she returned to the Ward.

A nurse approached her. 'Now he has improved a bit we think that if we can arrange Rob's medication carefully enough, it will be possible to leave a long enough gap for him to go home for part of Christmas Day.'

This was the first bit of good news they had had for weeks.

Immediately her two older children knew, they arranged a family get together at Alice's home, and James said he would collect them both the next morning, so that Anna could drink. The ward had told Rob that even he could have a drink so long as he did not overdo it.

Despite everything, it was a happy day – full of laughter. Brian said he would take them back, which meant James could drink too – and drink he did. He didn't realise it, but Brian was topping up his cider with vodka. The more he had the funnier he got. It seemed as though there was no tomorrow, and for all they knew, there may be no tomorrow for Rob.

During the week between Christmas and the dawn of 2000, they had a bleak time.

Rob was quite poorly again and seemed to be deteriorating, and the haematologist was concerned that he may not be able to keep Rob alive until Alice's baby was born in the July when they could go ahead with the bone marrow transplant. He was very frank with Anna. 'It will be touch and go over the next few weeks'

'Can Rob have a scan to see if the tumour is getting smaller?' asked Anna.

'It's too early,' said the haematologist. 'Chemotherapy might be shrinking it, but it will not necessarily show at this stage – and if it looks the same size you will only lose hope. And whatever happens, we should not lose hope.'

A mutual friend phoned Anna and told her that Patrick had got engaged. This only made all his lies the more abhorrent. He must have been with this woman all through the weeks he had tried to fight his way back to Anna – it was obviously something that had been going on much longer than he let on.

New Year's Eve arrived – the eve of the millennium - a time that they were dreading. They had no idea what the New Year would hold, but somehow doubted it would be anything good.

Alice's news about the pregnancy was tainted with the fact that she could not give her brother the bone marrow immediately. Instead of feeling elated about the baby, she felt guilt and wondered how she would cope if her brother died before the baby was born.

Anna too felt her daughter's pain. 'This should be the happiest time in her life,' she thought. 'How cruel the twist of fate can be.' And much deeper down inside, a darker fear that she was trying to hide. 'How will I feel about this baby when it is born if I lose my son because the baby is alive?' That was a thought too dreadful to contemplate and she felt ashamed.

The nurse came around to take orders for midnight drinks. 'I'll be bringing a trolley round – bit like an air hostess,' she laughed. 'You can have anything you like Rob – and also your mum if you allow her to - so you can toast in the new millennium.

Rob looked at Anna and grinned. 'Okay,' he said. 'She can have one too – we'll both have a gin and tonic – a strong one.'

Early in the evening Rob fell into a deep sleep, and Anna took the opportunity to go out to get some air. She walked to the top of the multi-storey car park that had a good view over the town and even as far as the hills in the distance. Firework parties had already started and feeling totally numb she watched the displays popping up in different areas, and thought about all the fun people were having. She looked over toward the part of town where she knew this other woman lived and thought about Patrick and his betrayal. 'He won't even be giving us a thought,' she said to herself angrily.

It was now 11.30 p.m. and she decided to make her way back to Rob's room. On the way down, she passed a man who looked dreadful. 'Great isn't,it?' he said. 'I've just discovered that my car has been broken into and my mother is dying in there,' he nodded toward the hospital.

'I'm so sorry,' said Anna 'life is so unjust.'

In a way that man helped her to understand she was not the only one with grief to bear, even if it was in a very different way. There would be plenty of people who were not enjoying the dawn of the millennium or looking forward to the year 2000. 'I am not the only one,' she kept repeating to herself all the way back to the ward.

At 11.50 p.m. the nurse entered the room as promised. She was pushing a trolley full of alcoholic drinks and was wearing a silly hat. The noise of the bottles chinking woke Rob up. He smiled when he saw her. 'Great I am not too late then,' he said.

The nurse stayed with them to see the New Year in – and they pulled a few crackers and toasted the midnight hour together and put on silly hats.

Then exhausted, Rob fell asleep again and Anna was left alone with her thoughts.

She had been stupid and was paying for it. She knew what her friends and family would have said if they'd known she had met Patrick again. And in her heart she had probably known all along that she could not trust him, but she had wanted that one last chance so much.

In a strange way she was now relieved that she did not have to pretend and be furtive any more – she had felt quite guilty sneaking out to meet Patrick that day – now she really was rid of him for good, and now she could concentrate once more on the people who most needed her. Rob – her eighteen-year-old son who once again was facing a death sentence – and Alice her daughter expecting her first baby but unable to feel truly happy about it – and James, faithful James, always the rock of the family.

She felt ashamed that she had allowed herself to be lured away once more by selfish need for nothing more than a puffed-up man who desired power over people with no thought or concern for their feelings or wellbeing. She now knew the meaning of true evil, and its name was Patrick.

CHAPTER 26 'COMPLICATIONS'
2000 - The New Millennium

T he first few months of the year 2000 were taken up with hopes being raised and then dashed, with many steps forward, and quite a few back. It seemed like a repeat pattern of when Rob had first been diagnosed two years earlier – but this time it was more difficult. There was no protocol or pre-recognised treatment for him – the haematologist admitted he was working in the dark with a certain amount of trial and error. The leukaemia had returned in such a rare form.

After a few weeks, they had been allowed home for brief times during the day in between treatments. But the bed always had to be kept available for Rob.

This caused the ward a certain amount of difficulty because as beds in the hospital generally were at a premium, the bed allocation sister would prowl round wards looking for any that were empty in any part of the hospital, including the Cancer ward – despite it being out of bounds to the general public or ordinary patients because of the isolation procedures.

So, when Rob was let out, there was an understanding. If the phone rang at home and the ward said 'get back straight away,' that's exactly what they would do. And if it was after the main entrance was shut, they would enter via A&E and creep back to the ward via the back route and get Rob into bed as quickly as possible.

In a strange way this added a bit of excitement to their restricted lives. It was a game of "beat the bed allocation sister" and a lot of hasty ruffling up of the bed and scattering of magazines around the room went on by the nurses before Rob and Anna got back – just to make it look occupied.

Once more Rob was in the cycle of chemotherapy, neutropaenia when the immune system dropped to nil, and then blood transfusions and a gradual return to normal – whatever normal was. Rob had forgotten by now.

Then one day, the Haematologist summoned Rob, Anna and Alice for a special consultation.

'We have a difficult decision ahead,' he said.

Anna sat in between her very pregnant daughter, and her failing son.

'If we use Rob's own bone marrow once it has been cleaned up by chemotherapy, then he will definitely see next Christmas, but most likely not the one after…' the consultant paused.

'Whereas if we use Alice's bone marrow, then Rob may not even see next Christmas – although he would very likely see the one after if he survives the first.'

There was a stony silence and neither Rob, nor Anna, nor Alice could bear to look at each other, but Anna was aware of tears rolling down her daughter's face, as indeed they were hers.

Put like that, they were suddenly flung into the turmoil of nothing being secure again.

The haematologist went on, 'that is because with his own bone marrow, even if cleaned up, eventual relapse is very likely. But there is a big risk of rejection when using his sister's.'

'There is however something else to consider,' continued

the doctor. 'A new form of bone marrow transplant that is in the early days of experimentation. That way a smaller amount of donor bone marrow is introduced, and not all of the patient's own marrow knocked out. It is a less risky procedure because the chemotherapy is not so drastic or dangerous.'

'I don't know what to say,' said Anna in what sounded to her a very small voice. 'How can we make such decisions – we need help to decide.'

'Well I intend to ring my mentor in London at the hospital where it will be taking place. I shall discuss it with him and let you know his thoughts.'

It seemed once more as though Anna was being asked to play Russian roulette with her son's life. How could any mother make that decision? Not even a computer could make the decision for them this time.

As they were about to leave the room, Rob turned and said, 'If we use my sister's bone marrow I hope that doesn't mean I will grow breasts.' He smiled slightly in an attempt to lighten the mood – however there was a certain amount of anxiety behind the comment as well as if it had been a question in his mind for some time.

The haematologist laughed. 'No chance,' he said. 'Don't worry, although you may end up with some of her DNA in you – but you won't be growing breasts I promise!'

Then he added 'however the police are finding it difficult when trying to hunt down criminals nowadays - bone marrow transplants can muddy the water a bit. Whereas naturally no two people have the same DNA, after a transplant it is not necessarily such a clear definition.'

Alice turned to her brother. 'No silly antics then when you recover,' she smiled through her tears. 'I don't want to be had up for robbing a bank or anything.'

Over the days while all this turmoil was going on, Anna had a reply from the virologist. He said that if she could get written permission from the doctor who had been in charge when the biopsy was done, and if they would send a sample up, he would definitely test it for SV40.

Anna wrote to the Consultant at the city hospital, and they duly arranged for this to be done.

It was soon after that she noticed the phones were playing up at home again. The same echoing sound and clicking as previously, and although there was no motorcyclist, there occasionally would be a car parked a little way up the road, with the engine running and two men inside. One had a pony tail and the other was continuously smoking. They were often talking on a car phone, and whilst loud enough to hear that it was an internal car phone, Anna could not hear what was being said.

She saw them talking to the postman shortly before he was due to put her letters through the door. He paused and riffled through the letters then shook his head while they waited.

'This is nothing to do with Patrick' she thought 'this is definitely something to do with the drugs company. It all went quiet while I stopped sending letters and reports out, and now it has started up again – ever since I heard from the virologist.

Then out of the blue, she had a phone call from a mutual friend of both Patrick and herself, with a message from him.

The friend told her 'he says he has been such a fool and

made the most terrible mistake – could he please have another chance.'

If she hadn't been so traumatised by so many things she would have laughed out loud. 'What again?' she said. 'No, never again – it has happened too many times now – he is playing very cruel mind games and I truly think he is unstable.'

'That is a sensible answer,' said the friend, 'even though I have to say I have never heard him sound so genuine before.'

'What happened to his other wonderful fiancée I wonder?' asked Anna. 'The one he was engaged to at the same time as me.' She tried to keep any anger out of her voice.

There was a pause. 'I gather he hit her, and the son threw him out.'

'No change there then,' said Anna. 'Now why doesn't that surprise me? – as the saying goes – a leopard never changes its spots.' For the first time she was genuinely glad that she was well out of it - all regrets behind her and still wondering how on earth he could have had her in his power for so long.

'I will tell him "no chance" then,' said the friend. 'I don't blame you Anna.'

'Thanks,' said Anna. 'I really don't want to see or hear from him ever again – you can tell him that too please.'

A week later, she received a long and detailed letter from the virologist explaining that he had not been able to detect any sign of SV40 in Rob's sample because the sample was 'very poor.' 'Might have had more luck with a better sample,' he said. Then he added 'I don't expect you to give up on your theory just because of the poor result – this won't be the end.' It was almost as if he was encouraging her to keep going –

perhaps giving her a hidden message. However, he added that other scientists were now following up on the theory, and it was expected that the vaccine would change at some stage in the future.

'Oh, and by the way' he said. 'I have been in touch with the Professor at the city hospital and we think we have finally discovered the meaning of those numbers that came with that rather unpleasant parcel a couple of years ago. It appears one set referred to one of the known contaminated vaccine samples of the 1970s, and the other was a more recent sample, as yet unproved. Very intriguing.'

Anna could hardly believe her eyes when she read that. It would appear all her hard work and worrying away at the problem and being a nuisance to scientists was having some reaction after all. And she was also pleased that she had not given into pressure and gone to the press and started a scare. She would have lost all professional support and respect had she done so.

There was one more ordeal for Rob before everything moved toward the bone marrow transplant from his sister. Rob had to undergo the procedure of collection of his own bone marrow in its 'cleaned up' form as a backup, just in case Alice's donation did not take. This meant another general anaesthetic and more surgery – albeit needles being introduced in to the sacrum to withdraw the bone marrow tissue, and not open surgery as such.

He eventually came back to the ward quite late that evening after the operation - returning just at the time that the day staff handed over to the night staff.

One of the day staff told Anna that if his blood pressure

dropped below a certain level he would need a blood transfusion urgently. The nurse said Rob had come back so late from theatre that the Path Lab had closed, and they had been unable to obtain any blood matching his to keep in advance of any trouble, so it would mean having emergency blood until the following day if a transfusion was required.

However, somehow this had not been passed on to or perhaps not been absorbed by the night staff, because later as his blood pressure plummeted to below the level Anna had been warned about, the nurse said that there was nothing written up in the notes about a possible blood transfusion.

As Rob deteriorated, Anna became more vocal and persistent, and eventually she was listened to and emergency blood which was not a match but was safe to use in urgent circumstances was rushed up to the ward.

Rob had a rocky recovery from that operation and it took its toll.

Eventually, he was allowed home again and it was a waiting game.

***

The weeks rolled by taken up with routine batches of treatment and recovery until the Spring and come and gone.

The day when the baby would be born was getting closer and soon he would be given his second chance at life.

A letter arrived from the Prime Minister addressed to Rob. The PM had heard of Rob's relapse and impending bone marrow transplant, saying he was so sorry about the news and extending his good wishes that all would be well.

They had no idea how the PM knew about this. They

reasoned it must have been someone perhaps from the Leukaemia Charity at the city hospital.

Then on June the 24th 2000, James married Sandra in a small country church. It was a happy affair, despite Rob being so poorly. He looked very thin and had trouble holding himself upright, but he still managed to be an usher and keep going for the festivities.

Laura had come to stay for the wedding and it was a double celebration because her birthday was the day before the ceremony, and she was able to spend time with her Godson Rob. As usual, her "way out" attitude cheered them all up immensely.

Exactly a week later to the day on the 1st July, Alice went into labour and produced a lovely daughter – five days before she was due. It had been arranged that should the due date arrive and no baby with it, they would induce the birth as time was so critical for Rob now. But, fortunately, this did not arise.

A week later still, Alice was admitted to hospital and her bone marrow taken. Because she was feeding the baby she could not have the more modern method of extracting bone marrow – a stem cell donation - when a machine similar to a kidney machine, washed the blood and sieved out the required stem cells. This was because that would need her to take a course of hormones to increase the bone marrow cells beforehand, and hormones would interfere with her milk for the baby. Therefore she underwent a full operation where the marrow was extracted from her lower back by introducing a needle many times. She was under a general anaesthetic, but the procedure made her back very sore for a while afterwards.

There turned out to be a positive side for the bone marrow

donation with her having been pregnant. The stem cell count was as high as 9 instead of the required 2, which meant she was able to give a really healthy marrow donation.

'It's worth it mum,' she said to Anna. 'I am just so glad that Rob is still hanging on and able to receive it.'

The marrow was frozen and sent up in readiness to the London hospital.

Rob and Anna followed and were admitted there toward the end of July.

Once again it was a viciously hot summer, just as it had been in 1997 when he was first diagnosed.

The room this time was on a special bone marrow transplant unit, and although it had only been opened for ten months, it was sadly lacking.

Anna and Rob were shown into a small room – as usual with windows that would not open since all the air had to be filtered. The outlook was appalling. The window showed a blank wall on the opposite side only about six feet away, so close that it was obvious the unit had been squashed in between two previous wards. Anna could only see the sky by craning her neck to look upward where there was a restricted patch just visible.

There was a small fridge (which on inspection had obviously not been defrosted since the opening of the unit and still had bits of food from previous patients stuck to the side as well massive ice deposits). The toilet roll was hitched up through the light pull in the small bathroom, and there was a basin full of the previous patient's hair lying in the bath!

They knew they would have to be here for about six weeks,

and it was not good to start off on the wrong foot by complaining, so Anna set to defrosting the fridge herself. Turning it off at the wall and using all the paper towels she could find to mop up the water as it melted. It took five hours to complete, despite the heat.

A cheerful male nurse entered the room. 'I can see you are used to being in hospital,' he joked.

She then asked him if he could take away the bowl of hair, and also asked if it was possible to have proper toilet paper in the new shiny stainless-steel contemporary dispenser on the wall, rather than the toilet roll looped around the light pull. She was told the hospital could not afford the right paper for the fancy stainless steel dispenser and were only allocated toilet rolls which had no proper storage space.

However, the nurse did take the bowl full of hair away.

This was the beginning of a nightmare. The senior nursing staff and doctors were lovely and efficient – however, the hospital seemed to employ a lot of agency nurses. Some could not speak English; one had no idea how to take a temperature and used to make up the reading before putting it on the chart; and another used to try to take a blood pressure reading without putting the whole head of the stethoscope on Rob's arm.

Aware that the nurse could not read the thermometer because she always announced 36.8 as she shook it down, Anna started to take Rob's temperature herself afterwards, and altered the chart if necessary. Even in a normal situation, a person's temperature rarely remained exactly the same day to day, and certainly not a patient who was ill.

The thermometer was not the new electronic version they

had grown accustomed to, but the old-fashioned mercury and glass type. This in itself would not have been a problem but there was no little container full of disinfectant to rest it in, which would have been normal nursing practice. Instead, after use the nurse used to just rest it sideways on the window ledge. In Anna's nursing experience this would have been a disciplinary offence.

At the end of the first day, Rob and Anna just looked at each other. 'Right I am taking charge of the basics from now on,' she said. 'I am horrified by what I have seen so far',

'Thanks mum,' said Rob. 'I know the consultant is good, but I don't think I am going to make it through this time unless you keep an eye on things.'

Later that afternoon, Anna took herself off to the local shops and came back with a toilet roll holder amongst other essentials.

After two days they had not seen a cleaner at all. At both of the other hospitals the wards had been damp dusted each day. Patients on a cancer ward were at particular risk of contamination, and in a bone marrow transplant ward, they were at their most vulnerable of all.

Eventually Anna sought out the sister and asked if there was a cleaner who should have been coming around.

The sister looked horrified. 'Hasn't she been in?' she said.

'No' said Anna

'I'll get that sorted straight away,' said sister and she did.

Anna often saw the cleaner with her feet up reading a magazine in a little room off the ward. Now that so many jobs were out sourced to private companies, the standards had dropped considerably.

Another problem Anna had was that there was nowhere to put their spare clothes. They were after all up in London for six weeks, but there were no cupboards, no drawers, nothing, so they lived out of their suitcases piled up in a corner which made cleaning the floor a major event. Whoever had designed the bone marrow transplant unit had omitted some very important factors.

However, Anna was just grateful that she was allowed to "live in" with Rob. This was a perk that would not have been readily available a few years ago, but now it seemed to be established that cancer patients reacted better if their relatives were allowed to stay alongside them where possible. It also relieved the pressures on the nursing staff, because relatives would often take care of personal hygiene and toilet care etc. as well as keeping an eye on them.

Despite the basic amenities not being up to scratch, the senior nurses were very efficient and helpful. As long as one of them came in to see Rob, Anna could relax.

Rob missed his first meal on arrival because he was sent to X-ray at lunch time. When he and his mother returned to the ward, they were met by an angry red-faced man, who they gathered by the accent, was from some mid European country. He was furious and told them off for not being there when the food arrived and said he would have to throw it away.

Anna and Rob were so surprised at Basil Fawlty (as they named him) that they wanted to laugh. He did not seem to grasp that it was a hospital - even when they explained Rob had been sent to X-ray and had no choice in the matter.

Much later they found out that the patients' meals were

made in a factory in Wales the day before required and shipped up overnight in refrigerated lorries, heated up on trolleys and then served up to the patient.

This was horrendous news. Anna remembered how food poisoning had swept through a nearby Navy Base when they had first tried (and then abandoned) this freeze and reheat method of outsourcing cooking. Bone marrow transplant patients were not supposed to eat reheated food at all, and here it was their only option.

Anna went out and bought a toaster as only staff were allowed in the kitchen – unlike the other hospitals where relatives could make fresh food for the patient. And anyway, later when she did go into the kitchen, there was only a microwave, and no ordinary oven. As patients were not allowed microwaved food, it could only be used for the staff. She asked the nurse she met in the kitchen why there was not a conventional oven, and he just waved at the shiny cupboards around the walls which took up the whole place and said, 'That is where they keep the patient's refrigerated meals now.'

She realised Rob would not only be fighting the disease, and the chemotherapy, but also a hospital which was so keen to cut down on costs they were putting their patients at risk.

There was a surprise phone call from Laura. 'Hello dear, how are you both doing?'

Anna explained what was going on and then added 'the room is not very large – if you can imagine a six-foot man lying on the floor I reckon you would be able to get one and a half lying one way, and possibly two the other.'

'Anna – why don't you just say 9 feet by 12 feet?' asked Laura.

'Because for some unknown reason I find it easier to measure by thinking how many six-foot men you could get on the floor,' said Anna with a laugh. 'You know I am never any good at measuring things, and have no spatial awareness.'

'You haven't been at those chocolate brownies again have you?' asked Laura, and they both broke out in peals of laughter.

No – she had not been at the cannabis cakes again, although she wished she could. Instead, she made do with a bottle of sherry which she hid behind the fridge.

Before starting the treatment, Rob was sent down for a PET scan. This was a new and very efficient scan that would pick up everything; however, they were not prepared for the result.

The registrar told them that Rob would have to have a full bone marrow transplant after all, and not the experimental and less dangerous one.

'But we were told by the consultant that I would be having the new half and half type of bone marrow transplant that wasn't quite so drastic,' said Rob.

'That was before we had the results of the PET scan,' explained the registrar. 'I am afraid there are still leukaemia cells lighting up in the region of the tumour – they have shown up on this scan where they did not show on the ordinary scan.'

So Rob was in fact relapsing for a third time already. This was very bad news. They had been told that usually the second period of remission would last about half of the time of the first remission. His first remission had been for eighteen months they thought, so on that basis he should have remained in remission for nine months this time. Obviously he was relapsing earlier than anyone expected.

It would be a hard and trying time for him - cooped up in a tiny room, suffering from 'cabin fever' and with them both having to watch out anxiously for his care since the agency staff were so untrained and unreliable.

But there was nothing they could do about it, and so settled down for the long haul and back to the regime of taking a day at a time.

CHAPTER 27 'ANOTHER HOSPITAL'
August 2000

The hospital was in the centre of an overcrowded and run-down part of London and it meant that there were no open spaces to retreat to in the heat, although Anna thought she could see a small park beyond the railway that ran along the back of the ward and which she intended to investigate as soon as possible.

Her other option was to walk into the steamy traffic zone of shops just down the hill, where the air was thick with fumes.

She managed to locate the medical library for the hospital, and arranged to join, having her photo taken and an ID badge made up so she could call in when the library was open.

Her quest to find the reason for Rob's illness became even more desperate.

'I just don't want him to go through all this again,' she thought.

Her panic was made worse when a nurse informed her that the current regime of chemotherapy drugs would completely block out his immune system and any fast-growing cells in a more direct way than anything he'd received before. This would also mean that all the cells' memories of previous vaccines would be destroyed too, and that he would eventually have to be re-vaccinated and immunised against everything he'd already had from the start of his life. He would in fact be left with the immune system of a new born baby, which is why they had to watch him so carefully during the first months and years after the transplant.

The impact of this news on her was twofold. In one way, she felt the chances were that the drugs would completely knock out any trace of the SV40, but on the other hand, he might be re-infected again if he had the polio vaccine and it was still being made in the same way.

Then they had some good news – Rob would not be allowed to have any live vaccinations, which immediately ruled out the British version of the polio vaccine, and the MMR which had recently been causing so much controversy.

'Why is that then?' Rob asked the consultant.

The consultant replied 'When the risks outweigh the benefits, the vaccines are not given.'

This made Anna think 'But surely, wouldn't this apply to any young baby too?' It was back to the theory of what is best for the "herd" must always be followed, rather than what is best for the individual and allowing the parent to choose.

There was another offshoot to all this. Rob would not be allowed to come into contact with any baby or person who had received a live vaccine for some time as this would make him vulnerable. It was known that some parents had accidentally picked up polio themselves when changing the nappies of babies who had recently had the live vaccine.

Anna asked the consultant 'What should we do about Alice's baby daughter?'

He replied, 'Alice should contact her own doctor and make sure the baby has an inactivated or killed version of the polio vaccine. This can be obtained from Canada as it's not available in the UK.'

Her research had showed her that Canada did not use a vaccine involving monkey kidney cells. She was also told that Rob would be able to have the Canadian vaccine too when the time came. It would be sent for especially.

She remembered again the professor from the leukaemia charity who had stated 'The SV40 virus has been found in a number of different solid tumours, including in people too young to have received the original doses of polio vaccine that were definitely found to be contaminated. No-one has any idea where this virus is coming from or how it can end up in solid tumours.'

At the time, she had not thought about blood transfusions as another possible avenue. But now, as the idea occurred to her, she wrote to the head of the Blood Transfusion service. 'Do you check blood for SV40 before it is harvested?' He replied 'No – we don't search for SV40 in blood donations. We are aware of all the controversy. Regrettably though there is no way we can screen for every sort of possible virus.'

She had sent copies of his letter to the various organisations who were taking her theory seriously, including the virologist, who very generously had kept in contact since their first meeting, and he always answered all her questions in full – even though he was extremely busy or abroad. Sometimes the replies were held up for a month or two. And some of them would be dynamite if ever released into the public domain.

Anna was aware how sensitive this information was, and that he was risking his own profession by being so honest with her. Tempting as it would be to alert the public to these comments, she was determined not to let him down in any way because he was one of those brilliant scientists who believed in the truth and who could not be "bought". To let others know what he had said would be a betrayal of his friendship and openness.

Rob was refusing to eat the hospital food – this was partly because the severity of his treatment made eating impossible and he could not stand the thought of food. But also, it was because both he and Anna had realised the food was being cooked a long way away the night before in Wales and transported in refrigerated lorries to the hospital ready to be reheated for the patients, including the bone marrow patients who should not be eating reheated food of any kind. Therefore, Anna tried to tempt him with whatever she could rustle up for him in the confines of their room.

She on the other hand, used to eat the food brought to him so it was not wasted. The "meal deliverer" they had named "Basil Fawlty" after the owner of Fawlty Towers in the famous sitcom, was always grumbling or ranting about something. This used to make them laugh and in the end, they were quite sad when he was replaced by someone else who was quite normal. "Basil" really had not cottoned on that in a hospital sometimes people couldn't eat what they had ordered, and sometimes the patient was called for treatment away from the ward, X-rays or even surgery! Anna and Rob were not sure where he thought he was – maybe some mid European prison, but certainly he did not identify with a hospital and lacked the compassionate manner one would expect. Even so they missed him and their daily amusement.

One day, shortly after Rob had been given a particular drug through the Hickman Line, he visited the bathroom. The nurse had left quickly after injecting the medication in through the lumen plug, so did not hear the crash as he fell back onto the basin. Fortunately, Anna realised something was wrong.

She rushed in. 'What's going on Rob?' she asked.

He laughed and said, 'Don't know, just suddenly lost it.'

She helped to get him back toward the bed, supporting him under one arm, and juggling the drip stand with the other.

Before he reached the bed though his legs gave out and she found herself bearing all his weight. Although he was so skinny he was still heavy in this unconscious state and difficult to manipulate into position.

She managed to get him back on the bed, and just had time to raise his legs and place them on the sheet when suddenly he was convulsed in a fit. His head contorted to one side, his neck twisted at an agonising angle, his body rigid in a line yet jerking. He was clearly unconscious and fitting dangerously.

Anna reached for the red pull emergency cord and immediately a nurse arrived, who pulled the cord again and suddenly the bed was surrounded by five nurses and three doctors.

Terrified, all Anna could do was to hold Rob's hand and reassure him. 'It's okay,' she said trying to sound calm. 'I'm here and they are looking after you – everything will be okay.'

She remembered well from her nursing days that even when unconscious, a patient can often still hear, and if he had any kind of knowledge what was going on she reasoned he was probably very frightened.

Rob had apparently had an allergic reaction to the drug they had shot up the line.

Anna could not help but ponder fearfully what could have happened had she not been there, and how long it would have been before he was found if indeed he would still have been alive. If he had recovered himself and come to and got back to bed, they may never have realised he had had a severe allergic reaction and given the drug again at some stage with more fatal results. There were no CCTV cameras to monitor the patients in this hospital and each was isolated in an individual room.

Over the next twenty-four hours he was monitored regularly at quarter of an hour intervals.

The fit gave Anna the excuse to insist to the nurses that he mustn't be allowed to have the thermometer under his tongue when taking his temperature – this was standard nursing practice when someone had fitted – and that he had to have it taken under his arm each time. It was too dangerous to put a glass and mercury thermometer under the tongue in someone who might lose control and clench the jaw and shatter the thermometer.

It was a couple of days later that Rob remembered he had received one dose of the same drug when he was at the local hospital, and it was soon after that he had started hallucinating that there were "black things" crawling up his leg, and he had kept trying to brush them away.

At the time they had not associated it with the drug and so no connection made but now they realised he must never be given it again.

Although it was a very difficult journey for them now being so far away, Alice and Brian drove up with the new baby. The baby was not allowed on the ward for fear of bringing in any infections, so Anna went out to the anti-room where Alice was feeding the newest member of the family.

It was so cruel that Alice could not have her mother's support at home at a time when she most needed it. But at the end of the day, Anna had to make decisions about priorities.

She gave her daughter a hug and cradled her granddaughter. 'I miss you so much Alice,' she said. 'Me too Mum,' said her daughter.

Then Alice said 'Mum I do hope Rob will be all right in here. When I was walking up the corridor to get to you, there were used and bloody dressings on the floor, and quite frankly, I felt I had walked into a third world hospital.'

'This is a very different environment from the other two hospitals I admit,' said Anna, 'probably because it's in London. Only yesterday as I went down to the ground floor I found myself walking ahead of two policemen, and there was a bed being wheeled in front of me with someone with a bandaged arm in the air hanging from a support, and two more armed police in front of that. Suddenly realised I was in the middle of a police escort for someone I found out later was a dangerous criminal!'

'Anyway, I agree,' continued Anna. 'The standards aren't the same as the city hospital or our local one. There was a time when any London hospital was renowned for its standards, but not all of them seem to be the same these days. I promise I will keep a close eye on your brother.'

***

Weeks passed, and it was now the day they had all been waiting for – the 19th of August. It would have been Anna's parents' wedding anniversary had they still been alive, and so there was now a double reason for remembering this date for ever. Rob's own and damaged immune system had been completely destroyed and he was ready to receive the bone marrow that had been stored, frozen and rushed up to the hospital as soon as Alice had given birth to the first grandchild. He was about to receive his second chance of life.

They had become very fond of the young Indian nurse who was preparing the drip for the momentous occasion. She was one of the nurses Anna trusted implicitly.

'Contrary to what a lot of people believe, a bone marrow transplant is not an operation as such,' explained the nurse who had entered the room with what looked like an ordinary bag of blood. 'But it is given like a blood transfusion and it will only take about forty minutes. The worst part is the drug regime preparing the patient beforehand, which you have already been through, and then afterwards when we are all keeping our fingers crossed that it takes. So enjoy this moment Rob – in a sense you are being born again!'

Rob looked embarrassed 'I don't think I want to go through it in exactly the same way as the first time.'

'This will be a lot easier,' laughed the nurse, 'and for your mum too'

Rob and his mother watched as the life-giving marrow started to drip slowly into the Hickman Line. They had seen so many fluids administered to his body in this way; it was strange to think they were now watching the climax to all the pain and suffering he had been through.

Anna had learnt that there was a danger of something called 'graft versus host' disease where there were four possible outcomes after a bone marrow transplant. The first and worst was that the new bone marrow would reject the whole of the host body it was being transferred to, and gradually all the main organs would shut down. The next outcome was where the new bone marrow settled in and could function, but the patient would always have to be on anti- rejection drugs and antibiotics for the rest of their lives. The third was the best possible outcome. That was when the transplant had taken over the immune system, and the body had integrated to the extent that eventually it could manage without anti-rejection drugs or antibiotics or fear of rejection of the host body and organs. The last possibility, which was as bad as the first really, was where the transplant did not 'take' at all and did not recognise leukaemia cells as aliens to be destroyed and therefore the patient relapsed.

She was told that there needed to be a certain amount of "graft versus host" reaction as it meant that the new marrow was in there fighting and would recognise and destroy any return of the leukaemia.

'In some patients,' explained the doctor, 'they may only show signs of this battle going on in their body in small ways – like an irritating or rough patch behind the ear.' In Rob's case it seemed to be his gums that would go white and get slightly swollen when the battle was in progress.

It was obvious which outcome they hoped for, but in the end, as long as it was one of the two that meant survival and no relapse, they would be very happy.

True to the word of the nurse, the whole amazing procedure was completed forty-five minutes after it had started.

There was a feeling of anti-climax afterwards, as though

something amazing had happened but there was no outward evidence.

'We should have a drink to celebrate' said Rob – so they each had a small drop of sherry from the bottle Anna kept hidden behind the fridge for self-preservation.

***

A few days later there was a setback.

Steve, one of the male staff nurses who was usually very jolly, came in with a serious expression and some bad news. 'Rob is testing positive for MRSA,' he said. 'I'm sorry Anna that this means you have to be confined to the room and not mix with any of the other patients or relatives.'

Anna's heart sank. MRSA invading a brand new and struggling immune system would surely mean that the battle was already lost. It was one of the diseases that was racing ahead of any of the anti-bacterial drugs and even in a well body could prove fatal.

For four days, she stayed captive with Rob, and he received different medication.

When the consultant came around on the fourth day she dared to ask 'Has he still got MRSA?'

The doctor looked puzzled. 'Oh no,' he said. 'We discovered three days ago that it was a false alarm.'

So for all that time Anna had been fretting for nothing. Bad communication had a lot to answer for.

***

Gradually Rob recovered his taste for certain things and he expressed a wish for fruit juice. This was a great leap forward, and so Anna got his favourite – grapefruit juice.

At the next doctor's round she announced this improvement and was surprised by the reaction. 'Weren't you told not to give him grapefruit juice?'

Anna felt as though she were being accused. 'No, not at all. I thought you would be pleased.'

'Problem is,' said the consultant, 'while he is on anti-rejection drugs that is the one thing he mustn't have – grapefruit in any form.'

'Why is that?' asked Anna.

The consultant looked at his registrar 'You tell her,' he said.

The registrar looked awkward and turned to the senior houseman 'you tell her.'

The houseman said to the medical student by his side 'you tell her, it will be good practice for you.'

The medical student looked vacant. 'I'm afraid I don't know.'

In the end, Anna realised that none of them knew the reason, and were not used to being quizzed about things.

Somehow the whole episode had reminded her of a sketch from a John Cleese sitcom again.

She resolved to find out herself, and after visiting the medical library, she discovered it was because certain flavonoids found in grapefruit interfered with the way the anti-rejection drug worked. It was apparently the only fruit flavonoid that had this affect.

She wrote it all down on a piece of paper and slipped it to

the medical student when she saw him on the ward. 'Now you can get some brownie points by telling them what they should have known in the first place,' she said with a smile.

Soon afterwards, the registrar swept in to the room accompanied by the medical student.

'Ah,' said the registrar. 'I can tell you the reason why Rob can't eat grapefruit.' He opened his mouth to continue, but the medical student nudged him and said, 'Actually it was Anna who told me.'

There was an awkward silence which seemed to last for a painfully long time as the registrar regained his composure and pride - and then the conversation went on as though grapefruit and flavonoids had never been mentioned!

***

On one of Rob's recovery days, he noticed a strong smell of solvent filling the room.

'Can you smell glue?' asked Rob

'Yes I can,' said Anna, 'very strong glue and it is getting stronger.'

They began to cough.

'We'll be asphyxiated in here if we don't get some fresh air,' said Anna, and against all the rules she propped open the door to their isolation room, and then went off in search of a nurse.

She was somewhat surprised to see a number of relatives each coming out of the single rooms with the patients following them, dragging drip stands and any other mobile equipment they were attached to. They too were trying to keep the doors open for air and each were demanding 'What IS going on.'

The fumes were becoming so unbearable that the staff arranged for all the rooms to be vacated, and all the occupants were herded to the only part of the ward which was not controlled by air conditioning. This was a cramped airless room (without opening windows) where visitors usually waited.

Together all the patients and their relatives huddled, 'exchanging bugs no doubt' thought Anna.

In the end, the Sister discovered that a builder working on the roof, had left a large open tub of solvent right near the intake for the air conditioning.

It took several hours for the fumes to disappear, since they were circulating in the system by then, and eventually, after the source had been removed, it finally died down altogether.

'Mum if I manage to get out of here alive' said Rob 'it will be a miracle.'

Thankfully, Anna still believed in miracles. And thankfully, the professor in charge of Rob's treatment as well as the medical staff and senior nursing staff were very professional. The team were only let down by many of the agency workers - domestic, catering and auxiliary nurses employed from companies outside the hospital and outside the NHS.

'When I was nursing,' Anna said, 'all the ancillary workers were part of the hospital team and were governed by their internal heads of department employed by the NHS. That was how the hospitals could keep a firm hold on the standards and whatever part you played - everyone had a strong sense of pride and commitment to the team. And what people don't realise is that their work is as important to the patients' welfare as the highest doctor. Trying to cut costs never pays off in the end.' Sometimes it was the domestics cleaning the ward that used to give the patients cheerful company and conversation when the nurses were too busy to stop.

Later that day she went down to the dining room as lunch had not arrived on the ward.

She was walking along one of the old corridors, when she saw a man she thought she recognised. He was the man with the pony tail she had seen waiting in the car outside their home, just before their telephone line had deteriorated. She was convinced they were being bugged at home.

'This is ridiculous' she thought 'I am getting paranoid, but I am sure I remember his face. In fact I shall never forget his face, and I am positive that man is the same one unless he has a Doppelganger.'

She glanced over her shoulder to see if she was being followed, but there was a crowd behind her now and she could no longer see him.

However, when she eventually got back to the ward a strange thing had happened.

'Your word processor has been taken off for checking,' said the nurse, 'a technician came and said he had to take it because it was electrical and had been brought into the hospital and they had to make sure it would not blow any of our fuses.'

'What did he look like?' asked Anna with a sudden shiver down her spine.

'Oh I don't know really' – said the nurse – 'average height, shoulder length dark hair tied back.'

Anna's heart chilled even more. So she had been right all

along.

Rob said 'he seemed genuine enough mum – was wearing an ID badge and everything. He says it will be returned to you as soon as possible.'

'Did he take all the discs?' asked Anna.

'Just the one in the machine' said Rob.

'Thank goodness for that,' she thought, 'That only had personal correspondence on it. The disc with all the research information, reports and letters is in my handbag.'

She checked, and yes it was still there. 'But,' she thought, 'that might mean that he will either target my home again, or might even come after me here.'

Anna decided not to go anywhere but stay put until the machine was returned. She also alerted James that the family home might be a target again.

'Are you sure you are not being too much of a Miss Marple?' asked James.

'Please listen James,' she said. 'I know I am on to something with this polio vaccine research, and I also know for sure that the man who took my machine away was the same one who was lurking outside our property in the car on more than one occasion.'

'OK mum,' said James, 'just to put your mind at rest.'

He paused and then said 'One other thing you ought to know, we have been having a few silent phone calls when we have been there to check the cats and post. And on one occasion Patrick was knocking at the door.'

Anna felt sick 'What did you do?'

'Sent him packing in no uncertain manner,' said James with satisfaction. 'Didn't give him a chance to tell me what he was doing there – just threatened to get the police if he didn't leave.'

So once more she was left feeling that maybe she was being watched and stalked for two possible reasons. Was it Patrick using a private detective, and why would that be anyway, or was it because the drugs company was getting agitated because of her research?

The following day, there was a knock on the door and the nurse entered. She was carrying Anna's word processor.

'He's dropped it back – said he didn't need to see you personally' she said.

'I bet he didn't,' thought Anna. She checked that the disc had been returned too. It had, but she would have no idea whether it had been copied. At least it hadn't been erased, but then that would have been a dead giveaway.

***

Soon, Rob was well enough to be left for longer periods of time on his own. Sometimes Anna would go down to the dining room for breakfast, usually consisting of a bowl of porridge. However, one morning, having loaded a large amount of hot porridge oats into the bowl, she moved ahead quickly, aware there was a long queue behind her. Not realising her shoulder bag strap had caught on the corner of the counter; she and the tray she was pushing came to an abrupt full stop, while the bowl of porridge carried on at great speed. In the confusion that followed, the jet-propelled porridge narrowly missed a consultant standing ahead of her. Despite her offer to deal with the problem, the kitchen staff insisted that they pick it all up off the floor in slow motion, which in turn held up the queue of people behind who were getting annoyed. Embarrassed she found herself looking around the dining room to see how many people had witnessed the gaff, and suddenly she caught sight of the familiar pony tailed figure sitting at a table. He was regarding her with some amusement.

She decided to stare him out – as if to say 'Leave me alone,' and eventually he looked away.

Anna was furious at this intrusion. She decided to face him out and went up to him.

'Haven't I seen you somewhere before?' she asked bravely. 'In Bournemouth?'

A brief look of annoyance crossed his face, as though she had found him out, but he soon recovered his composure.

'Never been to Bournemouth,' he said. 'Is it as nice as they say?' He looked straight into her eyes. Almost as if he was challenging her, but also it seemed he was playing with her.

Staring daggers at him, she moved as far away as she could to another table.

This incident unsettled her once more, and she decided to stay close to Rob again. She now had no doubt that she was being watched, and her movements followed.

***

Over the next four weeks, Rob continued to recover despite some very harsh drug treatments and setbacks.

Finally, the day came when he was discharged into the care of the Haematologist at the local hospital again.

Gratefully they packed up all their belongings and started

the exhausting journey home. One of Anna's old hospital friends had kindly offered to drive them home in her large estate. The friend was happy to do this as long as James came with her as navigator.

They had grown very fond of some of the staff, and also dependent on them in ways they had not realised, so it was surprisingly difficult to say goodbye.

Anna wondered how the staff themselves coped and whether they ever wondered about their patient's outcome.

Rob was adamant he did not want to keep in touch with the other patients who he had made friends with this time.

'It's just that I am afraid quite a lot of them won't make it through the treatment here mum,' he said. 'I would rather not know.'

And so, with a last look around the room that had been 'home' for the past six weeks, and with promises of keeping in touch with the staff, they left to start on the next stage of Rob's battle for life.

CHAPTER 28 'LOOSE ENDS AND CONUNDRUMS'
October 2000

I s our phone still bugged? Have there been any other signs that we are still being kept under surveillance?' Anna asked James anxiously as soon as she entered the home.

'I got the neighbours to look out,' he said. 'They saw two men in a car on a few occasions. Apparently, they seemed to be just hanging around for hours smoking and talking, but when they realised they were being watched they disappeared. Also, I gather there were no more signs of Patrick turning up. Our neighbours know what he looks like and were on the alert.'

So now mother and son were back home again, with a new lease of life.

It is said that there is a custom of tattooing a semi-colon on the arm with the date of a new start in life when someone had been given a second chance, but Rob decided he just wanted to get on with living, rather than remembering the past.

Somehow it would be disrespectful to those friends he had already lost to cancer and leukaemia and who had not been given that chance, despite earning it.

He had been saddened to hear that out of the six close friends on the Paediatric ward when he had first started on the journey, only two including himself remained alive. He felt an unreasonable sense of guilt about this, in the way that survivors often do.

Anna realised that her son's bone marrow was the same age as her granddaughter and also that her daughter and youngest son now shared some DNA characteristics as well (but not breasts as Rob had feared!)

The first three months of recovery were quite difficult. There were times when they had to return to the local hospital to be checked on, even admitted for short spells, to make sure everything was going well.

It was a highly vulnerable stage of the recovery. A fact that Rob's father did not seem to appreciate.

A month after the bone marrow transplant, his father was getting married again, to the woman who had tried to annul his parents' marriage so she could remain a Roman Catholic, according to the rules of the church. 'This would make us all bastards,' James had observed bitterly at the time. Their father wanted Rob there at the wedding with Alice and James.

'You can come and stay with us,' his father had said, 'and share a room with her nephew' ('her' being the bride to be).

It was hard for Rob to explain that he really was not up to the five-hour journey north to the place where his father and bride-to-be were living. Neither was it a good idea to share such close accommodation with a stranger because of the vulnerability of his immune system and the likelihood of picking up infection he would be unable to fight. He would be a long way from his medical support team and not have easy access to any other.

His father and future new wife seemed to take this as a snub, although it had not meant to be, and they refused to understand the difficulty. However, James and Sandra, Alice, Brian and the new baby Hannah would be attending the wedding to support their father, which Anna felt totally reasonable.

When they returned, she asked Alice how things had gone. Before her daughter had a chance to open her mouth, Brian interjected with 'Well the bride was wearing something feathered on her head, which made her look as though she had stuck her head up the backside of an ostrich.' They eventually stopped laughing, and Alice added 'I was very worried at the reception though mum, because they stuck us on a table with some heavy smokers and of course I had Hannah beside me in a carry cot. I was worried about her all the time as the smoke enveloped us. And to make matters worse, we were separated from James and Sandra who were on a different table. It would have been good to have their support.'

Anna was determined that Rob should think about his future now he was the other side of the bone marrow transplant. It would be very easy to slip backwards having had his GCSE exams and the A-Level exams ruined by his illness and relapse. And apart from anything else, it was healthy for him to turn his back now upon the past few traumatic years and get back into the swing of his peer group. Looking to a future would help him to heal more than anything she reckoned.

As so often happens in life, Anna's anxiety about Rob's future was laid to rest as the result of a chance meeting with a friend. Sometimes when life is in the darkest moments, a life belt is thrown out of the blue. The friend had just completed a Foundation Course. 'I can now do a degree if I want,' she announced. 'It has given me access to higher education that I could never possibly have dreamed of.'

Neither Rob nor Anna had heard of this type of

opportunity or open door into the future before. There were of course many different foundation courses, but if he could just find the right one, it would be the ideal chance to get him back on track for a degree course at University. He may be a couple of years behind the majority of the others attending, but Anna's friend proved that any age was acceptable, and it was not unusual.

So three months after the bone marrow transplant, when he had passed the first medical hurdle on the road to recovery, Rob attended an interview at the local University for a foundation course due to start seven months later – and was given a place.

Anna herself was also recovering. She was getting over the loss of support now she was no longer institutionalised. She had been in a safe cocoon all these years, with a medical team alongside her and Rob, and although at first being cut adrift from this support had been difficult to cope with, she now found her own confidence was returning. She took up various hobbies and joined groups and renewed friendships and became a voluntary worker at the local hospital. It was a world she felt she knew well.

At one of the follow-up medical checks they attended Rob was told that the haematologist felt it would be safe to try and take him off the anti-rejection drugs. This would also mean that he would no longer be permanently on antibiotics either. The reason antibiotics automatically went alongside the anti-rejection drugs was because the latter's job was to dampen down the new immune system to stop it attacking the organs within the host body. This in turn meant he was more susceptible to infections.

It was a trial run that worked. So Rob came off drugs

altogether. It would appear that a real miracle had happened, and his bone marrow transplant had had the best outcome possible, number four on the list of possibilities. The fact that he had been given only a 20 per cent chance of survival at the start of his journey, now faded away into the nightmare of the past.

Life was looking up for the whole family, and Anna was able to enjoy her new granddaughter too.

Inevitably the time came when Rob was called for the renewal of all his vaccinations and immunisations. When the chemotherapy had wiped out all the white cells, it had also wiped out all the memories laid down by vaccinations of how to kill off any invading illness such as diphtheria, tetanus, polio, measles, mumps etc.

But although Anna was nervous about any effects from any of the vaccines, she was consoled by the fact that the polio vaccine was to be imported from Canada and was a killed version made on diploid human cells, and not a live one made on monkey kidney cells. Also, Rob was not allowed to have the MMR as it too was a live vaccine. MMR by this time had received a lot of bad press about links to autism and the specialist who had come up with this theory, and who Anna had a certain amount of sympathy for, had been banished to America and disgraced.

She felt sure however, that he had probably stumbled across some truths that had been stamped on by both the drugs companies and the Government. He may not have followed proper protocol in testing his hypothesis, but the way Anna reasoned it was that he was a highly paid, highly respected paediatric consultant. Why on earth would he put his career and whole life at risk if he did not truly believe what he had witnessed in some of his patients, and if he did not feel he was working in their best interest? It would have been far easier to just sit back and keep quiet, rake in a good salary and have an easy life, but he obviously had concerns and a conscience.

And why would they now not give Rob the MMR vaccine? Because "the risks outweighed any benefits" they had told him.

Strange as it may sound, it all seemed to make more sense when Anna bumped into a naval officer she had known some years previously and who now kept goats. He said that having kept goats for a long while, he was well aware of some of the hazards. One of which was a virus that attacked goats, and which multiplied in the gut and thereby blocked out the absorption of an essential vitamin for the health and workings of the brain. This virus as a consequence used to send the goats quite crazy and made them behave in very odd ways; rather like mad cow disease. So there was a definite connection between bowel and brain and a virus blocking essential vitamins.

After all she reasoned, the measles virus multiplies in the gut and stomach, as does the polio virus, so there seemed to be an element of possibility that with the measles vaccine being live and able to multiply and with the fact that the vilified paediatric consultant had found large quantities of live measles virus in the stomach and intestines of children who had shown signs of a psychological reaction after the vaccination, that perhaps even if he had gone the wrong way about it, there may be some truth hidden there in his hypothesis. Perhaps a large amount of the virus multiplying in the stomach and intestines blocked the absorption of vitamins essential to the normal working of the brain - in the same way as the virus that upset the goats!

These thoughts affirmed her belief that, although it worked in a different way, if the polio vaccine was contaminated with SV40, then the monkey virus could piggy-back and jump species using the thin walls of the gut to gain entry to the immune system.

She had a phone call too from a friend she had not seen in years. Her friend was in fact a microbiologist who had worked for a while on vaccines for a drugs company in the past. This friend did not go into great detail with Anna, except to say that what she had learned about how vaccines were made during this period made her mistrust the whole system and she flatly refused to have any of her children vaccinated against anything.

That was an enlightening yet frightening piece of information and part of the jigsaw puzzle slowly piecing itself together. It was in contrast to the view of her friendly virologist from the World Health Organisation who had said he had willingly let vaccines be tried on his own children without obvious problems.

But then, there were other circumstantial reasons that made a child susceptible to cancers and leukaemia before the virus struck; so some children would be alright, and others not.

These stories from different directions reinforced Anna's belief that drugs companies were in it only for the money and would fight anyone or anything that posed a threat to their profits, and the Government had its mind set on herd protection only – and to hell with the individual and any risk they may be exposed to. She was sure that originally it had not been like that, but gradually over the years as the ethics of both Government and drugs companies had changed to a selfish motive, the scales weighed heavily down on the possibility that there were risks out there to everyone.

She felt helpless. Now that their own battle was largely behind them, she felt less inclined to stick her head above the parapet and make herself a target in some way.

So steadily she let go of the desperate research she had done and decided to leave it up to the Scientists she had explained her theory to. The baton was firmly in their hands now. She had no way of testing her hypothesis herself.

Gradually life picked up pace, and even Patrick receded into the black past which they were all trying to forget.

But just as Anna was relaxing again she discovered something odd had happened to the answer phone. The whole tape had been wiped clean, including the outgoing message. There seemed to be no possible explanation for this – except that somehow someone must have accessed the line from outside the building.

'So maybe even though I am quieter these days, we are still of interest to them,' she thought and once more her determination returned.

Then, she received some news which shocked her and turned her world completely upside down, knocking everything else out of her mind.

Her loyal friend Ruth rang and told her that she had heard from Patrick while Anna and Rob were in London. He had moved up to the northwest to join yet another woman and this time married her. Apparently, rumour had it that he had been banned from a number of dating agencies in the south because people he had been introduced to complained of his violence after a few weeks, and it was said he had even been investigated by the police in the case of a murdered prostitute. He had therefore turned to the internet and met this new target on one of the dating sites. It had suited him that she lived far away from his previous lives and anyone who knew him.

'He was obviously becoming more mentally unstable' said Ruth 'thank God you are not involved now.'

'When did he move away?' asked Anna, not knowing quite how she felt. It was a strange mixture of feelings. She was relieved that he was now well out of the way and not ever likely to resurface again in her life, but at the same time, there was a certain emptiness which she knew was crazy. She still remembered the better times and this news had dragged it all up again.

'Not that long ago,' replied Ruth, 'but I really don't think he could have been behind your most recent bugging experiences because apart from moving away – well – have you seen the news on TV at all?'

'I haven't had time,' said Anna.

'Be prepared for a shock then,' continued Ruth. 'You see his body has been found in a river.'

There was a stunned silence. 'Are you sure it was him?' asked Anna

'Quite,' said Ruth. 'They have definitely identified him. They showed his new wife on TV. She is in a terrible state. It is a suspicious death they say.'

'I wonder if she killed him in self-defence?' suggested Anna.

'At the moment they haven't arrested anyone – but he has upset so many people no doubt it will take a lot of interviewing before they find out,' said Ruth.

As Anna replaced the receiver, she felt a sudden sadness but at the same time a feeling of great relief. That chapter of her life was definitely closed now in more ways than one – the book had slammed shut once and for all. He could no longer haunt her and turn up again protesting his love for her and confuse her emotions - and yet she was still experiencing some sort of grief. Perhaps there was always grief for the past – no matter what it held – after all, there were always good bits as well as bad in most situations.

There was no need to tell the children, as they would no doubt discover it for themselves soon enough.

She even found herself wondering if perhaps his new wife had sons who had realised what he was like and had dealt with him.

But life had to go on and although she grieved in a way she could not understand, now her aim was to concentrate fully on getting Rob back to live his own life to the full.

She resolved to revive her research once more, but as the days stretched to weeks, and then the weeks to months, and Rob gradually recovered in stages of two steps forward, and one back, she found that the urgent quest that had taken up so much of her time during the critical period became less consuming.

Her interest was rekindled again though when she happened to be sitting next to a scientist at a private dinner party one night. When she told him about her theory, he said that there was now a ban on importing monkey kidneys from America for use in laboratories.

So she opened up her correspondence once more with the virologist who she had befriended all those years before, and who had so patiently answered all her questions, and listened to her endless meanderings. She told him what she had recently learnt and suggested it had something to do with her theory.

He wrote back and told her he wasn't sure about the import ban, but that there were changes on the way with regard to the polio vaccine. It was no longer going to be given as a live vaccine but would be inactivated and given by injection which would be safer.

This was certainly a step in the right direction – it made sense not to use live vaccine.

She was very relieved on receipt of his letter and decided to ring him. 'Does that mean they no longer use monkey kidney cells to grow the culture?' she asked.

There was a long pause. 'Well actually – they do still use monkey kidney cells for the British vaccine – but you know my view on that. I believe it is perfectly safe.'

Her heart went cold. So they had not really learnt anything then. The authorities were still letting finances override the common good of the country's children. It was cheaper to use monkey kidney cells to produce the vaccine than the safer human diploid route. She also could not but help wonder if the virologist himself was being 'leant on' in some way.

'I doubt that you will ever give up though will you?' he said. 'I am sure we have not heard the end of the story.'

Again, she felt she was being urged not to give up – otherwise why would he say that.

As she put the phone down Anna thought 'We're always led to believe it is the Third World that is used as the dumping ground for redundant or dodgy medicines. But here we are in so called "Great" Britain still putting our children at risk, while the rest of the Western World is given the safe form of the vaccine made from diploid human cells.'

***

Some while later she was watching the television. The drugs company that had tried to block her research was announcing that they were giving free help to countries where polio was still rife and causing real concern. 'They were working for the benefit of mankind!' it said.

The live footage they were showing was of children being given drops onto the tongue. 'They must be using the defunct vaccine that used to be given in drop form when the vaccine was live and that's now been replaced. Having to make a new inactivated vaccine which is given by injection, must have left the drugs companies with a pile of the old sort and they are offloading the live vaccine onto others less fortunate in an attempt to look magnanimous,' thought Anna with a mixture of disbelief and anger.

Troubled she looked out of the window. It was that time of year again. Late summer, early autumn, the time of year when Rob was first diagnosed and later again when he relapsed. She always felt unsettled when the sun was at that certain angle, it brought back bad memories. Strange how such subtle signs triggered the mind and tipped out its contents no matter how hard you tried to lock away those memories in little boxes.

But she had no energy left to fight. She had handed the information and the responsibility over to those scientists who knew so much more than she did and now she had to leave it up to them and trust that they would do their best. Some she knew were very honourable people who would follow what they believed was right no matter what the consequences. However, the drugs companies had undoubted power over many in the medical world who did not share the same ethics as the people she had been in touch with. She had achieved all she could and frustrating though it was, she had to now sit back and let things happen.

***

A full year had slipped by since Rob's transplant, and it was a real milestone. He had even applied to a University to study medicine and been accepted.

How strange that expectations and time can be shifted sideways and onto unexpected paths.

Life was to be embraced and lived to the full – every moment of every day.

They had all learnt that, but Rob was making sure that nothing he had been through was going to hold him back. Life was for the taking, and that he would do.

'Who knows mum,' he said. 'I might one day be able to help some teenager who is given the same sort of sentence I was. Living proof that miracles are possible.' He smiled.

Anna was pleased to hear this. Her son was indeed someone to be proud of.

And then a strange thing happened. She turned on the television. It had been nearly a year since Patrick's mysterious death and things had gone quiet.

But now, on the screen, the police inspector was asking for

witnesses and for anyone to come forward who might recognise the picture of a man which was then displayed. It had been established he had been the last caller at Patrick's house on the day that he was found face down in the river.

Anna stared in horror at the screen. The face in the photo fit picture looking back at her belonged to the man who had been following her all these months. The man, tall and thin with dark hair drawn back into a pony tail. Now there were answers she would never have, and her brain would be for ever trying to solve things that were impossible to prove.

'Perhaps he was nothing to do with drugs companies at all,' she thought. 'Maybe he was keeping Patrick under surveillance for completely different reasons.'

The ideas and possibilities rushed relentlessly through her mind and she felt completely mixed up. Maybe she would never find out the truth about who was interfering with their lives.

If it was that they were shadowing Patrick, nothing explained why the notes and information about Rob's vaccination records went missing, and nothing explained the parcel which contained both a red rose and a monkey kidney and batch numbers, or the attempt to snatch her research work when she stopped at that petrol station.

Was it possible that Patrick and the drugs companies were somehow interlinked?

A few years ago, her life had seemed so normal and she felt safe.

Now, it could never be the same and these questions were never likely to be answered.

But at least it appeared that somehow her persistence and enquiring mind had helped to change the safety of the polio vaccine – but sadly only halfway.

There would be no peace until she knew that monkey kidney cells were no longer used in any form of vaccine. To mix the DNA of any other species with that of the human seemed very dangerous.

She turned her computer on and wrote to the head virologist, the friend who had encouraged her so much over the years.

'Will you please let me know if ever they do dispense with the use of monkey kidney cells in vaccines,' she pleaded. 'I will always fear for the safety of the public while this method is still used.'

She waited hopefully for a reply for weeks, but nothing came.

And then, one Sunday shortly before Rob was due to start his degree, it was announced on the BBC news that the head virologist of a World Health Organisation had disappeared without trace. When named she was shocked to hear it was the scientist who had been so helpful and open with her, and she feared for his safety.

She remembered all the correspondence she was keeping safe where he had risked his own reputation by being honest and open with her about certain errors in the vaccination programmes. 'These letters really are dynamite now,' she thought. For his sake and safety, she must lock them away where they could never be found.

It then occurred to her that she had other sensitive

documents from other scientists who had found the monkey virus in solid tumours and no answers as to how it got there.

Anna shuddered at the thought of the many dark areas, dangers and secrets hidden within a civilised country and how they can affect very normal lives, especially of those gentle scientists who follow their own hearts and whose only concern is to expose the truth.

One thing Anna did know for sure now though was that she had to make her research and hypothesis about a possible link between the polio vaccine and leukaemia public. She owed it to the virologist for all his support – it was time to take matters into her own hands. But how could she do it?

Perhaps, just maybe, she could publish her research anyway...

ABOUT THE AUTHOR

Mary is a mother of three and grandmother to five. Since retiring, she keeps busy as a radio broadcaster, singer, guitarist, and author.

Mary has two other books currently published:
Green Smarties: Tales of a Navy Wife
&
The Nellie & Sybil Sagas, Book 1; a humorous look at how two friends have grown older, if not wiser.

Her books are currently available on Amazon and can be ordered through selected book shops.

Mary is also well known for her work on iKidz, a radio programme for Hospital Radio Bedside and singing at Pâtisserie Angélique in Westbourne.

Mary is an active member of the dialogue and performance group Doppelganger Productions whose members have encouraged her greatly.

37321536R00179

Printed in Poland
by Amazon Fulfillment
Poland Sp. z o.o., Wrocław